The Embezzlement Ledger

A Florian Fooks Murder Mystery

The Embezzlement Ledger

Shirley Arnham

A CIP catalogue record for this book is available from the British Library.

Ebook ISBN 978-1-7399186-4-4

Paperback ISBN 978-1-7399186-5-1

TABLE OF CONTENTS

CHAPTER ONE

"Wash, I've asked you three times now. When are you going to fix the back porch roof?" Janet Turner asked, walking into the sitting room of the house she shared with Bronze Canyon's sheriff and their two children. Midafternoon on a sleepy Sunday.

Wash Turner, sheriff of Bronze Canyon, relaxed in his favorite chair, feet up, reading the newspaper. Correction - sleeping behind the newspaper. At the sound of his wife's voice, he started up with much rustling.

"Wha'?"

Janet came further into the room and stood over him, arms folded. "The back porch roof?"

Wash's blank gaze turned up at her.

"You promised to fix it."

"Did I?"

"Yes." She looked down at him. "So?"

Wash growled. "You want me to do it now? Right now?" he snapped.

"Well, you're not doing anything at the moment, are you?"

Wash opened his mouth as if to say he *was* doing something and then closed it again. He threw the paper aside.

He stalked out. "I'm a sheriff, Janet, not a janitor," he tossed over his shoulder.

"Not in this house, you're not," Janet said to herself.

She went to the window and watched her disgruntled husband disappear into the shed. He reappeared some minutes later with a ladder, a hammer and a box of nails. He still muttered under his breath as he leaned the ladder against the back porch. Janet winced when the handle of the hammer rammed its way down the front of his pants. Nails were crammed into his mouth and the first few rungs of the ladder climbed. She smiled in a satisfied way. Only then did she turn away to attend to other things.
The afternoon became filled with the sound of furious banging as the shingles on the back porch roof were persuaded back into place. Then all of a sudden, something slipped, a yell, followed straight away by a panicked cry, a heavy thud and then a groan. By the time Janet rushed out, Wash was struggling to sit up, holding his left leg, pain etched over his face.

"Better get the doc. Think I've busted my leg."

Florian Fooks, reforming outlaw, bent to peer at the immobilized limb. Straightening up, he sniffed. "I reckon that's broke," he said, deadpan.

Having returned to Bronze Canyon from Boston yesterday, Fooks waited until the next evening to visit the injured sheriff.

"I know it's broke. It feels like it's broke. That's 'cos it is broke!" Sheriff Washington Turner snapped. "When ya quite finished, I didn't ask you here for ya medical advice." He put a hand on the splinted leg and closed his eyes.

Fooks put on his best innocent face. "No need to be like that, Wash." He couldn't quite keep the smirk off his face. "'Course me being in hardware. I coulda told you the proper way to use a ladder is--"

"Fooks," Wash growled. Pain etched over his pale face. He furiously waved Fooks into a chair.

Fooks pressed his lips together in sympathy. Janet had warned him. Wash's broken leg had pained him all day, and he was in no mood to tolerate Fooks' humor this evening.

Fooks sat and set his features to serious. "What can I do, Wash?"

Wash sighed. "I'm gonna be outta action for a while."

"Yeah, you will be," Fooks agreed, nodding at the leg.

"I'm in kinda a fix, Fooks. I mean, look who I've got as a deputy ..." Wash scowled. "Luke said he'd come outta retirement for the duration but him an' ... I mean him and Bart. Y'know, they don't get along."

Fooks pursed his lips thoughtfully and nodded. Luke Fletcher was Wash's predecessor as sheriff of Bronze Canyon. Before that, a U.S. Marshall, respected by lawmen and outlaws alike. Now enjoying his retirement, only occasionally called on to help out by Wash. Deputy Bart foisted on Wash as a favor for an old friend. The boy always willing, but none too bright. Not a recipe for a successful law enforcing partnership.

"So ..." Fooks' head snapped up. "No. Now Wash, you know I'd do anything to help..." He rose slowly. "But I've a wife and a little daughter ... Not to mention a business to run." Fooks paced. "Wash, I appreciate your trust in me an' all, but I just can't. I mean, I know nothing 'bout the law." He winced and twitched his head. "That is. From your side of the fence. No, really ..." Fooks came to rest with his back to Wash and stood hands on hips.

Fooks gave a deep sigh. "All right. I'll ..." He turned and saw the amusement on Wash's face. "What's so funny?"

Wash chortled. "Did ya think I was gonna ask you to stand in as sheriff? Ha, Ha." He put his head back and roared.

Fooks felt disgruntled now. "You mean you weren't?"

"No." Wash wiped his eyes. "Ask Florian Fooks to be sheriff? Oh no, Ha, Ha, Owh!" He held his leg.

"Ah." Fooks struggled. *Am I relieved or offended?* He returned to the chair, placing his hat over his knee with purpose. "So why am I here?"

Wash sobered. "I'll need to find a decent lawman until this heals up. So, the Capitol is sending one. Be here day after tomorrow." Wash looked at his friend. "Jus' thought I oughta warn ya, the man they're sending … he don't like outlaws who rob banks. His brother was a bank teller. Two months ago, someone shot and killed him in a robbery gone bad. Word has it, my stand- in is putting up most of the $5,000 reward."

"Oh." Fooks understood. This could be awkward, given who he was. Now he became serious. "Do I know him?"

Wash hesitated. "Yeah."

"Who?"

Wash swallowed hard. "Jack Priestly."

Fooks sucked air in sharply. Yes, he knew him. Priestly had been a sheriff in a town where the Guardian Wall Gang, his gang, had robbed the bank, getting away with $35,000. Priestly had raised a posse and given the Gang a hard chase. To make matters worse, the day before the robbery, Fooks had played poker with the man. A considerable amount of his winnings had come from the sheriff. Later, Priestly realized just who the lucky poker player had been and made it known he had vowed to capture him. Preferably dead rather than alive. Definitely no love lost there.

Fooks licked his lips and swallowed. "How d'you … I mean … I can avoid him for a while, but that could take months." He gestured at Wash's leg.

"Yeah, I'm sorry Fooks. It's outta my control."

Fooks nodded. "I know." He considered. "Perhaps," he turned back. "Perhaps if I talk to him. Tell him I've gone straight. Y'know first off. Try and reason with the man," he said, silver tongue winding up. "It's been years since the Guardian Wall Gang robbed the bank in Prelude. He can't hold a grudge that long. Can he?"

Wash's face told him Priestly could.

Fooks groaned and rubbed a hand over his face.

"What do I tell Mary?" *Oh Sheesh.* Just when he was making progress in living a law-abiding life, something like this occurred. He didn't want his secret to come out. Only a few people in town knew who he really was. Despite four years of living a law-abiding life (mostly) he remained a wanted man. He'd chosen to live in Wyoming, where statute of limitations didn't exist, because he liked Wyoming. Unless something dramatic and unexpected happened, he planned to remain living under his assumed name of Joseph Crane for the rest of his life.

"I'm sorry Fooks," Wash said. He regarded his friend with sympathy.

Fooks took this as a warning that his fresh start was still fragile and could easily break in an instant. He had to find a way out of this. Rubbing his forehead as he thought. He didn't know how to do it. Simply no idea at all.

CHAPTER TWO

A week later, Fooks was concentrating on the books in The Hardware Store's back office when he barely heard the outside door tinkle. He'd been away for weeks, sorting out his old partner's new life in the eastern city of Boston, and he'd expected to come back to loads of catching up to do. He smiled, tight-lipped in satisfaction, at the neat penmanship of his assistant's writing. *Russ has done a great job here. Better than my scrawl. Perhaps I should go away more often.*

"Mr. Crane." A yell came from the store. "Mr. Crane."

Fooks had left Ted, his other assistant, to mind the store alone. Wednesday afternoons were always quiet for some reason, so Fooks had no qualms about leaving Ted while he worked in the office at the back on the books. Fooks rubbed his eyes and sighed. He'd tried doing the accounts at home, but his toddler daughter, demanding as ever, kept interrupting. Rather ungentlemanly, he'd parceled her up and delivered her to her mother in The Hat Shop.

With the office blissfully quiet in comparison, he'd managed a full hour before this interruption. *Knew it was too good to be true.*

"Yeah?"

"Mr. Carmichael, to see ya. He's got a … thing."

Curious about the thing, Fooks stomped into the store. He took in the scene. The town's newspaper editor, Craig Carmichael stood, breathing hard at the end of the counter. Ted stood back against the shelves and then he saw the … thing. Pursing his lips, Fooks made his way down to the end.

"Hi Craig," he said, with a nod.

"Joseph."

"What's this?" Fooks waved his hand at the thing.

Craig's eyes flicked to Ted and then back to Fooks, who turned to his young assistant.

"Ted, how 'bout making some coffee please, huh?"

Ted nodded and slowly retreated into the warehouse.

Fooks turned back to Craig and gestured towards the thing meaningfully.

Craig managed a grin. "Oh, it's a …." He swept the canvas cover off to reveal a typewriter.

Fooks recognized the object, yet questioned its presence in his store. He smacked his lips and nodded. He could understand the secrecy, though. The identity of the author behind the stories Fooks wrote for the paper was confidential, and Fooks wanted it to stay that way for a while longer.

"Joseph, I've published twelve of your Florian Fooks stories now. They've gone down well and my readers are demanding more. I want to publish more and I know you've got more, but you have to admit your handwriting is abysmal. I'm having real problems reading it."

Fooks remained quiet. When telling a story, he ended up scribbling, so he didn't forget to get everything down. He nodded resigned.

"So, are you saying you won't publish anymore?" he asked in disappointment.

"No. I want you to learn how to type." Craig was emphatic. "This is an old typewriter, but it still works, and it'll do for a while until you get the hang of it. Then the newspaper will stump up for a newer model." He saw Fooks' interest but wasn't sure. "Here are the instructions." He handed over a pamphlet. "Play with it for a couple of days. See how you get on. I can't show you how it works right now, but you like a challenge. I'm sure you can figure it out."

With a smile, Craig let himself out. The open door catching on the tinkle and he turned, saying, "Oh, by the way, it's heavy. I'd put it in a cart to take it home if I were you. So long." He gave a cheery wave, leaving Fooks alone with the enormous machine.

Typing. For this, I gave up leading the Guardian Wall Gang?

After the store closed for the day, Fooks trundled the typewriter home in the small handcart the store used for local deliveries. He heaved it onto his desk. Craig hadn't exaggerated. Boy, it was heavy. Getting his breath back, he scanned around the little house, frowning. Where were Mary and Susan? *Thought they'd be home by now.*

He spied a note on the coffee table. In Mary's handwriting, it read,

Had an errand to run. Susan is with Wash and Janet. Back later.

Fooks grunted and dropped the note back. He turned and, hands on hips, he regarded the typewriter.

"Okay, let's take a look see." He settled himself at the desk in front of the machine and studied the instructions.

The afternoon became filled with mumblings and murmurings like, "*Lay the paper under the paper shelf (F)*—where's F?" After several attempts, he eventually succeeded in inserting a sheet of paper correctly into the machine.

"Strike the key with sufficient force and promptness to throw the type against the cylinder. Strike but one key at a time. Strike squarely, with equal, even touch ... Okay. Hey, I'm typing. Now what? *To return the carriage to begin a new line, pull the carriage-lever (170) toward you* ... Okay, so what have I typed? *The carriage may be lifted at any time to observe results* ...Ooh. Hey that's pretty neat."

Deep in concentration practicing typing when the front door opened, Fooks started. Old habits die hard and he put a hand to his chest, as if to still his rapidly beating heart. He glanced around quickly to confirm Mary and Susan. "Hi," said Mary, struggling to put Susan down.

"Home, Pappy."

Fooks grunted an acknowledgement.

"Sorry we're late." Fooks sensed Mary hanging up her coat and wrestling the child out of hers. "What's this?" Mary put her hands on his shoulders and smacked a kiss on his cheek.

"It's a typewriter," Fooks mumbled, frowning hard in concentration. *Why weren't the keys in alphabetical order?* He snatched up the pamphlet and thumbed through it until he came to a diagram at the back. *Placed so the letters most used are located to facilitate speed.* "They're hopeful, aren't they?"

"Seems complicated," Mary said.

"Yeah, 'tis." Key pressing.

"Don't you want to know where I've been?"

"Hmmm?" More key pressing.

"I've been to the doctor about something important. Aren't you curious to find out what about?"

"Yeah 'course'." Even more key pressing, followed by lifting the carriage and peering at the paper underneath. "Look, I typed that." He beamed proudly at her. "Mary, I can type."

"Yes, very nice."

"You didn't look."

"Yes, I did."

"What did it say?"

When she didn't answer, Fooks growled and turned back to the typewriter.

"Joe!"

"Just a moment, Mary, I'm trying to get the ...." He tailed off and pressed some more keys.

Mary sat down on the sofa and pulled Susan onto her lap. "Shall we tell Pappy about your new brother or sister?" she said, conspiratorially in Susan's ear but loud enough for Fooks to hear if he had been listening.

"No," Susan said with a giggle.

"That's what I think too. We'll just make it our secret, shall we?"

"Yes."

"What would you like, Susan?" Mary said in a loud voice. "A brother or a sister?"

"Sister." Susan was firm.

"Hmmm. Then we would really outnumber Pappy, wouldn't we?" Mary said, louder.

"Yes."

Fooks' back remained stubbornly turned away from her. Mary sighed.

"We could gang up on him. Do you think he'd like that?"

"No."

"I don't think so either, but if he doesn't turn round, he won't get any choice."

Fooks slapped the desk and spun around in his chair. "WHAT?"

Mary smiled at him smugly.

Fooks allowed the conversation to replay in his mind.

"Mary, what are you saying?" he asked. He wanted her to be clear.

"Remember, we talked about Susan having a brother or sister," she started. "It would appear she might be getting one," she beamed.

As it sunk in, a wide, double dimpled grin spread over his face. The typewriter now forgotten. For a moment, a flicker of anxiety crossed his face. He hadn't told Mary about Priestly coming. *Will she understand the implications?* He'd have to tell her soon, but not right now.

CHAPTER THREE

Two days later in her little house, Mary looked up from her mending and across at her husband, leaning on the mantelshelf, one foot up on the grate of the cold fire. A quiet evening. The kind she liked. Dinner over and cleared away. Susan down and asleep. *Just me and Joe.* Except he had been pacing up and down of their long living room for the past hour, only now finally coming to rest.

"Are you going to tell me?" she asked, biting off the thread. She'd been sewing patches on the knees of Susan's overalls. *Just like a boy.* What were they going to do if the child inside her was a boy? They be no stopping them.

Fooks looked around. "What?"

"There's something bothering you. Are you going to tell me what it is?"

"There's nothing bothering me," he said, a mite too briskly, but he took his elbow down.

"Yes, there is. I know you, Joseph Crane. Yours isn't the look of a man who's easy in his mind."

Fooks scowled, walked over, and threw himself onto the opposite sofa. Mary gathered up her sewing. She waited. *It'll come. I just have to be patient.*

"It's to do with Wash," he said, quietly.

Mary blinked. His answer wasn't what she'd expected. "What about Wash? He is all right, isn't he? It's just his leg that's broken—"

"It's not his leg. That's fine. It's—" Fooks broke off and swallowed hard. "The Capitol is sending someone to stand in as sheriff while he's laid up."

"I thought Papa and Bart were going to manage."

"Yeah, so did I." He rubbed his forehead. "The man the authorities in the Capitol are sending is called Jack Priestly."

Mary shook her head. The name meant nothing to her, but by the look on her husband's face, it did to him. "You know him?"

Fooks nodded deliberately. "Yep."

Mary widened her eyes. "Does he know you? The old you?"

Fooks' tongue explored his cheek, and he nodded again. "Yep."

Mary's eyes widened more. "So—"

"Yep." Fooks made a popping sound with the p.

"Oh." Mary pressed a hand to her stomach. An entire army of butterflies suddenly took flight in there. She gave a whimper, cast her sewing aside, and crossed to him. "What are you going to do?"

Fooks shook his head and looked away. "I dunno Mary." His voice came out shuddering. "I really don't know."

"Maybe he won't remember you. It's a long time ago now and you've changed."

"Oh, he'll remember me all right," he said and gave a bitter laugh. "I cleaned him out one night at the poker table. And the next night, we cleaned out the bank in his town. A man doesn't forget things like that. I hurt his pride. Twice." Fooks scrubbed a hand over his eyes. "I'm sorry Mary."

Mary moved to sit beside him and laid a hand on his arm. "When is he coming?"

"Two days."

"Then you've time to go." She swallowed hard. "And stay away until he's gone."

"I can't. I'm barely back from Boston and the bank wants the half yearly stock take done for the mortgage." He looked at her. "I have responsibilities here. You and Susan and the new baby. I can't just run off."

"And if you don't go and he spots you? What then?" Mary sniffed. "He'll arrest you." She swallowed hard. "Won't he?"

Fooks took a deep breath and played with her fingers. "I guess we'll face that if it happens. I intend to keep out of sight." He smiled faintly and patted her hand. "You're gonna be married to a ghost for a couple of months."

Mary shook her head. "You can't hide for that long. He'll spot you. Your name is bound to be mentioned around town and he's going to wonder why he's not met you. He'll come looking." She put a hand to her lips, her eyes watering. "And when he finds you—"

"He won't find me." Fooks deepened his dimples. "I've kept one step ahead of the law for years. I know what I'm doing."

Mary looked doubtful, but pulled herself up. "What do you want me to do when I meet him?"

"Just act natural."

"I'm not sure I can do that knowing—"

"You mustn't give me away." A flicker of pain crossed his face. "I'm sorry I'm dragging you into my life. That life. This was always a possibility, but I wouldn't do that for anything. And now it's here and we have to face it. We'll get through this. I promise you."

The look on his face told her he wasn't entirely convinced.

"Was that nice?"

After the stress of telling Mary about Priestly, the next morning Fooks decided he should take his turn at baby minding. The morning had gone well. He and Susan had played dolls and bricks and push along donkey. He enjoyed getting to know his little daughter again after his recent time in Boston. Fooks laughed at Susan eating her lunch and opening her mouth for more. Susan's attempts at feeding herself usually ended in an unholy mess. Responsible for being alone with her, he was taking no chances.

"More." Susan screwed up her face in protest when nothing more was forthcoming.

"All gone." He showed her the empty bowl.

"Let's see what Mama's left you for dessert." He stood up, tossing the empty bowl into the sink and crossed to the icebox. "What do we have in here?" He peered in and gave a gasp of surprise. "Apple." He set the pureed confection on the highchair tray. Intent on closing the icebox door and finding a spoon, he didn't hear the front door open.

"Howdy? Y'all there?"

Fooks scowled. The unmistakable Texas drawl of his father-in-law. *Great.* "In the kitchen, Luke," he called back. He set his features in greeting as an older man came in.

"Hello, sweetie." Luke rubbed his knuckle over his granddaughter's chubby cheek.

"Grampy." Susan giggled and squealed.

Luke straightened up. "Y'all heard about Jack Priestly?"

Fooks closed the icebox door. "Yeah, Wash told me."

"D'ya know him? Y'know from..." Luke waved his hand vaguely, "from ya previous ... occupation?"

"Yeah, I ran across him."

"Can he recognize ya?"

Fooks nodded. He took a deep breath and put his hands on his hips. "Fraid so. I haven't changed much since I last run into him."

"What are ya gonna do?"

"I don't know. Stay outta his way, I guess."

"For two months?"

"What else can I do?" Fooks hunched his shoulders and spread his hands.

Luke growled. "Difficult one. Ya'll have to take care he don't spot ya."

"Yes, plan to. I'm sure I can manage it. There's a lot of work to do at the store, which will keep me busy and off the street. I can duck around the back of town instead of walking down Main Street. The saloon is out for the duration, though. I'll be careful, Luke."

Luke nodded thoughtfully. "Anything I can do to help?"

"I've told Mary, and she understands why I won't be socializing for a while. She's terrified, though. Perhaps you can reassure her some."

"And jus' how can I do that?"

Fooks bit his lip. He was still proving himself to Mary's father, and this situation wasn't going to help any. Another reminder he wasn't exactly ideal son-in-law material. "I dunno," he said, shaking his head.

Luke sucked his teeth. "I'll give it some thought."

"Thanks." Fooks gave a slight smile. "Now, was there something else? I'm kinda busy."

Luke's eyes sparkled. "Mary asked me to stop in and see how you were doin'."

"I'm quite capable of looking after my daughter, y'know."

"Hmmm." Luke raised an eyebrow over at Susan. "Are you sure now?" he asked, amusement playing over his lips.

Fooks followed Luke's gaze. Unsupervised, Susan recognized food she liked. She'd plunged her hand in and had smeared apple around her mouth. Globs of the pureed fruit fell from her chin onto her dress. Fooks cursed inwardly. He'd forgotten to put the towel around her neck.

"No!"

Luke chuckled at Fooks' anguish cry. Fooks leaped forward and spun the bowl onto the kitchen table. Not before Susan had dived in again. She appeared to be enjoying the sensation of squeezing her dessert between her fingers.

"Well, if'n y'all got this, I'll be on m'way."

"Thanks." Fooks' sarcastic tone matched the disgruntled wince he flashed at Luke's retreating back. A roar of laughter emanated from the living room.

Fooks turned back to his daughter. "Thanks, Susan, for making me look bad in front of Luke. Now he thinks I'm not capable of minding you." He slumped and viewed the mess on the table and the baby. "He might be right," he said bitterly.

Susan reached for the bowl, a trifle too far for her. She screamed in frustration. "All right. All right. I'll get a spoon. And then I'd better clean you up. If Mama sees you like this, she'll have a fit." *Wonder if Priestly has to deal with stuff like this? I guess we'll find out in a day or two.*

Fooks walked into the store the next morning and saw his two assistants staring out of the window. He went to join them. "What are we looking at?"

"New sheriff just arrived," said Russ, the older of the two boys.

Fooks swallowed hard. Jack Priestly, here. *Sheesh.*

"Who is he?" He didn't want the boys to realize he already knew the man.

"Just walking along the street from the depot now, with Mayor Watkins. See?" Ted pointed at two men. One in a smart suit and sporting the mayoral chain of office. The other a middle-aged man with dark hair and long, bushy sideburns.

"Uh-huh."

Yep, that's him. So, he's really here.
"Are you gonna go say howdy, Joseph?" Russ asked.
Fooks sniffed. "Now, why would I do that?"
"You're an influential man in this town. Dare say he'll wanna meet all such folks sooner rather than later."
Fooks gave a brief laugh. "I'm not influential." He turned aside. "Naw, I'll meet him soon enough." *Not too soon, I hope.* "Give the man time to settle in. Now come away, you two. We need to get the store straight before stock taking tomorrow."
They groaned in unison.
Regular stock taking was a condition of Fooks' mortgage. It wasn't practical to do it too often, but he had to comply every six months. Meant closing for the day and working long into the evening, humping boxes, counting out every screw, nail and widget in the store. Not to mention recording and then reconciling to the ledger. The work often took him days, but now Russ could help him, hopefully now not so many.

CHAPTER FOUR

His first sense to came back – hearing. Awareness of voices, two women talking. Too low, he couldn't make out what they were saying. They were echoing and fuzzy, like he, or they, were underwater.

Then Fooks blinked his eyes open. Shapes and colors blurred around him. A blinding light off to his left made him close his eyes tightly and turn his head away. His head pounded, an all-encompassing ache, but where the pain originated, unclear. As he became more aware, the pain intensified. The brief glimpse had revealed a room he didn't recognize. Curiosity getting the better of him, he opened his eyes again.

This time, he squinted slightly and things gradually coalesced into recognizable shapes. He could make out items of furniture. Yet he still didn't understand where this room was. He raised his hand lend rubbed his eyes. His movements, slow and shaky. Looking at his hand, like he saw it for the first time. He turned it over in the air, inspecting. Yes, it was his hand. He knew it was. Yet it didn't feel like his hand.

He needed a drink, his mouth dry. Turning his head felt like an effort and hurt like the blazes. On the nightstand stood a glass and a flask of water. He tried to push himself up. Tried to get nearer to the precious liquid. He couldn't. Too weak. He fell back with a groan. Staring at the ceiling, he panted. Where was he? The room was vaguely familiar, but he didn't know why. Another groan. Louder this time. Perhaps one of the voices outside would come.

He became more aware of the rest of him. Something tight wrapped around his head. His hand ... yes, definitely *his* hand ... felt a bandage. Tentatively, his fingers explored its extent. A sharp gasp escaped him when he prodded a sensitive spot. *Stay away from there, Fooks, until you know more.* He raised the other hand and examined it. Trembling and weak, but his hands and arms didn't appear to be hurt. Further down, he saw underwear. *His* underwear. He recognized the loose thread hanging from the button of his henley. He smiled and pulled at it fondly.

Wherever this place was, he might have to leave in a hurry. Where were his clothes? He couldn't see them. Frantic searching made him dizzy. No choice but to fall back against the pillow and wait for the whirling to stop. He turned away from the sun shining through the gap in the curtains. He took a moment before he could push back the bedcovers and reveal his legs. Clad in long johns they felt okay. He shuffled to the side of the bed, intending to throw his legs to the floor.

The door opened, and he stopped. A young woman came in. She appeared familiar. Yet he couldn't place her. He went cold. Perhaps she had been on a train or in a bank. Perhaps she recognized him.

When she saw him, she beamed at him.

"Oh, Joe, you're awake."

He licked his lips. *Joe?* He really needed a drink. "Ma'am?" he croaked.

She came over swiftly, poured him a drink, and held it to his lips. Surprised at first by her informality, yet he felt comfortable with her and drank greedily.

She giggled. "Here. Easy now." She took the glass away and set it aside. He wanted more, and he reached for it. She smiled, nuzzling his hand away before he could reach it. "No. You can have a little more in a moment."

She placed the glass further away. "You've been unconscious for three days. Do you remember what happened?"

He blinked a no.

"You were in the store. You went to get something off a top shelf and the racking gave way. Pulled everything down on top of you." She straightened the bedcovers over him, pushing him flat.

Fooks blinked at her familiarity. What she had told him didn't mean anything. He shook his head, just a bit, wanting to avoid any dizziness like before and then winced. "Ma'am I don't ...." He studied her. She looked familiar. *Should he know her?* He cast around the room. "Where am I?"

"At home in bed, of course," she smiled.

"No, this isn't home." His brow creased. *Was this home?* It looked familiar, but he didn't have a home. Well, not a proper one. Not unless you called the leader's cabin at Guardian Wall, home. "Who are you, ma'am?"

"Mary." She straightened the bed covers again. "Your wife. In case you've forgotten."

He smiled at her, wide-eyed again. "Oh, no ma'am." He laughed gently, but politely. "I don't have a wife. I think I'd remember if I did." He smiled the full double dimple at her.

Mary gave him a sharp look and perched on the edge of the bed.

"Joe, that's not funny."

He could smell her perfume. He knew it. He just didn't know her. Yet she appeared to know him. *Why was she calling him Joe? Joe who? His name is ... mmm, yes ....*

"No Ma'am," he said. "Where's ...?" He swallowed hard. "My friend?"

Mary narrowed her eyes. "Your friend? I don't ...." Then she had an idea. "Do you mean Samuel?"

Fooks shook his head, wincing when it hurt. "I don't know a Samuel," he said.

"Yes, you do Joe," she said. She was firm. Her face had fallen from the delight of seeing him awake to one of uncertainty.

Fooks blinked and rubbed at his temple. None of this made any sense. "Oh, yes ...." He smiled weakly. *Go with it, Fooks, and see what happens.*

"You also call him Tobe or Tobias Swan," she stated firmly. "And he's in Boston. As you well know."

"No. No! Something's not right here," he cried. He tried to sit up. So weak, he soon gave up the struggle and fell back. Putting a hand to his head and closing his eyes, he waited for the wave of dizziness to pass. He didn't understand any of this. She knew Tobe as Tobias Swan? And he was in Boston?

"Tobias has been in Boston since we married," Mary said, as if reading his thoughts. "You went to see him."

Fooks groaned. "I don't .... know." He tailed off and shook his head. "I don't know .... who you are," he forced out.

Mary stiffened. "Do you know who *you* are?"

"Yes ma'am. I'm...." He took a deep breath. No discernible reason he should trust her; he just did. "I'm Florian Fooks, ma'am." He swallowed hard.

Mary sucked in a breath and stood up. "I think Doctor Albright should see you." She started for the door. Looking back, she saw his alarm. "It'll be all right, Joe. Just don't mention who you are and everything will be fine."

She left him feeling more confused. He flopped back, too weak to do anything else.

"Mary, you look like you've just seen a ghost," Janet Turner said, putting an arm around Mary's shoulders, when she emerged from the bedroom.

Janet had been minding Susan while Mary looked after Fooks. Which was understanding of her, as she had her own invalid at home.

"No. Not a ghost." Mary shook her head. "Joseph's awake but he … doesn't know who I am. He says he doesn't have a wife. Then he asked for Tobias." She looked at Janet as if she had all the answers. "Joe says his name is Florian Fooks."

"Well …," Janet began. "It is."

"I know." Mary sank onto the sofa and pulled Susan onto her lap.

"Pappy okay, Mama?" Susan asked, her little forehead wrinkled.

Mary smiled and pressed a kiss onto her daughter's head. "Yes, sweetie, he's awake now."

"Susan see Pappy," she said, wriggling to get down.

"No, not yet. He needs to see the doctor first. Just to check he's okay." Mary looked up at Janet. "Would you?"

Janet smiled and nodded. "Yes, of course. On my way home." Janet gathered her things and made for the front door.

"Thanks for looking after Susan."

"No problem." She gave Susan a cheery wave.

"Bye," Susan sang.

Janet pulled open the door to a deluge of rain.

"Janet, can Wash walk yet?"

Janet turned back, looking doubtful. "He can hobble about on crutches in the house. I doubt if he's up to going outside yet." She looked back at the rain. "And I'm not sure I want him to in this."

"Janet, please … ask him to come when the rain's stops. There's no one else. Joseph doesn't remember being Joe. If he remembers being Florian Fooks, he might remember Wash."

Janet nodded. "I'll ask him. It's not far. He should be able to manage if he takes it leisurely."

After the rain had passed, Wash crutched his way along to Mary's house and into the bedroom. He found Fooks struggling, with more success, to sit up.

"Wash?" Fooks queried, with a deep frown. "Washington Turner?"

"Ye-ah," Wash sighed when he sank into a chair by the bed and rested his crutches to one side. "So. You remember *me*?"

"Yeah." The silver star on Wash's waistcoat didn't escape his notice. "Always thought you'd go straight, eventually." Fooks widened his eyes. "And I see you have."

"Been sheriff here in Bronze Canyon these past eight years."

"What happened to you?" Fooks waved a hand at the crutches.

"Oh, fell off the porch roof while I was fixing it." Wash chuckled gently. "Ain't all plain sailing being law-abiding, y'know. As you're beginning to find out."

Fooks chewed his cheek. "Am I under arrest?" he asked. He spoke deliberate and nervous.

"Nope." Wash smiled. "What's the last thing you remember, Fooks?"

Fooks considered. "Robbing the 1st National in Sheridan. Tobias got stuck in the bars trying to get out." He couldn't resist the impish grin at the memory.

Wash leaned forward and put a hand on Fooks' arm. "Fooks. That was six years ago."

Fooks lost his grin. "No. That was...." He chewed his lip. Nothing afterwards came to mind. "Six?" He gasped. "Six years ago?"

"Yeah. Getting on for seven now I'd say," Wash said, pleasantly.

"Wash." Fooks said, scrabbling to get up in panic. "What's going on? I don't understand. Who was the woman? She said… she was my wife." He gulped, sinking back, realizing he wasn't going anywhere right now. "Have you ever heard anything so ridiculous?" He tried without success to smile.

Wash nodded. "When you were Florian Fooks, that *would* have been ridiculous." Then he added, with an amused expression, "but you ain't Florian Fooks. At least not anymore."

Fooks just stared at him.

Wash leaned forward. "You and Tobias came to me a few years back. You wanted to go straight, and you needed my help to do it."

Fooks laughed. "Tobe and me? No way."

"Well, you did. You've been living here in Bronze Canyon, Wyoming for the last four years."

Fooks stared at him in disbelief. "No," he said, shaking his head. "Why would we do such a thing? We're good at our job. Why would we give it all up?"

Wash smiled. "Because people like me are getting better at *our* jobs. Only a matter of time, Fooks, and you knew it."

"So, er…" Fooks cleared his throat and Wash reached to hand him a glass of water. It was cool, and it washed down the lump rising in his throat. "So, what do I do? Now I don't rob banks and trains anymore?"

"You live here, as Joseph Crane, where you own and run the hardware store. Mary is your wife and you have a little daughter, Susan."

Fooks blanched. "No," he said again, shaking his head. "I can't have." He rubbed his forehead. He felt sick.

Wash grinned ruefully. "You have a fine marriage, Fooks." He took back the glass before its contents spilled.

Fooks smacked his lips and focused on the ceiling when he found his eyes watering. It sounded idyllic, but it had hit a sore spot. A desire he kept firmly and deeply buried. That life just wasn't possible, being who he was. It could never happen. Now he was finding out it *had* happened, but he didn't remember.

He sniffed deeply. "Does … she … Mary know who …?"

"Yeah, Fooks she knows. Your silver tongue worked overtime to convince her you were serious 'bout giving up that life, but ya did. You're an honest man, Fooks." Wash smiled fondly. "You haven't proved her wrong 'bout trusting you yet."

Fooks looked stricken and rubbed his temple. "I don't remember," he breathed.

"You don't remember Mary at all?"

"No," Fooks wailed. He covered his face with his hands. "Wash, I don't recall any of it. It's like a … a wall in front of me. I know there's something behind it, but I can't get through it." He removed his hands, looking at Wash in anguish.

Wash winced. "Sorry to add to your woes, Fooks, but because of this," he indicated his splinted leg, "someone's coming to stand in for me. Ya know him. Jack Priestly. He arrived three days ago."

"What? Hell, I can't be here." He pushed aside the covers. He was getting up whether he felt like it or not. "Where are my clothes?" He appealed to Wash for help.

"Now hold on. Ya ain't going anywhere."

Fooks grunted a denial. He opened his mouth to speak when they heard a male voice outside the room. Wash said, "Sounds like the Doc has come to see you. Heads can be funny, so don't go rushing about. Just let him see to you before ya make any rash decisions. I reckon I better let him get in here." Wash collected his crutches, struggled up and started to the door.

"Say Wash, where's Tobe? The… Mary said he'd gone to Boston. What's he doing there?"

Wash smiled. "Tobias married the railroad heiress, Caroline Fairfield. They live in Boston. A story and a half by itself. They have an unconventional marriage, but he's doing all right. Starting a family too, by all accounts. You and Mary plan to go for a visit next Summer."

Fooks blinked. He put his head in his hands and groaned. He knew nothing of this. It was a nightmare, and his best friend wasn't even here to get him through it.

"It'll be all right, Fooks. Just take some time."

Wash laid a hand on Fooks' shoulder and gave it a reassuring shake.

CHAPTER FIVE

The doctor came, examined Fooks' head wound and checked the rest of him over. He'd seemed satisfied his physical injury was healing nicely but had offered nothing illuminating about his lack of memory. Although he promised to look the condition up and get back to him. Fooks, too overwrought with everything to press the point.

Early the next morning, Fooks woke feeling much stronger. He took himself off to explore the house. Finding the bathroom, he tended to his morning business, relieved he wouldn't have to endure the indignity of a bed pan anymore. That taken of, he looked in the mirror over the bathroom basin. Apart from the white bandage over his head, the face which looked back was him. Peering more closely, he saw fine lines and he frowned. *Don't remember them before.* He pulled at a tuft of brown hair. *Yep, still me.*

Coming out of the bathroom, he surveyed the living room. *So, this is my life now.*

The living room had an alcove, complete with an oversized desk. On it sat a typewriter. He had never seen one in a domestic setting. Fascinated by how it worked, Fooks idly pressed random keys. To his left, he recognized his own handwriting on a pile of papers. Absently he sat down to read.

He didn't understand what he read. It was a story of a gang of outlaws about to stop a train and rob it. Despite jumping about, making it confusing and difficult to read, things seemed to go okay. The events were familiar. Yet something felt wrong.

"That's not right."

He continued to read, hoping for answers. As he puzzled over the story, something brushed his leg.

Looking down, he saw a small girl in her nightgown, clutching a cloth rabbit. This must be Susan, his daughter. She had brown hair, lighter than his own, ruffled by sleep and gray eyes, the same as Mary.

"Pappy!" she cried, holding the cloth rabbit aloft by its long ears.

Fooks smiled. If he had any doubts, she was his daughter, the two dimples either side of her mouth cleared that up. Taking the rabbit, he studied it critically.

"Hmmm." Obviously much loved. He set it on the desk and smiled down at Susan. She giggled, grasping his thigh.

"Up, Pappy. Up."

Fooks hesitated. He had no experience of little children. How did you ...? Instinct told him how to pick Susan up. When she settled on his lap, she grabbed her toy and held it protectively. He laughed.

"I see Susan has found you," said Mary.

Fooks looked up. Mary hadn't bothered with a robe. While her nightgown wasn't exactly transparent, it showed enough to make him gasp. He swallowed hard, all too aware he wore just his underwear.

"Yes," he breathed. "What am I doing here?" His thumb rifled through the stack of handwritten sheets.

Mary smiled. "Oh, you're working on your next story for the newspaper. Craig... the newspaper editor, had the ones already published turned into a book for you." She went to the bookshelf by the kitchen door, searched for a moment, and then held out a book to him.

He took it with both hands, like a precious, fragile object. The gold lettering on the front said, 'Tales of an Outlaw, by Florian Fooks.' He stared at it in disbelief and then up at her.

"I think you are going to call the new story Train to Boulder," Mary said, indicating the manuscript. She stood close to him. He could smell her perfume. "This is your typewriter. Don't ask me how it works. You only got it a few days before your accident. You're still learning how to use it." Leaning over the desk highlighted her shape even more. He stared at her middle. She stopped. "What's the matter? Have you remembered something?"

His eyes rose slowly to her face, quizzically. "Are you …?" he began and swallowed hard, "expecting?"

She smiled and pressed her hands to her stomach. "Yes. You were sitting here, trying to work out how the typewriter worked when I told you." She laughed. "I don't know whether I annoyed you because I'd distracted you or delighted you because we are going to have another baby."

"I remember," he breathed.

"You do?" she asked hopefully.

"No, not exactly. I remember the feeling." He smiled weakly. "I think being delighted won out."

She smiled, blushing. "Yes, it did. We put Susan to bed early that night."

Fooks looked up at Mary and took her left hand. His thumb ran over the ring on her third finger. "I'm sorry I don't remember you. Or Susan." He shook his head. "I don't know how I could forget you. I'm so sorry," he said, sadly.

She touched his cheek. "It's not your fault. I'm sure your memory will come back. Perhaps reading your book will help. Doctor Albright is coming to see you again this morning. Later, if you're feeling up to it, we can walk around the town. There's no rush." She kissed his mouth softly.

There it was. An almost overwhelming desire to take her in his arms. It told him he cared for her and their child. Smiling down at Susan, he felt the wall separating him from them begin to loosen. He hoped spending time with them and reading his book might help him break through completely. Amazed when all of a sudden, he realized this was something he wanted to happen.

"I sent a telegram to Samuel... Tobias. He replied, saying Caroline was having a hard time with her pregnancy. He can't leave right now, but he'll try to get out soon."

Fooks frowned. "Who's Caroline?" *Some floozy, no doubt.*

"His wife. You've met her."

"His wife? Sheesh." Fooks blanched. "What's she like?"

"I don't know. You met her when you went to Boston recently."

Fooks growled, rested his elbows on the desk with his hands over his eyes. "I went to Boston?" He shook his head. "I don't remember."

"You can't expect everything to come back all at once." Mary rubbed his shoulders. "Dr. Albright said he'd look into your condition. Perhaps he'll have an idea which will help."

Fooks growled. "Let's hope so.

Fooks sat in the wing-back chair later that morning, waiting for Dr. Albright to arrive.

"How are you feeling, Joseph?" Dr. Albright asked when Mary let him in. Mary returned from closing the door to sit beside Fooks.

"Confused."

"To be expected." He put his doctor's bag down beside his patient. "Mind if I examine your head wound?"

Fooks shrugged. "Go ahead. That's something you *can* treat. Right?"

Dr. Albright leaned over to find the end of the bandage. "It's what I'm more used to treating that's true." Fooks winced when the doctor unwound the bandage and peered at the wound underneath. "Hmmm, seems to be healing well. Think I should leave this off now. Just don't go anywhere dusty. Try to keep it clean for the next week."

He stood back regarding Fooks, rolling up the bandage while he did so. "I've done some research into your condition. Want to hear what I've found out?"

Fooks indicated the sofa opposite.

"I believe it's called Focal Retrograde Amnesia." Dr. Albright tucked the bandage away in his bag. "As I understand it, you know your name, where you were born. You remember your childhood and early adult life. Is that correct?"

Fooks nodded, lips tightened into a thin line.

"But you don't remember anything from about six years ago?"

"That's right. I don't remember coming to Bronze Canyon. Or…" He reached for Mary's hand. "Or Mary." Mary rewarded him with a wan smile.

"You can remember what happened this morning?"

"Yes, I played with Susan." Fooks glanced at Mary for confirmation. She nodded, and he smiled back in relief.

"Makes sense. It means you can form short-term memories and you'll be able to learn new things."

"Not sure I want to learn *new* things, Doc. Quite like to remember the *old* things."

Dr. Albright smiled. "That could come in time. With retrograde amnesia, it's difficult to remember faces, names, places, dates and some things which happened during the time you've lost. It *can* come back, Joseph. I can't promise, of course. Or tell you how long. Talking to people about events, sight of something familiar, a happening which triggers a memory. You may not get everything back, but most should return. Enough for you to function in the here and now."

"But why six years though? Seems such a random amount. Why not everything?"

Dr. Albright pursed his lips. "That's a reasonable question. The fact is, there is so much we don't know about how the brain works. Did something happen to you six years ago? Something traumatic perhaps?"

Fooks shook his head. "I don't know."

"Who would know, Joe?" Mary asked. "Wash?"

"Possibly. I can ask him, I suppose."

After Albright left, Fooks sat, tapping his fist against his lips, deep in thought. Mary returned to the sofa and watched.

"It doesn't sound too bad," she said, trying to be positive.

"Maybe not for you. There's so many things I want to know and neither you nor anyone in this town can tell me," he said bitterly. *And I've Priestly to worry about as well. The sooner I'm clear headed the better.*

He shook his head. "Are you sure Swan couldn't come? He's the only person who can tell me if anything happened to me six ..." He continued in a shaky voice. "Six years ago. And other things I want to know."

"What is it you want to know?"

"Why we gave up being outlaws? What happened? Whose idea, was it? Why did we choose to come here to Bronze Canyon?" Fooks put a hand to his forehead. "I need to know all these things before..."

"Before what?"

Fooks gazed at her. "Before I can get on with my life." He swallowed hard. "Please, will you telegram Swan again?"

Swan paced in his suite at Ardmaddy. He had a dilemma. He held a telegram from Mary Crane. It had arrived a short time ago, causing him to worry.

Yet through the connecting door that led to his wife's suite, came the muffled sounds of a woman in childbirth. The cries cut through him. Had done since early this morning and it was now evening. *There must be something wrong, surely? Did it usually take this long?*

He ran his hand through his hair, anxious to know the outcome and also in concern about the pain he'd caused his wife.

He came to a halt and smoothed the crumpled paper. Reading the few words again, he tried to glean more information from them than the simple words.

Joseph hurt in accident more than first thought. Lost memory. Urgent you come.

This was the second telegram from Mary. It must be serious. Swan had so many questions. What sort of accident? How badly hurt? What did lost memory mean?

From next door came a loud wail. How could he leave at a time like this?

Swan continued pacing. What would Fooks do? Fooks had said he'd left when Mary neared her time. Leaving to help their former associates, Brad and Sid overcome a murder charge. What did Fooks say? He'd missed his daughter's birth. Well, that wasn't going to happen to him. His son or daughter was being born right now.

But then what? He couldn't leave right away. Caroline would need him. What if there was a problem? With either the baby or Caroline? Small babies die suddenly. So do mothers. Swan shook his head. No. Decision made.

He came to a stop again. "Sorry Fooks, I know ya need me, but I can't leave right off." He took a deep breath. "Cowdry!"

Swan's valet appeared from the dressing room, where he expected him to be.

"Yes, sir?"

Swan swallowed. "Need to send a telegram, Paul. Urgent. Will you take it, please? It's kinda personal."

"Yes, of course, sir."

Swan nodded and moved to his secretariat. "Okay. Thanks. Give me a few minutes, so hang around." He sat down and reached for a sheet of paper. Hand on forehead, he wrote something, scribbled it out and began again. He tried several times until satisfied with the result. "Here. The last one."

Cowdry took it as the sound of an infant's cry came from the next door. Swan and Cowdry swapped glances, the former halfway to his feet.

"Congratulations, sir," Cowdry said, with a beam.

Swan returned to his seat with a bump. "Um. Wow."

It felt like hours before the connecting door opened. A smiling doctor stood there, wiping his hands.

"Mr. Martin, would you like to see your wife and son?"

CHAPTER SIX

Fooks felt a hand on his shoulder and it squeezed. He sat slumped in the wing-backed chair at home, one hand over his face, the other held a crumpled telegram. He'd been sitting, lost in thought, for over an hour.

"Are you okay?" Mary asked, moving around his chair to sit beside him.

When Mary gently pulled the hand away from his face, he sighed.

"Yeah, I guess," he said in a tired voice. He looked down and straightened out the telegram. "I'd hoped he'd come y'know." His bottom lip trembled.

"I know." Mary gave his arm a reassuring shake. She teased the telegram from his hand and read it. "He has a boy. I always thought he'd have daughters."

Both their eyes strayed to Susan playing on the rug in front of the unlit fire.

"Guess he dodged a bullet there," Fooks said, with a faint smile.

Mary laughed. "She's not that bad," she whispered, leaning in. "Maybe we'll have two by the end of the year."

Fooks sniffed and looked at her with interest. *Here's a question I should know.* "Do you have siblings?"

Mary shook her head. "No. I think Papa was away too much."

"Tobias is the closest thing I have to a brother. Closest thing to any kinda family I got left." He paused. "Until I met you, I guess."

"You don't talk about your parents or your childhood."

Fooks looked down. "There's a reason why."

Mary leaned in. "Tell me. It might help."

"I doubt it."

"Talking might trigger something."

He ran his fingers through his hair, wincing when they brushed a sensitive spot. Seeing her determined face, he tilted his head to one side. "Perhaps."

He sat for a long while staring at a spot on the floor and then he began. "I lost my folks during the War. Fighting hadn't really impacted Kirby. One day, my parents were coming back from town. Deserting soldiers took pot shots at them. Killed my Pa right off." His tongue explored his cheek. "Ma wasn't so lucky. They used her cruelly afore they killed her."

Mary gasped. He looked away, smacking his lips.

"Tobias' folks had died the year before of smallpox and my folks took him in. My Pa was the headmaster of a prestigious boy's school. The first one in Nebraska. The school had closed 'cos of the War, but the trustees allowed us to stay. It was our home. And now I didn't have one." He idly picked at the seam of his pants. "I guess that's why…" He smiled at Susan, and then scanned around until he met Mary's face. "I'm happy here. I know I'm happy here." Fumbling for her hand, he added, "With you. And Sue."

The child looked up at the mention of her name and gave him a hard look. Mary laughed. "She doesn't like her name shortened."

"Really?" he grinned; glad his mood was lightening. Mary nodded, and he patted her hand. "I'll try and remember. I'll add it to the list." He looked far away. "It's becoming a long, long list." Then he rallied. "Tomorrow, will you take me to The Hardware Store? I oughta see how I'm making my living now."

The next day, Fooks and Mary stood on the boardwalk outside The Hardware Store just before it closed for the day. Conscious of Priestly at large, Fooks had wanted to wait until just before closing.

So, this is what I'm doing with this new life.

An odd collection of goods stood outside The Hardware Store. Brooms and tools in barrels, tin baths, watering cans, buckets, wooden crates containing jars and bottles. Lanterns hung from hooks above the boardwalk. Baskets, washboards and thick coils of rope hung from nails on the wall. Outside cluttered, difficult to reach the door. *Must speak to someone about that. Customers need to get in.*

"So, this is it, huh?" Fooks, arms akimbo, regarding The Hardware Store, critically. My life now. Sheesh.

"It looks a mess, but it's tidier inside. Let's go in," Mary said, pushing down on the door handle.

Fooks entered slowly, and stared around in awe at the Aladdin's cave inside. Counters ran either side of the store in front of wooden and glass display cabinets. Step ladders leaned in the corner for access to the higher shelves. He wasn't sure what all the things were, but he supposed he must know. *Must be in there somewhere.*

At the back, a boy stood behind a further shorter counter. Mary acknowledged him when she walked in. He returned a nod and a brief smile, but his eyes didn't leave Fooks.

"This is Ted," Mary said.

Fooks grunted. He continued to scan around the store. In front of Ted stood a scale, with its big pan for weighing out nails. On the back wall behind him were rows and rows of miniature drawers, all labeled with their contents. To the left, a door.

Fooks looked up. A collection of lamps, hung from the ceiling, some more ornate than others. Everywhere stacked with something. At first glance, a cluttered mess, but on closer inspection, an organized assemblage grouped by use. Household, decoration and handyman. "Guess I sell just about anything you can think of."

"Yes. Just about."

He felt Mary's eyes on him as he moved behind the back counter. Ted moved out of his way. Fooks ran his hand thoughtfully over the surface, feeling the grain of the well-worn wood. It felt familiar and comforting. He pulled out a drawer, labeled two-inch screws, and nodded. Two-inch screws were what it contained. He shut the drawer with a slam and moved on to the door.

"What's through here?"

"The warehouse," Ted said. "I'll show you." He led the way.

Fooks turned to Mary. "Is this where I had my accident?"

"Yes." Mary joined him at the door and her light touch on his back nudged him forward when he didn't move.

The warehouse, although not huge, towered to double height. An office stood to his left. It had no door, and its glass window looked out into the warehouse. Inside, he could make out a desk with a hefty leather-bound ledger and a stack of supplier catalogs, a chair and a filing cabinet. An older boy rose to his feet. Fooks stood in the doorway, his eyes straying immediately to the small safe in the far corner.

"This is Russ, Joe."

Fooks' eyes shifted to Russ and he nodded. "Any problems while I've been ... away?"

Russ grinned. "Nothing I couldn't handle." Then he sobered under Fooks' stern gaze. "Everything is running fine. I'm getting the paperwork up to date."

"Good." He noted the paperwork on spikes or hooks. Everything appeared tidy and organized. *'Course it is, it's my office.* "I'll try and get in tomorrow."

With another nod to Russ, Fooks turned to inspect the warehouse, craning his neck up to the ceiling. Here were rows of racking holding tins of paint in every imaginable color and size, oil and varnish. Coils of barbed wire, tarps in neat folded piles, animal traps. On top were lengths of lumber. *How do I get them down?* The pair of ladders to one side might provide the solution. *Risky though.* The warehouse contained everything needed for gardening, farming and ranching.

Ted hovered in the background until the tinkling bell from the store announced the arrival of a customer. He sped off.

"Over here."

Fooks followed Mary to a section of racking, bare of items. On the wooden floor below, clear evidence of blood.

"This section came down and fell on you."

He shook his head. "Not quite," he murmured.

"What do you mean?"

"I was climbing. Up there." He gestured to the top. "I fell. Pulled the racking away as I came down."

"You remember? Oh Joe, that's wonderful."

"I was stupid." He shook his head in disgust, wincing. "I've seen enough. Can we go home now?"

He walked away without a backward glance.

CHAPTER SEVEN

Fooks was determined to accept his new life. He'd realized almost immediately he had a decent thing going here in Bronze Canyon. Given the amount of time elapsed since his last clear memories, he doubted he could return to the life he knew. He felt a moment's regret. *Sure had some good times.*

All he had to do was get to grips with being Joseph Crane. He found it a bit easier the more he thought on it. Still felt odd though that he, Florian Fooks, genius master criminal, should have settled for something so mundane as a shopkeeper. Ah, but it wasn't so unthinkable. Made such a perfect disguise. *Sure gonna miss it, but this is me now. Let's get on with it.*

Nearing the end of his first week at store owning, one morning he took the back way along to The Hardware Store. Although anxious not to run into Jack Priestly, today he walked with a jaunty, happy stride. The sun shone and not too hot. He had a newspaper to read and a job to go to. A fine day to be alive. And free. *Free? Wow, that's a thought.*

The Hardware Store stood in the middle of a row of three. Going in through the warehouse was a possibility, but the rear door looked shut. *Yeah, so I'm a little late today. Those boys shoulda unlocked it by now.* No choice but to go around to the front and risk Priestly spotting him. Reaching the end of the alley, he edged cautiously out. *Sheesh, I look suspicious.* Not too many people about. *Have to risk it.*

He arrived at the door of the store and stopped. A man leaned against the wall outside, idly kicking mud from his boot against his woodwork.

"D'you mind?" Fooks said, sarcastically and with a deep frown of disgust. The answering glare at first one of hostility before the fella, with some reticence moved away.

Fooks watched him for a moment as he sauntered further down the boardwalk. He was just about to enter the store when the fella paused, lingering outside The General Store, and glanced across the street. Fooks followed his gaze to another man standing on the corner. This man with reluctance, speedily diverted his attention elsewhere.

Fooks narrowed his eyes. He could spot suspicious behavior when he saw it. *Why are they acting that way? What are they up to?* All of a sudden, they became more furtive. Fooks scanned around to see why. Coming towards them down the street was the deputy. Wash had told him about him, his name Bart Harker, smiling and tipping his hat politely at passing ladies. Bart sported his deputy's badge. The two men turned away abruptly, avoiding his eye line, and pulling their hats down low.

Fooks chewed his lip, casting around, seeking some explanation. Further down the street, another two men stood by six horses. He stared more closely. The reins were looped loosely over the hitching rail. *All right, I guess I know what you're up to.*

"Morning, Joseph," Bart said with a grin.

"Yeah, morning. You must be deputy Bart. Wash told me about you. Got time to step in for a moment? Something to show you."

"Doing m'rounds—" Fooks took his arm and forcefully propelled him into the store. "Well, okay if ya insist."

Once in and the door shut, Fooks turned to him abruptly. "Listen, Bart, the bank's about to be robbed."

"What?"

"Duck out back and get Priestly. Quickly."

"How d'ya...?"

"There's no time to answer questions. Do as I say." Fooks slapped him on the back and pushed him towards the back of the store.

Although not the brightest, Bart recognized the urgency in Fooks' voice. He nodded and went off as directed.

Fooks remained at the door, keeping to one side but watching the street.

"What's going on, Mr. Crane?" Ted asked, moving around the customer side of the counter.

"Keep back, Ted."

Fooks felt around under the counter. Instinct told him, or a surfacing memory, that a concealed drawer lurked there. In it he found his Schofield and a box of ammunition. For a second, he wondered why they were there, but then he realized. Having a gun in the house with an inquisitive child wasn't a sensible idea. The store, a much better place to keep it. *Good thinking, Joseph Crane. Exactly what I would do.*

He fumbled to load the gun in his haste, spun the cylinder, and pulled back the hammer. He cracked the door and took up a watching position again.

Russ appeared from the back. "What's going on? I just seen Bart..."

Russ stopped at Fooks' frantic wave to be quiet. He looked at an anxious Ted for answers. Ted shrugged.

It happened fast. One minute, the street was quiet and normal. The next all hell broke loose. Cries of alarm, shouts of protest, running feet, horses whinnying. Fooks dashed out. The first of two men exited the bank opposite. Sheriff Priestly and Bart ran down the street, intent on blocking the robbers' escape.

The two men holding the horses mounted up and dragged the other four horses, intercepting the robbers, right in front of where Fooks stood. *Well, this is a first.*

"Wouldn't if I were you," he yelled at them.

"You ain't my mother," came the reply from the first.

In answer, Fooks fired a shot into the air.

The first robber's foot found a stirrup, but the noise of the shot spooked the horse and it bucked around, forcing him to hop after it. He executed an undignified roll onto the animal and kicked him forward into a full gallop. The two already mounted men tore after him.

Behind them, the other robber carried a bulging canvas bag. The two watchers joined him. They located their horses and performed similar dances.

Sheesh, I'm gonna have to shoot someone here. Hope my aim is true. Fooks made his decision. He fired at the man carrying the loot. Hit him in the shoulder and nicked the horse's neck as the bullet continued on its way. The man tried to get on, but the horse streaked away, galloping up the street after its stable mates.

With a hand clasped to his shoulder, the man attempted to juggle the haul and simultaneously get on another horse. When that failed, he tossed the bag to one of his accomplices and held his hand outstretched, expecting a lift up.

"Thanks, Petey. Be seeing ya."

The rider sped away, only to have his mount shot from under him. He landed with a thud and lay still.

The left behind robber, Petey, cursed, and tried to run, one hand holding his injured shoulder.

"Nope," said Fooks, leveling his gun at him. "Suggest you give up now."

Resigned, Petey stopped and raised his hands, one higher than the other.

Down the street, Bart checked on the fallen rider and shook his head. Priestly moved forward and grabbed the reins of the last robber's mount. A risky move. The horse reared and bucked. The robber tried to pull out his gun, but the horse's movements made it hard to do. Priestly seized the opportunity. He shot the robber's hand. Priestly yanked the panicked animal under control, pulling the reins from the man's bloody grasp.

"Okay, get on down son."

The robber faltered.

"Do it before I shoot ya outta the saddle."

The man gulped and kicked free of the stirrups. He dropped to the ground, nursing his injured hand.

"I've got the money, sheriff," said Bart, running up, holding aloft the canvas bag, only to trip over his own feet, staggering before righting himself.

Fooks allowed himself a brief smile when he saw Priestly roll his eyes. Now he had a problem. When Priestly saw him...

"You!"

CHAPTER EIGHT

Okay, let's go along with this for now.

Fooks dropped his gun to the ground and kicked it away. He raised his hands. Priestly grinned before gesturing that Fooks should walk in front of him. Fooks kept his hands high as Priestly marched him at gunpoint along to the jail. Out of the corner of his eye, Fooks saw Mary standing at the door of The Hat Shop, holding Susan, watching on anxiously. By her side stood her assistant, clutching at Mary's arm.

"Pa-Pee," Susan squealed, reaching out a hand to her father.

All Fooks could do for them was offer a weak smile of reassurance before stepping up onto the boardwalk. He paused for a moment for Priestly to open the door. With a final look back over his shoulder, he took a deep breath and entered the jail.

Inside, Priestly accepted the money bag from Bart before gesturing to the larger of the two cells. Three townsmen had rounded up the two injured bank robbers, now subdued and compliant, and were bringing them in.

Fooks stood to one side while they were herded into the big cell. Bart stood ready to lock the cell door.

"Thanks gentlemen. Buy you a drink in the saloon later."

With a nod to Priestly and a confused look at Fooks, the good Samaritans left.

"Get the doc sheriff, I can't feel my arm," one of the robbers complained.

Priestly snapped. "Yeah, yeah, I'll get him. Soon as I get this one under lock and key." He waved his gun at Fooks. "In."

"I just helped you stop a robbery," Fooks told him. "I wasn't part of it."

"We'll sort out the details later. Now in."

Fooks glared at him hard, before huffing, and turned to walk into the smaller cell. Bart delayed locking the door.

"What's going on sheriff? Why have you arrested Joseph?" Bart asked, confusion wrinkling his brow. "He helped stop the robbers from getting away."

"Go get the doc Bart. Before those two shed any more blood over my nice clean cell. And be quick about it. *You* get to clear up what they spill."

Bart looked at Fooks for answers.

Fooks sat on the bunk, leaning forward, elbows on thighs, rubbing his thumbs. "Do as he says Bart," he said, in a murmur. *How am I gonna get out of this one?* He shook his head, working his jaw as he thought. *And Mary and Susan saw. Damn.*

Bart hesitated before making for the door.

"The keys!"

Bart stopped, realizing he still held them in his hand. "Sorry sheriff," he said, slapping the big key ring into Priestly's hand.

Priestly dropped them onto his desk. He holstered his gun before walking forward. Stopping out of arm's length from the bars and regarded Fooks.

"Well, well, well. At long last you're finally where you belong Fooks."

Fooks kept his face expressionless. He wasn't about to give Priestly the satisfaction of knowing just how much his stomach churned.

"Did he jus' call him Fooks?" one of the injured men said to the other.

"I dunno." The other gasped, shaking his head. "I hurt Davis."

"Yeah, so do I. He did. I swear he called him Fooks. Can only mean one man Petey. Florian Fooks. Whoo hee. In the same jail as you an' me. Now that's something to tell. Ain't it Petey?"

"If you say so," Petey said, with a groan, rolling onto his back on the cot, clutching his bleeding arm.

Fooks and Priestly continued to glare at each other.

"You're making a mistake Sheriff. I'm not who you think I am. Ask Wash." Fooks swallowed hard. Asking Wash was risky. Wash had agreed to him being here in Bronze Canyon, but he never said he'd lie for him. If Priestly spoke to Wash, he'd be in a difficult, if not impossible, position.

"We'll see," Priestly said, before turning away. "Right now, ya causing me a lot of paperwork, so I ain't about to do ya no favors Fooks."

Fooks rolled his eyes. *Sheesh, save me from lawmen looking to make a name for themselves. They're the worst kind.* Then devilment took him. "Open up this here cage and there won't be no paperwork."

Priestly sat behind the desk glowering at him. "Shut up Fooks."

Fooks lay down on the bunk and put his arms behind his head. "Only thinking of you sheriff. Got your best interests at heart."

"I don't wanna hear another word outta you."

Fooks nodded and closed his eyes. He had a lot of thinking to do.

As soon as Fooks and Priestly disappeared inside the jail, Mary turned to her assistant and thrust Susan into her arms. "Look after Sue."

Mary hitched her skirts and took off at an unladylike run towards Wash's house. She didn't know if he could do anything, but he needed to know. With a bit of luck, her father might also be there. Nothing like the habits of long in the tooth retired men. Luke would come along at eleven and bring Wash up to date about anything going on in the town. In the main just gossip, but Wash, feeling isolated, welcomed the visits.

"Wash! Papa!" Mary ran around the back of the house and there they both were. Sitting on the porch, laughing as they sipped their coffee.

When Mary leaped up the step onto the porch, Luke rose to his feet, coffee cup in hand.

"Mary, what on blue blazes is wrong?"

She stood for a moment, taking deep breaths, a hand pressed to her stomach. *Hope I haven't hurt the baby*. She allowed Luke to take her arm and lower her into a seat. He handed her a glass of water.

"It's Joe. Sheriff Priestly's arrested him," she managed to blurt out between gulps of air and swallows of water.

Luke and Wash swapped glances.

"What happened?"

Mary shook her head. "I don't know precisely. Some men tried to rob the bank. Joe helped stop them. Sheriff Priestly—"

"Does he think Fooks was one of them?" Wash asked.

"I don't think so." She sniffed and wiped a hand under her nose. "I think... I think he recognized him." She bent over and sobbed into her hands.

Luke put a hand on her back. "Oh, Mary I'm sorry."

"Now we don't know for sure that's what it was," Wash began, as running feet sounded along the side of the house.

"Sheriff! Sheriff!"

"Round the back Bart." Wash rolled his eyes at Luke Fletcher.

Deputy Bart was a solid kid and willing to do most things asked. Just not too bright thinking for himself. Wash, the sentimental man he wouldn't admit to being, kept Bart on. He also knew he could call on Luke if a real crisis came up. As the former sheriff of Bronze Canyon, Luke Fletcher was the ideal man to turn to for help. However, he despaired of Bart and never missed an opportunity to urge Wash to find someone else.

Bart appeared on the back porch.

"Sheriff, I ran all the way," Bart panted. "Ya gotta come."

"Bart, I'm not going anywhere." Wash pointed at his splinted leg, resting on a box.

"Oh, yeah, sorry, forgot." Bart gave a nod at the leg, bit his lip at Luke, then tipped his hat at Mary. "Ma'am." Then hopping from foot to foot, he continued in a rush, "It's Joseph. Sheriff Priestly's locked him up."

"Calm down and tell us exactly what happened. Mary says someone tried to rob the bank."

"Robbers tried to. We stopped 'em. Me and the sheriff. Got two of 'em locked up. And we got the money." Bart flashed a pleased look, then sobered.

"Whoa up there Bart. Start at the beginning."

Bart gabbled out the story of the foiled bank robbery, interrupted by Wash and Luke wanting to clarify a particular point.

"Then Sheriff Priestly saw Joseph, said 'you' and arrested him. I dunno who he thinks Joseph is, but he seems pretty certain. I mean Joseph's Joseph, isn't he?" Bart hopped from foot to foot. The two men swapped glances.

"Yes Bart," said Mary vehemently. "Joseph is Joseph."

Luke levered to his feet. "I'll go. I made myself known to Priestly a few days ago. He knows who I was. See if I can't sort this out."

Wash flashed him a weak smile. Mary twisted in her seat. "Papa, what can you do?"

Luke looked thoughtful. "I have an idea. Might work. Might not." He smiled. "Won't know unless I give it a try, will I?" He placed a reassuring hand on Mary's shoulder as he passed.

"Come on Bart. Let's get on back to the jail."

When Bart and Luke reached the sheriff's office, Doctor Albright was already treating the prisoners for their injuries. Priestly stood guard outside the door of their cell, just in case they attempted to overpower the good doctor.

Priestly scowled at Bart. "'Bout time ya got back here. Where have ya been all this time?"

Luke stepped forward with a raised hand. "My fault Sheriff. He ran into me and told me what happened," Luke said. He gestured to the cell containing Fooks. "Why have you arrested him? He wasn't part of it."

Priestly grinned. "Nope, but he is a bank robber. The worst kind. The successful kind. Law's been looking for him for years. Sizable reward too. This capture will make headline news." He chuckled. "Can hardly believe it."

"He's my son-in-law."

"Ya son-in-law?" Priestly's eyes popped. "He's—"

"Joseph Crane. He owns The Hardware Store. Married to my daughter Mary."

Priestly laughed. "Then you've had the wool pulled over ya eyes big time. He's Florian Fooks, the despicable leader of the Guardian Wall Gang." Priestly drew himself up and smiled smugly. "Wanted dead or alive and now locked up tight as a drum in my jail. What d'ya think to that?"

Luke stepped closer. "I think me an' you need to talk." He glanced at the occupied cells and Bart. "Step outside Sheriff." It was an order, not a request, and Priestly protested. "Now." Luke's tone brooked no argument.

Priestly reluctantly followed Luke out and around the corner of the building into the alley. Luke glanced up to check the position of the sun. *Don't want the sun in my eyes. Don't mind in Priestly's though.*

"Ya ain't telling me I'm wrong," Priestly started, in his defense. He crossed his arms. "I know he's Florian Fooks."

"Joseph Crane," Luke emphasized the name, "has lived quietly here in Bronze Canyon for the past four years." *Probably best not to actually* acknowledge *that he* is *Florian Fooks.*

"What? Does Turner know?"

"Yes. Turner knows."

"Then I'll have his badge." Priestley's outrage, muted somewhat by tugging on the brim of his Stetson to shield his face from the sun. "He should have locked him up. Florian Fooks is the biggest crook this side of the Mississippi."

Seeing Priestly was working himself up. "Just a minute Priestly." Luke snagged the man's arm as he walked away. "Joseph Crane is a model citizen. No trouble."

"Don't matter. You of all people, should know I can still arrest him. Wyoming doesn't have any statute of limitations."

Luke nodded. "Joseph Crane likes Wyoming. Livin' here quietly, mindin' his own business. He's built a life here for himself. A devoted family man. I can't fault him, Priestly." Then seeing there was nothing for it, Luke pressed on. "Perhaps he has done some bad things in the past, but everyman deserves a second chance and I'm supportin' him."

"He'll get a second chance after he's served his time in prison."

Priestly walked away, but Luke caught his arm again. "Now listen Priestly. If ya do, you'll destroy my daughter's life, and I'm not about to let ya do that."

Priestly squared up to Luke. "And how are ya gonna stop me?"

"I'm appealin' to ya sense of fair play. Joseph's lived a straight life for four years. He oughta get some credit."

"Then he can take his chances in court. Maybe the judge'll take it into account."

Now Priestly walked away, tipping his hat to a passer-by when he emerged from the alley. Luke watched him for a moment before following him back into the jail.

CHAPTER NINE

This could be interesting. That's Mary's pa. Wonder what he thinks he can do?

Fooks looked up as Luke and Priestly returned to the jail. He met Luke's eye with a question. Luke nodded. He waited until Bart had shown Dr. Albright out, before turning to face Priestly. "Supposin' there was a way to resolve this," Luke said, talking to Priestly but keeping his eyes on Fooks.

The two injured captives in the next cell lay prone on their bunks. Albright had given both something for pain and they were out of it.

"Resolve this?" Priestly barked, spinning around. "There's nothing to resolve. He's going to prison. That'll resolve this."

Luke stepped forward, a finger to his lips. "If there was somethin' he can do for you, wouldn't that change your mind about sendin' him to prison?"

Priestly narrowed his eyes. "What are you getting at Fletcher?"

Luke turned to Bart, who stood hovering by the desk. "Give us a moment, Bart. Time to do ya rounds. Make sure everythin' is locked up tight."

"Now just a minute Fletcher." Priestly protested. "Ya can't order my deputy about."

"On ya way, Bart."

"Yessir."

Bart stumbled out.

Fooks raised an eyebrow, pursed his lips and nodded. *Okay so the old man's got some clout.*

When the door shut behind Bart, Luke turned back to Priestly. "Figure ya wouldn't want him hearin' what I'm about to propose."

"Okay, what ya got?" Priestly folded his arms.

In his cell, Fooks moved to the bars, intrigued. *Does concern me so reckon I've a right to listen.*

"Heard tell ya brother was murdered in a bank heist not too long ago. Seems to me it's takin' a toll on ya. Not thinkin' straight." Fooks' knuckles tightened around the bars watching Luke continue to talk with Priestly. "If he can find out who done it an' perhaps bring those responsible to justice, now wouldn't that be worth somethin' to ya?"

Priestly chewed his bottom lip. His eyes flicked from Luke to Fooks and back again. "Sheriff at Mudwater Flats, Dakota Territory, suspected the Smedley Gang but dismissed them, as it didn't seem likely. They don't as a rule range that far north." He shook his head. "Done no robberies in that part of the territory previously. No reason for them to start now."

Fooks lifted his head in interest. *A mystery. I like mysteries.*

Priestly stared at a spot on the floor. "Sure, I want the men who done killed Arnold. Put up some of the reward money myself." Then his eyes widened in realization. "But I'm not prepared to let *him* go to find out."

"He's probably the only one who can confirm if it was the Smedley Gang." Fooks rolled his eyes. Luke ignored him, continuing with, "there's a network of thieves, ya know. Gossip. Hearsay. A word here, a word there. A man of *his* reputation and place in the hierarchy, he'll find out without too much trouble."

Priestly bit his lip, considering. "You can do it?" The question to Fooks, brusque.

Fooks shrugged. "Nothing to lose. Can give it a go. If," He gave Luke a meaningful nod. "If I get something in return."

Luke gave a slight nod and turned to Priestly. "Y'all forget 'bout him livin' quietly here in Bronze Canyon. Out of the way. Doing no harm to anyone—"

Priestly raised a hand to get Luke to stop. "Okay. I get the message. He's reformed."

Fooks winced, dropped his head, and smirked. *We'll see about that.*

Priestly raised his chin. "If I let him go, he can just ride off and we'll never see him again. I'm not about to take that chance."

Luke nodded. "He won't." He gave Fooks a hard stare. "I can guarantee it."

"How?" Priestly demanded.

Yeah, how?

"I told ya he has a wife and a child." Now Luke sucked his teeth. "He'll not abandon them."

Fooks false smiled at Priestly when he stared at him.

"What gives ya that idea?"

"Because I'll be goin' with him to make sure he comes back to her."

Fooks stiffened. *Hell no.*

Priestly said he needed some air. Taking the cell keys with him, he left Fooks and Luke to talk.

Fooks chuckled. He stood facing Luke, bars in between them. "He don't trust you."

Luke grunted. "Man's under stress. Don't blame him."

Fooks grunted. "I kinda do for putting me in here." He rattled the bars of his cell in emphasis. He frowned. "How come he even listened to you? Who are you?"

Luke stroked his chin and smiled ruefully. "Guess Mary forgot to tell ya, I used to be a U.S. Marshall afore I retired ten years ago." He chortled when Fooks swallowed hard.

Sheesh.

Fooks shook his head and cleared his throat. "What's this deal you've pitched to him?"

"I had to offer him somethin'. Seems to me this is somethin' ya can do without too much bother, an' he'll be obligated to ya."

"Yeah, but you're forgetting. Apparently, I haven't been an outlaw for six years," Fooks said, doubtfully, then widened his eyes. "I'm out of the loop."

Luke gave a rare grin. "Somehow I think you'll manage."

Fooks scowled. "How well do you know him?"

"Personally? Not at all. By reputation? A little."

"You're not filling me with confidence here." Fooks turned away from the bars.

Luke watched him pace the six steps down the length of the cell beside the low bunk.

"Would ya rather spend ten years in prison? 'Cos that's your choice. Priestly isn't gonna just let ya go."

Fooks about turned. "No, I don't wanna go to prison." His face lightened hopefully. "You could break me out?"

Luke, glaring at him, gave him the answer.

Fooks turned away again with a sigh. Then he stopped and said, over his shoulder, "Say I agree to what you're proposing and he lets me out. How can you be sure I won't just get the drop on you?"

"Like I told him, ya won't abandon your wife and child."

"Sure of that, are you?"

"The man I know wouldn't."

Fooks stalked back to the bars. "Yeah, but I'm not the man you know."

Luke drew himself up. "Reckon deep down inside, ya still are."

Fooks scowled. "You're putting an awful lot of faith in me, old man."

Luke faced Fooks through the bars. "I may be old now, but I was a lawman for a lot of years. I learned how to judge a man. Figger I haven't lost the skill."

Fooks nodded. "Are you up for this? Dakota is a long way from here. I'll be riding hard and fast." Before Luke could answer, he went on. "I'm bound to do and say things you as a former lawman might find, shall we say, questionable?"

"My concern is for my daughter. Mary took a chance on you and so far, ya ain't let her down. And you're not gonna, are ya? Especially now she's in a delicate condition again."

Fooks rubbed his cheek. "A different man is responsible for that," he said, quietly.

Luke took a step closer to the bars. "No. It's the same man. Just a different guise is all. Look, this mess ya in isn't your fault, but only you can fix it. My plan offers you a chance to do that. Priestly might just go for it if I go along with you. He knows my reputation." Luke paused. "Knows I'm not easy to lose. Plenty tried. Not many succeeded."

"Your reputation is ten year's outta date."

Luke sniffed. "Fine. It's your decision." He walked away. "Good luck in prison."

Fooks glowered. Then rolling his eyes ceiling wards, he called Luke back.

"Wait up."

Luke had reached the door. Now he turned, one hand on the door handle.

"If Priestly agrees, I'll try what you suggest." When Luke walked back, Fooks added, "But you aren't coming with me."

Luke straightened and came back. "Way I see it; Priestly won't allow ya to go alone. You'll need someone with you." Luke looked thoughtful. "He could go with ya himself, of course, but he'd havta resign. I doubt if he'll head out on his own. If he was goin' to, he'da done it afore he took this job. 'Sides, he'd lose out on all the plaudits from capturin' you. Even if he was prepared to forgo that, either way would leave Wash in a fix. Bronze Canyon might jus' get someone else. Someone I can't do a deal with to get ya outta there." Luke considered. "The choice is yours Fooks. Me or him?"

Fooks raised his chin. "What if I took Bart?"

Luke laughed. "Ya really wanna spend weeks alone with Bart?"

Fooks stared at him, then puffed. The hapless deputy tried hard, but not someone you wanted to rely on. "No, I guess not."

"Listen Fooks, ya're a clever man. I'm proposin' a way outta this mess you find yaself in. I'm not that bad a fella, y'know and there might be situations where y'all need a retired U.S. Marshall." He glanced sideways when the street door opened. Fooks stiffened. Priestly. "What's it gonna be?"

Fooks glowered. "You're not really giving me much of a choice, are you?"

Luke smirked. "Nope."

Priestly stood for a long while in the middle of the jail. First looking at Luke, who had taken a seat expectantly, and then at Fooks, who had laid down on his bunk, hands behind his head. Fooks feigned indifference to the conversation which would determine his fate.

Priestly moved to stand behind his desk. "All right Fletcher, you've got a deal, but I have some conditions of my own."

Luke straightened. "All right. Name 'em."

Priestly's back was to the cells, and he glanced over his shoulder towards Fooks. Turning back to Luke, he hesitated. Then he straightened. "All right, ya go with him, but here's the thing. Like ya say, there's a camaraderie amongst thieves. If it is the Smedley Gang, or whoever, I want Fooks to go after them and bring 'em in. I figger they've spent the money by now, but if there's any left, bring it back."

On his bunk, Fooks pursed his lips. *Okay, I'll see what I can do. I'm not putting my life at risk, but the money might come in handy.*

Luke glowered. "The men ya want are killers Priestly. Fooks and me could get--"

At which point, one of the bank robbers gave out a loud snore. The other, roused some, let out a groan. Fooks scowled. He'd prefer it if they weren't aware of this conversation. When the snoring increased and became in stereo, he nodded. Both appeared to be asleep. *Great, here's me, hoping to get some shuteye.*

Priestly laughed at Fooks' disgusted face. "Yeah, save me a dilemma, won't it?" Then he sobered and shrugged. "Real sorry if you stop a bullet, Fletcher. You were a good lawman, but in doing this, you've hitched ya horse to his wagon. Take it or leave it. No skin off my nose. I'm happy with the kudos from capturing one of the biggest thorns in the law's side this side of the Mississippi. Shame Swan ain't with him. No idea where he is, I suppose?"

"No," Luke said, with a growl.

"Pity." Priestly glanced again at Fooks. "I'll settle for just Florian Fooks. Ain't much to look at, is he? Always thought he'd have more of a presence, y'know?"

Cheek.

"Guess that's why the law never caught him." Luke took a deep breath. "All right Priestly you've got ya terms."

Priestly turned to the cell. "Let's wake him up and tell him the good news." Fooks pretended to start when Priestly rattled the cell door.

"Sure hope you don't go into the hotel business," he grumped. "If that's the way you treat the guests."

"Get over here. Now."

Fooks sat for a few moments on the edge of the bunk, rubbing his hands over his face, before levering up. He gave the occupants of the other cell a hard look before he moved to stand at the bars.

Priestly wriggled his jaw back and forth, glancing from one to the other. "If I let ya outta here, are ya prepared to go after the men who killed my brother? Under Fletcher's strict supervision, of course."

Fooks pulled a face.

"Do I have your word?"

Catching Luke's hard gaze, Fooks nodded. "Yes. You have my word. I'll find the men who killed your brother." Then he false smiled at Luke. "And I'll have Mr. Fletcher with me to make sure I do."

Priestly stroked his chin, still considering. "All right." He straightened up and hitched his pants. "Goes against my better judgment, but... ya have two months. Turner should be up and about by then, ready to resume his duties." He turned to Fooks. "So, if ya ain't back by then, I'll be free to hunt you down." He squared up to Fooks across the bars of the cell. "And believe me, I won't stop until I get you and put ya where ya belong." A beat. "In an unmarked grave."

Fooks chewed his lips, and with a glance at Luke, he gave a nod of acceptance.

Luke motioned to the cell door. "Let him out." He gave Fooks a slight grin. "We ain't ridin'. There's a train at 3.30."

Priestly glanced at the clock. "That's an hour from now. I expect you to be on it. Both of you."

CHAPTER TEN

Great to be free. Thanks, old man.

Fooks walked out of the sheriff's office behind Luke, crossed the street, and stopped on the opposite boardwalk outside the saloon. He gave a deep sigh and circled his shoulders and swung his arms. Then cracked his neck from side to side, gave another sigh and smiled at the blue sky in pleasure. Several passers-by greeted him. *No idea who you are.* He nodded and smiled.

Luke turned back when he realized Fooks no longer followed him.

"What are you doin'?"

Fooks stood, hands on hips. "Just being glad to be alive old man. Time for a beer. Or two."

"We haven't got time for a drink. Priestly gave us an hour to get on our way."

Fooks grinned. "We've got time." He turned, intent on entering the saloon.

"Oh, no ya don't." Luke caught his arm and steered him away. "Y'all comin' with me so I can pack a few things.

And then we're goin' to tell Mary we'll be away for a while."

Fooks scowled as Luke frog marched him along. He offered a false smile in reply to more greetings and almost skidded to a stop when one man tried to engage Luke in conversation about the bank robbery.

"Can't stop now. We've gotta get on our way," Luke said forcefully, tightening his grip on Fooks' arm.

"Is this what it's gonna be like?" Fooks asked as Luke hurried them away.

"Yes," Luke said, roundly.

Sheesh.

Luke kept hold of him until they reached his home, two rooms above the barber's shop. Fooks found himself pushed into a chair in the sitting room while Luke went into the other room. He sat for a few moments, looking around with disdain. He must have been here before, but it didn't look familiar. *Is this all he's got to show for all those years of chasing crooks? Much more affluent a lifestyle being one of those crooks.*

He ran a hand through his hair, longer than convention, falling over his collar and into his eyes. "You know I meant to get my haircut last week. Think I'll go do it now while I'm waiting." Fooks levered up. Slamming back down again when Luke appeared at the bedroom door. He held underwear in his hands and his face was like thunder.

"You just stay right there Fooks. I got ya outta jail, didn't I? Least you can do is behave yaself."

Fooks held his hands up. "Okay. Okay. I'll stay put."

Luke nodded, satisfied he meant it, turned back, then stopped. "D'ya remember that?"

"Remember what? I've got kinda big hole in my memory right now."

"Before your accident, ya told me you planned to stop in after your haircut."

Fooks frowned and chewed his lip, considering. "Guess it does seem familiar." He ran a hand over his hair.

"I need a cut, but…" He pressed his lips together. "Probably best to leave it until this has healed." He waved a hand at his head. "Perhaps they'll be an opportunity while we're away."

Luke grinned. "Ya finally acceptin' we've got to do this?"

Fooks looked away. "Yeah, I guess." When he looked back, he said, "D'you have a plan?"

"Start at the scene of the crime."

Fooks looked doubtful. "Mudwater Flats is way north in Dakota. Take days to get there."

"Yep," Luke said, with a nod. "Best get started then." He turned away again, then had a thought. "D'ya know Smedley?"

Fooks shook his head. "Don't think so. Do you?"

"Heard a little about him. Nothin' good. Nasty piece of work. I'll fill ya in on what I know about him and his Gang on the way."

Mary rushed to her husband's side when Fooks and Luke walked in to the house. She clutched his arm, looking concerned.

"Oh, are you all right? Did the sheriff hurt you?"

Fooks shook his head. "No." He looked uncomfortable, with Mary clutching his arm. "We've got to go away for a while." He carefully extracted himself and turned to Luke. "You want to explain it to her while I go pack?" He stalked away to the bedroom he'd used since his accident.

"Papa?" Mary looked at her father for an explanation.

"Come an' sit down."

Luke led her over to the sofa and sat down, holding her hands. He explained in short what Priestly expected.

"But Papa, you're not up to a journey like this. You retired years ago."

"I know Mary. I know." Luke patted her hand. "It was the only way. Priestly was all for sending him to the

Capitol. You know what that'd mean." Luke shook his head. "I couldn't stand to see ya unhappy, not when there's somethin' I can do to prevent it."

"Papa, this is dangerous. Supposing—"

"We'll come back Mary. I promise."

"He's not himself yet."

Luke grinned. "Might be the best thang right now. Reckon it's Florian Fooks he needs to be."

"But Papa—" Mary screwed up her face.

Luke glanced at the bedroom door for a sign of movement, but dropped his voice to a whisper. "I'll look out for him."

"Who's going to look out for you?"

Luke smiled. "Sweetie, I'm old enough an' ugly enough to take care of myself. I've had plenty of experience, remember?"

"That's not the point."

Mary said no more when Fooks appeared, saddlebags over his shoulder, hat in his hand. He made to walk towards them, then stopped. He hovered in the doorway to Susan's room, smiling at the sleeping child. Then he turned abruptly.

Fooks stopped in front of the coat stand and pondered on the charcoal gray hat sitting atop. Mary watched him take down the battered disaster he called a hat. He hadn't worn it since he'd returned from Angelworth, almost eighteen months ago. Comparing it to the one he already held for a moment before flicking his eyes up to meet Mary's.

"This is Fooks' hat, Mary." With care he replaced his usual hat on top of the coat stand. "I'm gonna need to be *him* for a while. The other fella won't cut it." He placed the worn and holed item carefully on his head, and about turned. "Gotta get going Fletcher. If we want to catch the train for Omaha," he said, brushing past.

"Yeah, I know. Be right there."

Luke gave Mary's hand a reassuring squeeze before following.

The plan was to travel by Union Pacific railroad to Omaha, then change for St Paul, where they would change again for a railroad which would take them north to Dakota. A convoluted route, not direct, but quicker and more comfortable than riding. The first part of their journey through Nebraska, Fooks slept propped up against the window, hat covering his face. After the last few days, Luke couldn't blame him, respected his privacy, and let him sleep.

The journey in total took them over a week, with delays, time table mismatches and overnight stops. On the way, Luke did as he promised and told Fooks what he'd heard about the Smedley Gang.

"Mudwater Flats wasn't the first heist where they've killed an innocent bystander. The first time I think it was a genuine accident. Don't--"

"If you're gonna make a career outta robbing banks, you have to accept folks may get hurt. And that you might be responsible. Greed trumps any moral dilemma you might have." Fooks sat backed against the window, one leg bent up across the bench, foot dangling over the side.

Luke leaned forward; conscious they weren't alone in the carriage. "Your Gang didn't shoot anyone in any of your jobs."

Fooks grinned. "Didn't have to with me doing the planning." He looked away to stare out of the window at the passing scenery and sobered. "Shooting someone is a whole different game. One I didn't want to get into." He looked back. "So, I plotted and planned and hoped I'd covered all the bases. Could never rule out the possibility though. Too many unknown variables. There's always the chance something unexpected could happen. Always the chance one of us would get hurt or killed. That kinda constant stress wears you down, eventually."

"So, is that why ya decided to get out?"

"I don't know. I've no idea what caused us to make the decision we did. Swan and me must've had some kind of discussion but," he shook his head at the ceiling, "I just don't know." He shifted until he sat on the bench proper. He leaned forward. "Tell me more about the Smedley Gang."

"They've killed three people, including Priestly's brother, as far as I know. One of 'em..." Luke put his head down, swallowed hard, "... throat slashed ear to ear."

Fooks frowned. "Doesn't sound like it happened during a heist. More a deliberate act to me."

Luke twitched his head. "Yeah. Fella who got it had allegedly used his fists on a soiled dove Cole Smedley was partial to. Dunno any more than that."

"That's enough."

"Other man dead was from a posse which gathered after a job the Gang pulled." Luke studied his son-in-law. "Goin' up against them isn't gonna be easy. You up for it?"

Fooks glanced out of the window, sucking his teeth. "I don't like killers," he said, quietly. "Wouldn't have 'em in Guardian Wall. Some sneaked in from time to time. Showed them the door real quick. Cole Smedley the leader?"

Luke shook his head. "His younger brother, Robin, is the leader. Cole is the strong, silent type."

"Who else?"

"Two others. Dunno their names. Sheriff at Mudwater Flats may know. It's more his territory."

Fooks sighed. "I guess we find out when we get there." *Sure wish Tobias was here with us.*

Finally, they alighted at Mudwater Flats, in the northern part of Dakota Territory. The town stood on the banks of the Goose River.

"Hope I never have to see a train again." Fooks muttered to himself, as they trudged along Main Street, towards the hotel. Late in the day, with the town winding down. A procession of men made a bee-line for The Lonely Steer saloon, pumping loud music out into the street. Hurrying to get out of the light drizzle falling.

"Somehow, I always thought ya had an affinity for 'em," Luke said, and pressed his lips together to stop the threatening smirk.

Fooks threw daggers at him. "Don't push it old man. I can still light outta here."

Luke followed Fooks into the first hotel they came across. He stood silently by his side, raising an eyebrow when Fooks requested two rooms. Fooks took his key and left without a word, before Luke finished signing the register.

CHAPTER ELEVEN

The following morning, Luke and Fooks had eaten breakfast and were ready to start their day. The tension between them of yesterday seemingly forgotten. Pausing in the hotel lobby, with Fooks about to shrug into his thick Mackinaw jacket, he laughed, deep and husky. "You want me to go over to the sheriff's office with you? *Me*?"

"Gotta problem?"

Fooks widened his eyes. "Yeah." He jacked a thumb at his chest. "I'm me."

Luke shrugged. "Ya don't look like you."

Fooks scratched the back of his head, sensed the conversation about to get even more ridiculous. Mastering his patience, he turned to the older man. "Now listen Fletcher. I don't go willingly into a sheriff's office." Then he frowned. "Why d'you want me there anyway?"

"You might think of questions I can't."

Fooks held up a forefinger and waggled it under Luke's nose. "Uh huh. Nice try. You were a lawman. You know the questions to ask." He shook his head before waving a hand dismissively. "You don't need me. I'm going to the mercantile to stock up on trail supplies. If I'm already done when you're finished, I'll be in the library we passed yesterday." He moved away.

Luke followed him. "Library?"

"Yeah, they have back copies of newspapers. See if I can find out any more than what your sheriff will tell you."

Fooks positioned his hat carefully and stalked out of the hotel entrance, conscious of Luke's eyes on him. Luke hurried after him and caught his arm. "Wait up."

Fooks turned abruptly, his face like thunder, and angrily threw off Luke's hand. They squared up to each other in the middle of the boardwalk, pedestrians glaring at them as they side-stepped around them.

"I think ya oughta come in with me," Luke said.

"And I've told you no," Fooks said through gritted teeth.

"If ya there, it'll save time me not having to repeat the conversation. I'll do all the talking. You just stand there and butt in if there's something ya wanna know."

Fooks stood, hands on hips, looked at the sky and let his tongue explore his cheek. "How can I put this in words you'll understand?" He pressed his face in Luke's almost touching noses. "NO."

He started to walk away when footsteps sounded on the boardwalk next to them.

"Is there a problem here fellas?" a soft but firm voice said.

As both turned to face the newcomer, Luke smiled. Fooks stiffened. Although he was the first to recover, flashing a dimpled grin. "Howdy, sheriff, no problem. We were ..." Fooks glanced at Luke, "just discussing which one of us was gonna come see you. Need some information on a recent bank robbery." He finished with a pleasant smile.

The sheriff flashed them a doubtful look. "You bounty hunters?" he asked.

Luke shook his head. "No sir. Perhaps we can discuss this in your office?"

The sheriff continued to look doubtful. "All right," he said, cautiously. "It's over there." He tossed his head behind him. On the other side of the street stood his office. Then he turned and strode towards it.

Fooks scowled at the retreating back. Luke grinned ruefully at him. "Can't refuse an invitation like that." He nudged Fooks' arm and the full force of Fooks' outlaw leader's glare fell on him. Luke, unperturbed, added, "Can we?"

Luke set off after the sheriff. Fooks turned the outside of his jacket so the lining showed and draped it over his arm. He was pretty sure the jacket wasn't mentioned on his dodger, but his folk law talked about it. Red, with an unusual green plaid, when black was the more common other color. *Why haven't I bought a new jacket by now?*

"Are ya comin'?" Luke called.

Fooks scowled and trailed along in their wake.

Luke soon sized up the caliber of lawman they were dealing with when they entered the office. A middle-aged man, running to fat now but once, whip taut.

"Howdy, Sheriff," Luke greeted. "I'll be in your town for a few days. Jus' thought I'd come an' introduce myself. Professional courtesy."

The sheriff was on his way to his desk. Now he looked around. "Professional courtesy?"

Luke walked forward to face him over the desk. "Luke Fletcher. U.S. Marshall." He held out his hand. "Retired, now, of course, but I always like to check in with the local law when I'm in a new town."

The sheriff nodded and chewed his cheek. "I've heard of you," he said, shaking hands. "Lyle Gomez."

Luke nodded at the recognition. *Name still means something. Good to know.* He gestured to Fooks, who hovered just inside the door. "This is my son-in-law, Joseph Crane."

Gomez grunted in Fooks' direction, who gave a curt nod.

Gomez gestured Luke to a chair. "What brings you to Mudwater Flats?"

"We're on our way North to look over a prize bull." Luke rubbed his chin. "Heard ya had a bank robbery a few months ago."

Gomez sat. "Yeah," he said, cautiously. "What of it?"

Luke sniffed. "From what I heard; somethin' didn't smell right."

"Four-man gang. Well known, but not in these parts." Gomez tossed his head. "Why the interest?"

"Heard they shot the teller."

Gomez stiffened. "That's not common knowledge. How d'ya know?"

"He was the brother of a friend of mine." Luke raised his head. "Knew I was comin' this way. Asked me to look in and see if I can find out any more than the sparse details, they informed him about. Seems to thank you had an idea who the gang was." Luke pulled out the chair and sat.

"So did I. One customer in the bank heard them call each other Rob and Cole. Fits for the Smedley Gang and their descriptions stack up. Except this isn't their turf, but I can't think who else it could be."

"Who shot Arnold Priestly?"

Gomez drew back, leaving his forearms on the desk. He drummed his fingers for a moment.

"If I'm right, the description fits Robin Smedley. His brother, Cole, wasn't too happy 'bout it, by all accounts."

"Who were the other two?"

"Frankie Chronister and Sam Hegarty."

Behind him, Luke heard a sharp intake of breath from Fooks.

Gomez leveled a glance in his direction before getting up and pacing to a filing cabinet.

"Ya right. There is something that don't smell right." He shook his head, taking out a thin file. "But I'm jiggered if I can figger out what it is." He slammed the drawer shut and spun the file in front of Luke. "This is my report for the bank's insurance."

Luke read. It didn't take him long. A single sheet, written concisely sticking to the facts in dispassionate terms. "The bank staff co-operated. The Gang got the money. They were leaving. So why did Smedley suddenly turn and fire at Priestly?"

"That's what I can't figger out. He had no reason to. Don't make sense."

"Not to us, no. What d'ya know 'bout Mr. Priestly?"

Gomez clasped his hands. "Not much. Worked at the bank for nigh on two years. Family man. Wife and kid." He shrugged. "Nothing remarkable at all."

"Ever been in trouble with the law?"

Gomez took back the report. "Never so much as squished a bug far as I can tell." He sighed. "Nope. It's a mystery, and that's a fact."

Both men got to their feet, Gomez to the filing cabinet, Luke glanced at Fooks who rolled his eyes. Taking advantage of the Gomez's turned back, he made a hurry up motion.

Luke responded with a calm down action. He turned aside to stare pensively at the notice board where the Smedley Gang's posters were prominent. Studying the descriptions, committing them to memory. *Jus' like all times.* To one side were two more posters. For Florian Fooks and his partner, Tobias Swan. Luke read these two, noting the descriptions. Dark brown hair, brown eyes, average build for Fooks; light brown curly hair, blue eyes, medium stocky build for Swan. *Can fit most men, I guess.*

"Surprised these two are still up there. Haven't heard nothin' 'bout them for years," he said, waving his hand at the noticeboard to explain his interest.

Gomez joined him to look at the two posters. "Yeah, I reckon they're dead, but they came with the latest batch of dodgers. Bounty on both of 'em is reduced. Still look mighty fine up there though."

"Awh, they're long gone." Luke turned to Gomez and offered his hand. "Thanks for the information, Sheriff."

Fooks stared at his wanted poster for a moment, nodded at the sheriff, and swiftly followed Luke outside.

"What's the plan?" Luke asked, immediately the door shut on the sheriff's office.

"Get a drink," Fooks said, with a growl, and stalked off toward the nearest saloon.

"We've only just had breakfast," Luke protested, sighed but seeing there was no arguing, followed on.

In the saloon, several tables at the back had customers finishing up breakfast. A girl scuttled about, busy refreshing coffee mugs. The bartender making a great show of polishing glasses, ready for the day ahead. He blinked in surprise at Fooks' sharp request for whiskey at this early hour.

"Two?" he asked when Luke arrived.

"No, just coffee for me." Luke leaned his elbow on the bar and looked at Fooks, who stared straight ahead.

The bartender reached under the bar and placed a shot glass in front of Fooks, then turned away in search of a bottle. He waved to the girl telling her she had a customer for coffee at the bar.

Fooks threw coins on the bar while his glass filled. He downed the drink in one, swallowed hard at the rawness, but motioned for another, tapping the pile of coins to show he had already paid. The glass duly refilled, and the bartender moved away. Fooks hesitated, downed the second drink in one, set the glass on the bar and closed his eyes, letting the strong liquor slid down his throat.

"Feeling better?" Luke asked.

"Yeah." Fooks opened his eyes. He took a deep breath and puffed it out slowly. "Don't say it."

"Say what?"

Fooks looked at Luke out of the corner of his eye and shook his head. "Just don't say it."

Luke's confusion was interrupted by the girl bring mugs and the coffeepot. After she had gone, Fooks picked up his mug. "Sit over there and talk." He twitched his head to a corner table.

When they were settled, Luke broke the silence. "Did ya know any of the names Gomez mentioned?"

Fooks took a sip of coffee before answering. "Know Sam Hegarty some. He rode with Guardian Wall for a spell."

"D'you know where they hang out?"

"Probably find out." Fooks widened his eyes. "You're not thinking of riding in there?"

"What d'you suggest?"

Fooks rubbed his cheek. "Get Sam Hegarty on his own and talk to him. Ask him why Smedley killed the teller."

"He may not know."

"Is a possibility."

"I noticed ya got cheaper," Luke said into the next silence.

"Yeah, I saw that It's just plain downright insulting."

"I'd say it's a good thang."

Fooks scowled and folded his arms tightly across his chest. "Cheek of it. Don't they know I'm the best? I deserve an appropriate price."

"Now don't go getting' all bent outta shape. It's still dead or alive."

Fooks grunted. "That's something, I suppose."

"Few more years an' I 'xpect even that'll go." Luke went on, "That's what you want."

"Hell no." Fooks thumped the table with a fist, then bit his thumb and looked away. "Yeah, I guess so." He shook his head and looked back. "I dunno Luke. It's hard being two people and trying to keep them straight." He passed a hand over his eyes. "I dunno who I am half the time."

Luke patted Fooks' arm and leaned forward. "You're doin' all right. This mission we're on is a complication, that's all. Once it's over, you can get back to bein' Joseph Crane."

"Can we trust Priestly though? He knows where I live. If he snitches, Wash will get into trouble. Not to mention I'll be thrown in prison."

"I trust the man. He let ya go. Wouldn't 'ave gone for it if he was gonna renege on his word. Y'know, my grandpa used to say. Some chance is better than no chance. I like to think there's some truth in it."

"Wish I had your optimism."

"Ya do usually. One of your better qualities, from what I can see." Luke sipped his coffee. "What's the next move?"

Fooks didn't speak for a long while.

"Find Hegarty and see what he knows."

"D'ya know where to find him?"

Fooks chewed his bottom lip. "I have a few ideas." He tossed his head. "We'll need to ride to Grassy Heights. You up for it?"

Luke's face fell at the prospect of getting on a horse. "Yeah, have to be."

Hope so, old man.

CHAPTER TWELVE

"Been wonderin'. What makes a man become an outlaw?"

Later that morning, they'd picked up horses and were on their way, planning to cover the twenty miles to Grassy Heights before the end of the day. The days were rapidly shortening as Winter approached. With a marked drop in temperature, neither fancied riding in an unknown country after nightfall. Fooks wondered briefly whether his now sedentary lifestyle had made him soft. Deciding in the end, he'd always liked a soft bed and a hot meal.

Luke looked across at his son-in-law. Fooks shifted uncomfortably and a wince crossed his face. Riding didn't figure much in his life these days.

"Lots of reasons. In my case, I kinda fell into it." Fooks settled for a moment, then began to talk. "Me and Tobias sorta just drifted into it. Fell in with a bunch of boys our ages who were just trying to survive the same as us. We split at one point and I wound up alone in Guardian Wall. It's the sorta country that's always attracted the rougher element. A half Mexican fella by the name of Pete de Leon headed it up then and was already getting a name for itself.

He ran a tight ship. Loyalty, discipline, rule of law. Pete installed this in all his gang members and they respected him for it."

He smiled. "'Cept one young fella kept questioning him a lot. Not in a challenging sorta way. Just in a learning sorta way. Seemed to get away with it too. Only some of the fellas didn't like it. This smart mouthed kid getting all their leader's attention."

"You?"

Fooks grinned. "Who else? I hadn't been there long when who should come riding in one day but Tobias Swan and Wash Turner."

"I wasn't aware Wash rode with the Guardian Wall Gang. Or any gang for that matter."

Fooks wrinkled his nose. "He didn't. Wash was never a member of the Gang. Wash knew Pete, so the Gang accepted him. I don't know any more about their relationship and don't figure it my business to ask."

Luke nodded.

Fording a fast-flowing stream took all their concentration for a few minutes. When they reached dry land again, Fooks continued.

"Came as a real shock to both of us to meet up again after all those years in a place like the Wall." He shook his head. "I was fully into gang life. I was a crook, and I was proud of it."

Fooks dropped his head. "Wash and Swan had run from some trouble they'd got themselves into and Guardian Wall was the place they sought refuge. Wash hadn't planned to stay. When the trouble died down, Wash would be leaving. I knew Swan wanted to leave as well." He chewed his bottom lip. "I did something I now bitterly regret. I didn't want Swan to go. I'd missed him and didn't want to lose him again. So I had a long talk with Wash one night. When Swan woke the next morning, Wash had already been gone some hours." He dropped his voice. "I took the option of leaving as well away from him."

"It's not something I feel good about. I can't tell you how many times I've apologized to him, but I'm glad he stayed. He wanted no part in the robberies, so made himself useful looking after the horses and gear.

"One time we all rode out. Swan didn't come with us and he wasn't party to the plan. Anyway, something went wrong, and I came back alone in a hurry. Pete and some of the others were captured. I told Swan later; it was possibly my fault."

"Was it?"

Fooks shifted in his saddle. "Yeah. Got too cocky. Anyway, the rest of the bunch were coming after me so Swan and me left. In the nick of time, too."

"Where did you go?"

"I figured the gang were on our trail and we had to take steps to lose them. We went south. Swan was all for keeping on going, down to Texas, but I insisted we stopped in Denver. We went to see David Culley."

"Who's he?"

It took a moment before he spoke again. "I told you Swan and me split. I went to Utah. To find a man Ma met on the ship coming over. He was calling himself David Culley, and I lived with him for a while. He knew a man who ran a ranch in Texas. So, he sent us there."

He sighed. "We settled into ranch work. Spent a year or two down South." Fooks chewed his lips. "But I had a hankering to see Wyoming again. Texas is too hot for me and all that dust gets everywhere."

"Tell me about it," Luke said, with a growl.

Fooks' forehead wrinkled in irritation at the interruption. "Anyway we quit. Took our pay and headed North. Back to what I was good at."

Fooks fell silent and pensive.

"What's in Grassy Heights?" Luke said after a few moments, jerking Fooks out of his reverie.

Fooks stared out across the wind-swept prairie. "News of Sam Hegarty. He can tell us about the Smedleys. I'm not fool enough to ride into their hideout. Unannounced. Even if I knew it." He glanced across at Luke. *And certainly not with you in tow.*

A particularly strong gust of wind got under his hat. He snatched at it before it could sail away. Sweeping his hair back, he plonked the hat back on, and gave the stampede straps a yank to tighten them under his chin. "Sam was sweet on a girl in Grassy Heights. I hope she's still there." Fooks twitched his head from side to side. "But there might be a problem."

"What?"

Luke fought his own battle with wind and hat.

Fooks bit his lip. "So was I."

Here goes. Wonder if anyone will recognize me?

Fooks walked into the saloon in Grassy Heights, striding up to the bar as if he owned it. The bartender blanched when he saw who it was. "Don't want any trouble Fooks," he said quietly, polishing the bar in front of him. It was still early and quiet. The evening crowd hadn't turned out yet.

Well, Mike does. Can't of changed that much.

Casually stripping off his well-worn and tight-fitting gloves one finger at a time, Fooks was in no hurry to reply. Luke, a step behind, stood beside him, looking at him expectantly. That man looked up at the bartender and smiled pleasantly. "Won't get any. Two beers please, Mike."

Mike chewed his mustache for a moment, sized up Luke, before turning around in search of glasses.

Luke frowned a question at Fooks, who shook his head.

Mike eyed them warily. He filled one glass, then the other. Foam running down the sides, he placed them in front of his customers. "On the house," he said through gritted teeth.

Fooks glanced up in surprise from counting the coins in his hand.

"Ya likely only be needing the one. I can stand it." Mike moved away.

Fooks picked up the nearest jug and raised it at Mike's retreating back. "Mighty good of you." He took a sip and nodded to Luke. "Let's find a table. We might be in for a long wait."

Luke followed, noting Fooks chose a table in a corner, which gave him a view of both the front doors, the bar and the smaller door at the back of the saloon. And away from the hurdy-gurdy endlessly playing.

"Why did he think you might cause trouble?"

Fooks pulled a face. "Dunno."

"He knew who ya were."

"Yep."

Luke seeing, he wasn't going to get any more out of him about Fooks past, tried for a question more relevant. "Who are we waitin' for?"

Fooks didn't answer at first. Instead, he took out his pocket watch and flipped it open. "'Bout half an hour," he said, shutting the watch with a click and returning it to his top pocket.

"For what?"

"Girls." Fooks raised his glass to his lips. His eyes sparkled above.

"I thought we were comin' here to find Hegarty?"

"We are. The girl I told you about, she works here. Find her, we find him."

"It was years ago. Times change. Folks move on."

Fooks chewed his lip. "Yeah, I keep forgetting," he murmured, with a frown. He glanced across at the bartender. "He might know."

Luke followed his gaze. "Didn't seem too friendly to me."

Fooks wrinkled his nose. "Mike's okay. Jus' need to work up to things with him, that's all. Let's wait an' see."

Luke made a face. "Mary said ya can be infuriatin'. I thought she was exaggeratin'." He took a pull of his beer. "Guess not."

"You agreed to let me handle this my way. You don't have to be here Fletcher."

"I'm here to look out for my gal's interests, Fooks."

"Then you're not gonna like what happens when Lorelei appears."

The two men stared at each other hard. Luke jabbed his finger on the table in front of Fooks. "You remember ya a married man."

"Bet it never stopped you," Fooks said with a smirk, taking a pull of beer.

"I was faithful to my wife Fooks," Luke said in a growl.

Fooks nodded. "Good to know." He set the glass down and drew his index finger through a pool of condensation. "I don't intend on doing anything Mary would be upset about. It may look like it, but I won't mean it."

"Whether ya mean it or not, ain't the point. You made a commitment to my gal. Forsakin' all others."

"And I don't remember," Fooks said, raising his voice and attracting attention from Mike and the other customers. Noticing, Fooks leaned towards Luke and hissed. "Stop pushing me. I get it, but I can't remember. Cut me some slack, will you?"

Luke drew back, nodding. "Ya right, I do forget ya don't remember things. Not sure what ya do remember and what ya don't." Not exactly an apology, but near enough.

"That's the problem. Neither do I." Fooks glowered. "Just don't react."

CHAPTER THIRTEEN

Fooks sat up straight when the back door opened and five girls came out at a run. The other customers hooted, hollered and clapped at their arrival. Fooks scanned each girl's face.

"Well?" Luke asked.

"Nope. Let's ask. Drink up, old man. I'll order more beers." As he spoke, Fooks dimpled and motioned to the nearest girl, who came over, swinging her hips.

"Well, hello stranger. What can I do for you?" she asked, ruffling his hair in a suggestive way.

Fooks put a hand around her waist and drew her close. "Have company right now, but maybe later. Right now, two more beers."

He let her go, letting his fingers run down her smooth, bare arm when she moved away.

"Coming right up."

Fooks eyed her up and down, appreciating the bare arms and shoulders, the short skirt and black stockings. Luke cleared his throat meaningfully.

"Relax. I'm not gonna act on it. We want information."

When the girl came back with two foaming beers, Fooks pulled her onto his lap. She laughed. "I thought you said later, cowboy, but we can go upstairs now if you like." She stroked his cheek.

"Haven't been in this town for a while. You must be new. What's your name darling?" he said with a grin.

"It's Rosie and I'm not *that* new. I know my way around." She leaned in to nuzzle his neck.

Conscious of Luke's eyes on him, Fooks chuckled. "Oh, I bet you do." He pushed her away a little, one hand caressing her hip. "First, Rosie, I need some information. Is Lorelei still here?"

Rosie sat up sharply, causing Fooks to grunt. "Lorelei? You don't mean Lorelei Morales?"

Fooks smiled. "The very same. Is she here?"

Rosie pouted. "Sure, but she don't entertain the customers no more. She's management now."

Fooks' face lit up. "Ah, that's fine 'cos its business I wanna see her about. Can you tell her Fooks is here and would like to see her?"

"Fooks?"

Fooks widened his eyes and nodded.

"Sure, but what's in it for me?"

Fooks laughed and plucked at the strap of her dress. "When I've finished my business with Lorelei, perhaps you and I can take care of some business of our own," he purred.

Rosie was satisfied and moved off his lap. "I'll go see if she can see you."

Fooks nodded a thanks and she walked away. He took a sip of his new beer and then noticed Luke watching him.

"You look like you're sucking a lemon old man. Quit it."

Wow, she hasn't changed a bit.

A mature, statuesque woman came out of the back door a short time afterwards. The olive skin spoke of her

Mexican heritage but the bright blue eyes and white blond hair, in a thick plait over her right shoulder, told a different story. Her dress a sparkling silver, the square neckline showed off her ample bosom, fitted to a trim waist and clinging to her wide hips. The fishtail hem, frilled at the bottom, cut high in the center, showed off a shapely knee. She sashayed her way over to them.

"Well, well, well, if it isn't Florian Fooks," she said, placing a hand on his shoulder.

Fooks brought his eyes up level with her bosom. "Lorelei, you're looking well, I see."

"I'm grand. Where have you been hiding yourself?"

"Oh, here and there. Can we talk in private, Lorelei? I've something to ask you."

Lorelei flicked his chin playfully. "I don't do that anymore, but," she leaned down and kissed him on the mouth, "but perhaps for you I might make an exception."

Fooks, aware of Luke's hard stare, sobered. "It's a business matter, Lorelei."

Lorelei straightened up. "Sure, whatever you say. Come out back. Just." When Luke rose, she held up a finger. "You."

Fooks scraped his chair back, holding out a warning hand to Luke, stilling him. He positioned his hat with care before following Lorelei.

Once in the office, Fooks swept off his hat and pulled Lorelei into a fond embrace. Lorelei laughed. "You're forward, Fooks. Not seen hide nor hare of you for years. I thought for sure you were dead."

Fooks held her tight. "Been lying low."

"Must be very low."

"Yep." He released her, and she walked away.

"Your friend out there. He smells of the law." She turned on her heel. "Is he?"

"Retired."

"Strange company for Florian Fooks to keep. Where's Swan?"

"Back East."

Lorelei widened her eyes. "Now that is a surprise."

Fooks looked up in false astonishment. "You mean me turning up outta the grave wasn't?" He scanned around the office and nodded. "Looks like you're doing all right for yourself."

"I saved hard. When a half share of this place came up, I was able to buy in. I run the girls and the other entertainment." Lorelei put a hand to her hip, accentuating her figure. "This isn't a chance social call. You want something Fooks. I'm not sure I'm going to like it."

Fooks pursed his bottom lip and walked forward to her. His hands went to her hips, and he pulled her to him. "We'll see," he said, with a purr, his lips brushing hers. "Need your help, Lorelei. How about it?"

Lorelei uncoiled his hands and he let her. "What d'you need? I'll consider it if it doesn't cost me."

"It won't. Looking for Sam Hegarty. Any idea where he's at these days?"

Lorelei turned away. She unstopped a decanter and poured two drinks. When she turned back, she held one glass out.

"Depends. What d'you want him for?"

Fooks accepted the glass and took a sip. He grimaced at the roughness of the liquor. "Heard he was running with the Smedley Gang. Pulled a job in Mudwater Flats a while back. Teller got shot."

"Ah. That."

"So, you know about it?"

"I heard."

"Know where Sam is now?" Fooks asked casually, keeping his eyes on Lorelei.

"Might. What do you need him for?"

"Just to talk, that's all."

"He probably won't want to talk to you. You aren't exactly on his Christmas card list Fooks."

Fooks took a big mouthful of whiskey. *Sheesh, that's awful.* Masking his revulsion, he said, "I'm aware of it.

Figger after all this time, he might be looking more favorably at me."

"I doubt it Fooks," Lorelai said, sipping her drink. "Sam holds a grudge and doesn't forget. Or forgive."

Fooks straightened. "I'll take my chances. Now where is he?" His tone, noticeably harder.

"My, this must be real important."

"'Tis."

"Mind telling me?"

"Nope."

Lorelai fingered the neck of the decanter. "Will you hurt him?"

"Don't plan to. You still sweet on him, Lorelei?" He waved a hand around the office. "Can't see how he fits in to your new life."

"I was never sweet on him."

Fooks raised an eyebrow.

"He's my half-brother. My little half-brother. Just looked out for him, that's all. And I thought I was." Lorelei took a sip. "'Till he started running with the likes of you and Swan."

Fooks dithered before draining his glass. Then set it down deliberately to show he had finished. "I threw him out of Guardian Wall. Can't take any responsibility for what he did afterwards." He hooked his thumbs in his gun belt. "Now, Lorelei please. I just wanna talk to him. That's all."

"Just talk?"

"Just talk," he said, with a nod and a tight-lipped smile.

Lorelei took a deep breath, her bosom threatening to spill out of her dress. "Very well. The Smedley Gang's hideout is near Bitter Creek. You can find him in town most days. At the Lonesome Inn."

Fooks smiled and unhooked his thumbs. Placing his hat carefully, he turned away to the door.

"That's it? You haven't got time to stick around? For old times' sake."

Fooks smiled. "Thanks Lorelei." He opened the door. "Be sure and give my regards to Rosie."

With a grin, he left. Standing outside, he sobered and pulled on his gloves. With a determined nod, he returned to the saloon. He caught Luke's eye on the way through and a tip of his head signaled to Luke they were leaving. Luke scraped his chair back and threw a few coins on the table, covering their drinks before joining Fooks at the door.

Fooks held one of the bat-wing doors open, allowing Luke to pass. In doing so, he glanced back, saw Lorelei standing, arms folded by the back door. With a nod and a wink, he pushed on through.

What to do?

Fooks threw an arm over his head, fingers rubbing together. Frustrated that sleep eluded him tonight. Early start in the morning and he should be fresh. Although only a relatively short ride, getting started would be slow for both he and Luke. The clock on the town hall struck midnight. The saloon would be winding down soon. Lorelei would still be there. The even sound of breathing from the other bed told him Luke was asleep. Perhaps he could get dressed and sneak out.

Sometime later, he walked into the now deserted saloon. Mike, the bartender, stood counting bills on the bar.

"Just about to close up Fooks."

"I know. Is Lorelei still here?" Fooks pointed to the back door and continued moving towards it.

"Yeah, she's still here."

Fooks smiled tight-lipped and tipped his hat. "Goodnight Mike."

He found the office door and knocked, opening the door before Lorelei called come. She sat at the desk. She smiled when she saw him, standing in the doorway.

"I'd just about given you up."

She glided to the table, which held the drinks, filled two glasses, and held one out to him. He blanched. *Shoulda brought m'own bottle.*

Fooks shut the door. He tossed his hat onto a chair, walking forward. He ran his fingers through his hair. "Wasn't sure I was gonna make it. But I didn't want Rosie." He took the glass in one hand, his other hand snaked around her waist, pulling her tight against him. The smell of lavender rose from her closeness. A smell he remembered with relish. "I want you," he murmured, before his mouth descended on hers. He ground out a kiss, leaving them both breathless.

"No one's heard of you for years and you suddenly turn up and think—" He cut her off and this time when her arms snaked around his neck, she added, "Perhaps thinking isn't what I do best."

He pursed his lips. "That's debatable, but there's a time and a place for everything. Right now, I don't want you to think." The drink he downed in one go, and set aside the glass. With both hands moving over her hips, he growled appreciatively. "I got to remembering how," he looked at the ceiling as he thought of an appropriate word, "stimulating our nights together were. I figured the intervening years might have added some to our already comprehensive knowledge." His mouth and body pressed against her again.

When he let her up for air, Lorelei smiled. A manicured and polished fingernail drew a line down his cheek, passing over a dimple hiding in the stubble and around to his chin. "It would be interesting to find out." Her expression changed to one of annoyance at the knock on the door.

"Got the takings Lorelei."

"Just a moment Mike." She turned her attention back to Fooks. "Let me lock the takings away and then you and I can get down to some serious discussions."

Fooks let her go with a nod and took a seat. She called the bartender in. Mike held out the stack of bills to Lorelei. He eyed Fooks suspiciously.

"Takings were good tonight, I reckon."

"Thanks. 'Night now."

Mike shot Fooks another glance before shutting the door.

"He still don't trust me, do he?" Fooks said, getting up and reaching for her again. His lips traced over her neck and shoulder. He plucked at the thin shoulder straps of her dress.

Lorelei turned in his embrace. "Patience. Don't look Fooks." She waved the stack of bills in front of his eyes. "While I lock this up."

Fooks chuckled. "You think a Cassan Webb 1865, single dial, three-digit combination would stop me? I could crack it in m'sleep."

"Turn away Fooks." She tapped the bills against his chest and said more firmly, "Maybe you can, but there is such a thing as temptation."

"Oh, I'm tempted all right." He eyed her up and down, appreciating the view. Then he raised his hands in apology and backed away. "All right. All right. I'm looking away. Closing my eyes, too. How's that?"

A doubtful Lorelei went to the safe. She bent and went about depositing the takings. As she shut the door, he came close behind her.

"I thought your eyes were closed?"

"Oh, they are," Fooks assured her. "My sensitive fingers and my imagination are working overtime. It's just like seeing." He turned her in his arms as she straightened up. "Now saloon business is taken care shall we get down to business of our own?"

His fingers traced the V of her dress, starting in the small of her back up to the straps. He pulled them from her shoulders. She stopped him, hand against her bosom.

"Not here. Let's take this upstairs, where we can be more comfortable. I've a feeling it's going to be a long, long night." She kissed him gently.

CHAPTER FOURTEEN

Fooks leaned against the wall for support, panting hard. His shirt, unbuttoned, hung out of his pants. In his hands, he clasped a bundle of underwear, boots, gun belt and hat. He passed the back of his forehand over his brow and wiped away the sweat he found there. In the dim light of the hall, Fooks remembered previous occasions when he and Lorelei had come together in the night. Exciting woman. She had fired his blood all right. Yet tonight, something had stopped him.

Lorelei went behind the screen and changed into a negligee while he undressed. He hadn't got to his socks before she appeared. *Why hadn't he taken them off first? He usually did.* When his hands moved over the silky garment, feeling the voluptuous body underneath, oh boy, the flame of desire still there all right. Her kisses were hot and fiery and he'd responded in kind. Yet when she sat astride him and allowed him to slide the straps of her negligee from her shoulders, bearing her charms to his gaze, a pair of sparkling gray eyes floated into his mind.

At first, he pushed the image away, but it persisted. Even when his fingers and lips moved over Lorelei's body, the eyes were still there. And lips. Lips he suddenly recalled kissing and wanted to do so again. Needed to do again.

When he stopped his caresses, Lorelei asked what was wrong. His hand lingered on her breast. When he looked down, it felt like it wasn't even his. Horrified, he jerked it away. *So that's why he hadn't taken his socks off. Cold feet.*

"I'm sorry. I can't do this." He pushed her vigorously from his lap and tossed her unceremoniously onto the bed.

Gathering up his belongings, he fled.

Now here he stood outside the room, feeling like a rat. A lothario. Ashamed. Guilty.

He stumbled away, down the back stairs and out into the cool night. Where he slumped onto the nearest bench and put his head in his hands.

Sheesh.

Reminiscences of Lorelei had morphed into a burning desire for another woman. Sleep would still elude him tonight, but this time for an entirely different reason. He was a married man. A man married to a woman he now wanted so much.

"Oh Sheesh."

"Problem, cowboy?"

Fooks scrubbed his eyes and sniffed. Moonlight glinted off the badge the man wore on his vest.

Trying to stay calm, his voice faltering as Fooks replied. "No sheriff. Just resting a spell."

"Is that alcohol I smell on ya breath?"

"I've had a drink or two." Fooks widened his eyes. "I'm not drunk, sheriff if that's what you're thinking?"

"That's exactly what I'm thinking. Look at the state of ya." The sheriff drew his gun. "Ya're given me no choice cowboy, I'm arresting ya for vagrancy."

"No, I've a room at the hotel. I'm traveling with Mr. Luke Fletcher. It's his usual practice to introduce himself when he arrives in a new town. Didn't he come see you earlier?"

"Yeah, he did, but I'll be doing U.S. Marshall Fletcher a favor by keeping ya outta harm's way. On your feet now."

Fooks had no alternative but to stumble to his feet.

"Do yaself up properly, man."

"Well, I know I'm not fit to be seen at a church social but—"

"Won't tell ya again. Do ya shirt up."

Fooks fumbled with the buttons. Difficult to see, even in the moonlight. The slight swaying of his body made it look like he was more intoxicated than he was. Fooks didn't help his situation because when he'd finished, the buttons were out of alignment.

"Now pick up ya things." The sheriff snatched away Fooks' gun belt. "I'll take that."

Hugging the rest of his clothes to his chest, they proceeded across the street to the opposite boardwalk. Fooks stubbed his toe with a thud on the rough planks.

"Owh! Could ya at least let me get m'boots on?"

"Hurry up then."

Fooks sat down on the edge of the boardwalk and pulled them on with difficulty. He gave the sheriff a disgusted look. "Really, I'm not drunk."

"Get up. Let's go. Haven't got all night."

With a grunt, Fooks rolled up and gathered his things. "You're making a mistake."

"I don't think so. Now get."

When Luke woke the next morning and saw the other bed empty, he groaned. What he'd tried to prevent had happened. He thought he'd headed it off when Fooks had retired last night.

"Musta snuck out in the night."

He lay there, contemplating how he would explain this to Mary. Then he had a thought. A quick glance around the room told him Fooks' saddlebags were still there. He hadn't left town. But perhaps he was still with her. Luke had to admit, Lorelei Morales was one heck of a woman.

"Can't lie here all day."

Luke began by checking Fooks' bed. Nope, stone cold. Hadn't left just before he'd awoken. Luke set about getting himself ready to face the day, whatever it might bring. Nearly finished when he heard a knock on the door.

On opening it, he caught a quick image of a woman, before his head snapped sideways and his cheek exploded in a burst of pain.

"You rat. You no-good excuse... Oh!"

When Luke faced forward again, his hand on his cheek, there in front of him stood Lorelei Morales, her hands covering her mouth. Above, her eyes widened in horror.

"Oh, sir, I'm so sorry. Stan downstairs told me room ten." She glanced at the number on the door. It said ten. "There must be some mistake."

"Yeah, I ain't who ya think I am. Isn't he with you?" Luke rubbed his cheek and puffed. She'd packed quite a punch.

Lorelei dropped her hands and drew back her shoulders, forcing her ample bosom to strain at the buttons of her blouse. "He was."

Luke puffed again at the sight. He shook his head. Partially to dispel the vision and partially to counteract the ringing in his head. He held out his hand, inviting her to step in.

"Are you okay, sir? I'm so sorry. Is there anything I can do?" Lorelei became contrition personified.

"No, I'll be all right." He inspected his face in the mirror. Beginning to redden, but it'll die down. Eventually. "I haven't seen him this mornin'. When was the last time *you* saw him?"

"Last night. About one thirty, I suppose. The saloon had just closed and ... he visited with me." She paused. "Briefly."

"What do you mean?"

A faint tinge of red appeared on Lorelei's cheeks. "It means we were getting down to it, but then he left. Suddenly."

Inwardly, Luke smiled.

"I came to tell him what I thought of him."

"Oh, ya made that very clear." Luke held his cheek.

"Again, I'm sorry. I didn't expect anyone else to open the door."

"I know. I know. No harm done, Miss Morales. I'll live. And I'll be tellin' him what ya think of him." *Although perhaps not in the exact same way.*

Lorelei gave a tight-lipped smile and nodded. "I should go."

Luke let her out.

When the door opened again a short while later, he was pressing a cold cloth to his cheek. In stalked Fooks, tired and disheveled. He had all his clothes on now, gun belt slung over his shoulder.

"I wondered where ya'd got to," Luke said casually.

Fooks threw off his hat. He slipped the gun belt from his shoulder and flopped onto his bed.

"Sam is in Bitter Creek, half a day's ride from here. Gonna sleep for a couple of hours and then we can get going. All right, old man?"

"Care to tell me what's going on?"

"Nope."

Fooks closed his eyes, hands clasped over his stomach.

"Wanna tell me what's goin' on now?" Luke asked.

He'd shot fleeting glances at the younger man riding easily at his side for some time. Fooks looked drawn, as if he hadn't slept all night. And quiet. Sure, he could be taciturn at times, especially since his accident. Lot to take in and deal with. Luke could understand that, but this felt like something different.

Thankfully, the wind had died down since the other day. Replaced today by a blistering sun. With hardly any shade, this featureless landscape held no respite. The ride to Bitter Creek was turning monotonous.

Fooks started. "Going on? What d'you mean?"

Luke glowered. He'd seen how Fooks had reacted to the saloon girl and later when the madam appeared. A history there, all right. Ordinarily a man's desires were none of his business and he wouldn't pry. Yet Fooks was his son-in-law, and he owed it to Mary.

"Woke up in the night," Luke said. He made a conscious decision to keep facing out front. "Ya weren't there."

A moment before Fooks answered. "I couldn't sleep. Went for a walk." He tossed his head. "Didn't intend to be so long."

The muscle in Luke's cheek trembled. "Where did ya go?"

"Just around."

"Meet anyone?"

"Yeah." Fooks gave his attention to the countryside they rode through. "Sheriff doing his rounds."

"He recognize ya?"

Fooks shook his head. "No," he said. "Gave him no reason to look more closely at me. He thought me just a drunken cowboy."

"When I spoke to him, he seemed a competent fella. Ya new dodger was on his wall."

Fooks gave a weak grin. "I'm on most sheriff's walls. Kinda like a fashionable wallpaper."

Luke saw Fooks grit his teeth, but he seemed determined to press on. "So where were ya all night? Ya weren't hungover when ya came in this morning, so I don't figure ya were sleeping one off."

"Sheriff arrested me for vagrancy. Spent the night in jail."

Luke pressed his lips together to stop the smirk. He didn't entirely succeed, and Fooks noticed.

"Still, I'm surprised he didn't put two and two together."

"Like I said, I didn't give him any reason to look too closely. Just laid down on the cot with m'hat over my face and went to sleep." Fooks licked his lips. "Suppose it's only what I deserve," Fooks conceded with a scowl.

"I didn't say a word," Luke said innocently.

Luke weighed up his next words. He faced the front again. "Ya didn't go back to the saloon, then?"

Fooks took a deep breath. "Yes." When Luke whipped around. "I've nothing to apologize for, old man." With that, he flicked his horse into a lope.

Luke watched him go for a moment before urging his horse to follow. To his surprise, when he caught up, Fooks stopped. They sat facing each other, horses swishing their tails at the change of tempo.

Fooks chewed his bottom lip. "I knew Lorelei … before. She and I had a brief thing. She's a lotta woman."

"Could see that."

"I went back to the saloon to see her." Fooks swallowed and turned his head away. "There was a lot of kissing and a little squishing, but …" He sighed. "I didn't go through with it. I couldn't." He pressed his lips into a thin line and faced the front. "I didn't cheat on Mary. Now I don't intend to say no more about it." He peered at Luke closely. "Something wrong with your face, old man?"

"I had a visit from Lorelei this mornin'. She thought I was you."

"Oh." Fooks winced. "Sorry."

When Luke nodded, Fooks neck reined his horse around and set off again.

Luke brought his horse alongside and they rode at a walk. Breaking the silence, Luke chuckled. "Been a long time since a woman slapped my face. Brought back memories."

The corners of Fooks' mouth twitched into a smile. The atmosphere now improved, and they rode along more comfortably.

"So, you knew Lorelei and me hadn't---"

"Yep."

Fooks turned his head to look sharply at Luke. "Then why ask?"

"Wanted to hear it from you."

Fooks nodded. "Yeah, figgered that's what this was leading up to."

"Can't blame me. Mary's my daughter and if you've done wrong by her, then--"

"I love Mary, don't I?" The question, abrupt and firm.

Luke softened his stance. "Yeah, ya do."

Fooks nodded again. "Thought so." He looked away. "Wish I could remember, Luke."

"I'm sure in time—"

"Yeah."

"Ya're making a success of The Hardware Store. Folks in Bronze Canyon like ya. Might even stand in the town council elections next year."

Fooks gasped out a laugh and shook his head.

"You're doing a great job of reformin', Fooks, don't knock it." Luke studied the man across from him and hesitated before adding, "Mary and Susan, are ya life."

A faint smile fluttered over Fooks' lips. "Yeah, it's kinda nice having a family again," he said, in a whisper Luke could barely make out. "Think I'd like to get back to it soon."

Before Luke could ask him to repeat, Fooks added, "We've gotta get on with this first."

"Ya say ya know Sam Hegarty?"

"We had a difference of opinion."

Luke raised an eyebrow. "Over Lorelai?"

Fooks looked at him sharply. "That was part of it." He faced front again, but Luke could see the muscle in his cheek twitching. "Not sure I'm gonna get a pleasant welcome. Or," he said, softly and paused, "a very co-operative one."

CHAPTER FIFTEEN

The two weary men were at last stopped and sitting at a table in the Lonesome Saloon, in Bitter Creek early evening. Nominally only half a day's ride from their last stop, their way had become blocked by a landslide. The route around added two extra hours to their journey.

"Is he here?" Luke asked.

"Nope."

"Sure, ya likely to recognize him? Been a while."

"Not to me, it's not."

Luke bobbed his head, conceding the point. Reaching into the top pocket of his shirt, he took his glasses from their case. Glasses perched on the end of his nose; he pulled out the menu card from its holder.

Fooks watched him. It was a risky move for Luke to be in this lawless town. Lorelei was right. Even after ten years of retirement, he did smell of the law. *Suppose it's something that never leaves you.* Luke appeared unconcerned as he studied the menu. Like it or not, Fooks felt a responsibility for him. Should he have insisted he stay out of town? *Aw, well, too late now.*

"Anything good?" Fooks asked.

Luke tucked his glasses away. "Yeah, there's pie," he said, with a rare smile.

Fooks lifted his beer to his lips to hide the smirk forming there. A moment later, he slouched back in his chair, running a hand through his hair. Looking around, there were a few other customers. No music blared. *Place is kinda restful.*

"Sure, feels pleasing to stop moving. I'm feeling it. How about you?"

Luke grunted. "Just one more ache and pain to add to those I got already. Haven't ridden this hard or far for a lot of years. Don't suppose you have either."

"No, I guess I haven't." Fooks scanned the room again. Despite what he'd said, would he know Sam Hegarty again? It may not be too long to him, but in reality, it was. Men change.

"How long do we wait?"

Fooks turned back and leaned on the table. "Lorelei said he's here every day. It's early yet. Guess we'll have to wait."

Fooks drew the menu towards him and studied at it. Just the two options for the main course and he knew one of them. "Looks like two pies."

A short while later, and to their surprise, they tucked into two tasty meat pies. Fooks nudged Luke's hand. When Luke regarded him over the top of his glasses, Fooks nodded at the man who had walked in. A thin man, with slicked back black hair and considerable dark stubble. His tan buckskin jacket showed signs of patching and dirty in places. Hat brown and holed from wear and misuse.

"That him?" Luke asked, in a murmur.

"Yep."

"How d'ya wanna handle this?"

"He's on his own."

Hegarty walked to a table in the far corner where men played poker. They asked him to join, accepted him, and he threw his hat down before dragging out a vacant chair.

Fooks pulled a face. He wormed a fingernail between his teeth. "Let him get settled first. Then I'll go talk to him."

Supper plates cleaned and cleared away, Fooks sat back, looking in Hegarty's direction.

"Time for some stimulating card play," Fooks said, getting up.

Luke's hand shot out and clasped Fooks' arm. "Joseph Crane don't play poker."

"Joseph Crane isn't here," Fooks said in a hiss.

"Yes, he is. Listen to me. He's not willin' to risk his livelihood, nor his marriage on gamblin'."

"I keep telling ya, I'm not Joseph Crane," Fooks snarled. "Right now, I'm a man who's got a reputation as a gambler and I'm gonna play me some cards." He roughly shook off Luke's hand. "Go back to the hotel if you don't wanna watch."

Leaving Luke glowering, Fooks walked away to the poker table. Within a short while, Fooks grinned and pulling out a chair opposite to the man flagged as Sam Hegarty.

Play typical of small-town poker. No high stakes. Average level of ability. Fooks was finding it hard not to win too much. *A challenge of sorts, I suppose.*

"Don't I know ya from somewhere, mister?" Hegarty asked, as Fooks raked in yet another pot. *Better make it the last for a while.* One player had already left with an annoyed expression.

"Sure."

Fooks recognized the question for what it was. Hegarty knew him. He was just feeling him out. Fooks concentrated on making a pile of bills. "Everyone knows me." He grinned. "I'm a bad poker player's worst nightmare." He was rewarded by Hegarty's wince. *Yeah, he's certain now.*

For the next few hands, Fooks became conscious Hegarty kept throwing him glances when play allowed. Fooks kept an eye on him, just in case he got antsy.

Showing no sign of noticing, Fooks concentrated on *not* winning.

Fooks fanned the cards in his hand so only he could see. Eight of spades, Ace of spades, Ace of clubs. *Surely not?* Queen of diamonds. *Hmmm, possible.* Eight of clubs. *Yeah, dead man's hand.* Fooks closed the cards, hesitated, and dropped them on the table. "Fold."

With a hand to his lips, he watched with interest while the game continued on in front of him. Would anyone beat his hand? Should he have folded? In the end, his proved the best option. He wouldn't have beaten the winning hand, and he'd saved himself twenty dollars. Sign of a fine poker player. Knowing when to fold or not. Fooks smiled inwardly. *Yeah, that's me.*

The loser raised his arms above his head and yawned.

"That's me fellas. Gonna call it a night."

"Yeah, me too."

With no contenders for their seats and with now not enough players, the table finished. Fooks stacked up the chips and cards belonging to the house. Reluctant to leave until Hegarty decided what he was going to do. He didn't look up when Hegarty scraped back his chair and went to the bar.

On the pretext of returning the playing cards and poker chips, Fooks scooped them up into his hat. He came to stand next to Hegarty at the bar and emptied the contents onto the countertop. He positioned his hat carefully on his head, conscious Hegarty eyed him as he did so. With a polite smile, he slid the cards and chips across to the bartender when he served Hegarty.

"Thanks fella," the bartender acknowledged, pouring out a shot of whiskey for Hegarty. Fooks stood at the bar, pulling on his gloves. He waited until the bartender reached the other end of the bar and out of earshot. Then, watching Hegarty in the big bar mirror, he said in a low voice, "Talk in private?"

Hegarty swirled his drink, then downed it in one. "Ya gotta room?"

Fooks' reflection nodded. "218. Five minutes."

He turned and walked away, pushing through the swing doors and left them flapping.

Fooks answered the door when the knock came. Luke had taken himself off somewhere, so he had the room to himself. "What d'ya want, Fooks?" Hegarty asked, before fully in. He looked around nervously. "Ya on ya own?"

"Hello to you too, Sam." Fooks shut the door and moved to the table. "Drink?" Fooks held out a bottle of whiskey. Hegarty snatched it from him and wriggled the stopper free. Fooks watched Hegarty take a long pull and wiped his mouth dry on his sleeve. He took the bottle back before turning away to fill a glass for himself. "How ya been?" he asked offhand.

"Running with the Smedley Gang these days. Real profitable. Smedley knows his business." Hegarty continued to scan around the room. "Swan not with ya?"

"Not at the moment."

Hegarty blinked with interest. "Ain't heard nothin' 'bout ya for years. You two had a falling out?"

Fooks gestured to the bed behind Hegarty, before seating himself on a straight-backed chair. He crossed his legs casually. "Tell me about what went down in Mudwater Flats." He took a sip and waited.

Hegarty frowned. "Why d'ya wanna know about that?"

Fooks leaned forward, elbows on his knees. "Not interested in the job. I want to know about the shooting. Let's just say it's for old time's sake. Smedley is giving us law-abiding bank robbers a bad name killing innocent tellers. Don't enjoy being lumped in the same bracket." He dropped his voice, putting some menace in to it. "Now why?"

Hegarty pressed his lips together. "Fella was warned not to move. He moved. Smedley don't take kindly to his instructions not being adhered to. Stickler for that, he is."

Fooks sat back and shook his head. "Uh-huh. You'd got what you came for. You were leaving. Eyewitnesses said Smedley turned back and shot him without provocation. Why?"

Hegarty gestured to the bottle.

Fooks bent his arm back behind him to retrieve the bottle. All the while not taking his eyes from Hegarty.

Another slug loosened Hegarty's tongue. "I don't know for sure, but Smedley and Priestly had something going on," he said. "If Smedley finds out, I told ya—"

"What was going on?" Seeing Hegarty looking doubtful, Fooks added, "I've no plans to run into Smedley and even if I did, I have no intention of telling him anything. It's my business. Now what was it all about?"

Hegarty sighed. "Dunno the exact details. All I heard is Priestly fed Smedley money from time to time."

"Was he blackmailing him?"

Hegarty responded with a shake of his head. "Don't think so. When they met, Priestly never looked like a man under duress. Know what I mean?"

Fooks' tongue explored his mouth. "So, you think they were in cahoots in some way?"

Hegarty gave a tight nod. "Last time they met, there was a lot of shouting."

"What were they shouting about?"

Hegarty shook his head. "Couldn't hear. Didn't wanna. Me and the others made ourselves scarce."

"Where did Smedley and Priestly meet?"

"Sometimes in town. Sometimes at the hideout."

Fooks widened his eyes. "Priestly rode out to you?"

"Didn't ride. Came in a buggy, but yeah, he came to the hideout."

Fooks rose and paced to the window. He paused to straighten the closed curtain before returning to the center of the room. With a sigh, he turned on his heel and set off back to the window again.

Hegarty watched him for a moment, took a long pull on the bottle, then replaced the stopper with a firm slap.

"If there's nothing else, Fooks, I'll be on my way." He placed the bottle on the nearest surface and stood up. Fooks turned and moved to stand in front of Hegarty.

"Not quite." Fooks drew himself up, hooking his thumbs in his gun belt. "How long did this arrangement between Smedley and Priestly go on for?"

Hegarty shrugged. "Couple of years. No." He put a hand to his lips, thinking. "Less than. Eighteen months tops."

"And you don't know what it was all about?"

Hegarty shook his head and held out his arms. "All I know Fooks is Smedley went to Grand Forks, piping the First National there and when he came back, he was flush with money. Said he had an inside line on a source of funds."

Fooks rubbed his cheek. "Curious. Did no one ask him where he got the money?"

Hegarty laughed bitterly. "Ya don't know Smedley, Fooks. Not the sort of question ya ask. Not if ya want to survive unscathed."

Fooks rubbed his chin and turned aside. "And this went on for eighteen months, you reckon, and then suddenly..." He faced Hegarty, "then something happened." He looked thoughtful. "Something changed their arrangement. And you don't know any more?"

"Only that Priestly moved from Grand Forks to Mudwater Flats. Took up his job as chief cashier of the Trail County Bank."

"When?" Fooks walked forward to loom over him.

Hegarty gulped. "Not long after Smedley came back from Grand Forks. We never did do the job."

Fooks gasped. All was becoming clear, but he needed to think on it some more before Luke returned.

"Good to see you again, Sam." Fooks stuck out his hand. "Hope there's no hard feeling 'bout the way you left Guardian Wall."

"Naw, your schemes were too complex for me, Fooks." Hegarty stood and took the hand. "I like things simple." He nodded. "Give my regards to Swan."

When Luke returned, Fooks filled him in on what Hegarty said. While Luke prepared himself for bed, Fooks sat in the hardback chair, deep in thought.

"Gonna tell me what ya thinkin'?"

Fooks looked up in a start. Luke, now in bed, smiled ruefully. Fooks sat forward, elbows on thighs, rubbing his thumbs together.

"I've gotta plan, but I haven't worked out all the details yet."

Luke propped his head up on an elbow. "Tell me. Maybe I can help."

"May be. My guess is Arnold Priestly was embezzling his bank. Can't be sure without getting a sight of the bank's books."

"And how do we do that?" Luke asked, doubtful. "We can't just march in and demand to see their books."

Fooks grinned smugly. "No, *we* can't but a bank examiner can."

Luke shifted uncomfortably; aware he probably wasn't going to like what he heard next.

"Don't look at me like that, Luke. I warned you before we started out on this enterprise, I might do things you'd not like."

Luke climbed out of bed, flicking the covers roughly back into place. He stood over the reforming outlaw. "Jus' what do ya have in mind?"

Fooks looked up and pulled a face. "Just some harmless impersonation. Nothing too serious." Then when he saw Luke about to object, went on, "You don't have to be involved. I can handle this."

"I want to know a mite more about ya plans before I can agree," Luke said with a growl.

Fooks stood up and took a step closer until he and Luke were face to face. "This is my life on the line here and you don't get to vet my plans. We do it my way or not at all." His voice, low and ominous.

Luke drew himself up. "Ya need to stay within the law."

"No. I don't. I'm an outlaw. The clue's in the name." Fooks shook his head and he bit his lip. He was finding it hard to deal with this man, this lawman. "Jack Priestly was a fool to agree to us doing this. I can just as easy ride outta here and forget the whole thing. No skin off my nose."

Luke held his ground. "But ya not gonna are ya." Could have been a question, or a statement of fact.

Fooks stared at his father-in-law. "No." He licked his lips. "I gave my word. I may be a lot of things, but I don't break my word." He gave Luke a further hard stare before turning away.

Luke relaxed and regarded the stiff back. "What have you got in mind?"

Fooks looked over his shoulder and sighed. "I know someone who can get, or forge, a bank examiner's credentials."

"For here in Dakota?"

Fooks smiled. "Yes, and we have something on our side. Arnold's bank is a territorial bank. Reporting and inspection are not so onerous as a national bank. Arnold must have known this when he made his deal with Smedley." He shook his head. "Didn't want the complication."

"How d'ya know these things?"

"Made it my business to know 'bout the workings of banks. Didn't wanna hit one if there was an inspection taking place, did I? Or *before* a big deposit is due. Afterwards is the time, providing security isn't stepped up."

"But—?"

"I know. I know *most* outlaw gangs don't think like that. They hit when it's convenient for them. The Guardian

Wall Gang isn't like most outlaw gangs." Fooks twitched his head. "Not the way I run it, anyway." He walked away.

Luke pursed his lips. "Guardian Wall Gang has lost somethin' since you stopped runnin' it." Fooks turned on his heel. "Strictly small time now."

Fooks grunted and turned away, undressing. "That may change," he muttered. "Right." He nodded decisively. "Here's what we're gonna do. Tomorrow, you go back to Mudwater Flats and speak to Arnold's wife. Find out if she knew anything 'bout his activities. My guess is she does." He grinned widely. "And you, as a lawman, with your advanced interrogation skills, are ideally suited to find out what we wanna know. Ask about the Smedley Gang and Sam Hegarty. Mention of those two names just might crack her."

"And what are you gonna be doin'?"

"I'm gonna go and confer with an associate."

"I'll come with ya—"

"No. I need to go alone for this. He can smell a lawman from a mile away. Makes him nervous. If I turn up with you ... let's just say it'll look bad. For me."

Luke drew himself up to protest further, but Fooks held up his hand. "I'll come back. Didn't I jus' get through telling you, I don't go back on my word?"

"Yes, but—"

"No buts, Fletcher. We haven't got time to argue. Time is one thing we don't have. It's beginning to run away from us. I go alone. Final."

In emphasis, Fooks bounced into bed, turned his back, and drew the covers over himself. End of discussion. He heard Luke growl and get back into bed. Fooks smiled. He'd make sure he left before the older man surfaced.

CHAPTER SIXTEEN

Fooks stepped off the train at Wahpeton a day later and made for the ticket office. He smiled when he saw the harassed ticket vendor. Artie Shaw said the name plate. Trying to sell tickets to the long line of customers before the train departed again. Fooks swung his saddlebags to the floor and joined the line. *I can wait. Artie might be more receptive if he's flustered.*

He crept closer to the head of the line, smiling and tipping his hat politely whenever anyone made eye contact. Three customers from the front, Artie spotted him. His face falling as he lost track of counting out change.

"Hurry, man. The conductor's about to start up," the unhappy customer barked.

"Yes sir. Sorry, sir."

Artie's fingers fumbled with ledge bills, counted them correctly this time. He looked relieved when the next customer simply asked for a timetable. The woman immediately in front of Fooks wanted a ticket for the departing train but also had an inquiry about where to change. Artie dispensed the ticket, but information on the change required him to check paperwork.

"Why don't you ask the conductor, ma'am?" Fooks suggested. "Here, let's get you safely on board. I'll help you." Fooks bent and picked up the matron's bag and flashed her his most dazzling smile.

"Why thank you, young man." He'd instantly charmed the matron. "Most kind."

Fooks saw her to the steps of the nearest car and handed in her bag. He nodded to the conductor, who blew his whistle. "All aboard!" Giving the matron a cheery wave, Fooks returned to the now deserted ticket office. Artie stood anxiously behind the grill. Fooks greeted him with a grin.

"Hi ya Artie. Long time no see. How you doing?"

"I suppose this ain't a coincidence." Artie gave a furtive glance around, before leaning over the counter. "What d'you want Fooks?"

Fooks spread his arms with a look of innocence. "What makes you think I want anything?"

Artie tapped a pile of timetables into a neat pile. "Cos you're Florian Fooks an' you never do anything without a reason," Artie said with a hiss.

Fooks smiled at being caught out. "You know me too well, Artie. I do need something."

"I don't do what you used to pay me to do anymore."

"You don't know what it is yet."

"If it's you asking, then I don't want to know."

Artie creaked the grill of his position closed, but Fooks shot out a hand, preventing him. He lost his smile. "I need this, Artie, and you're the only one who can help me in the time." He leveled him with a hard stare. "For old time's sake, huh?"

Artie sighed and looked around again. "I'll listen to what you've got to say, but I ain't promising." He patted the timetables again. "Not here. Macy's Boarding House, seven o'clock. It's a respectable house and Macy is particular about timekeeping."

Fooks nodded as another ticket clerk entered the room behind Artie. Quick thinking, Artie shoved a timetable at Fooks. He nodded and tipped his hat.

Fooks charmed Macy of Macy's Boarding House to rent him a room, saying he was a friend of Mr. Shaw's. After an excellent supper, shared with Macy, Artie and the two other boarders, Fooks persuaded Artie outside. They sat on the porch in comfortable steamer chairs.

"I didn't expect you to take a room," Artie said, immediately they were alone.

Fooks shrugged and lit the cigar he'd purchased specifically for the occasion. "Why not? Beats staying at the hotel." He grinned, sending pungent cigar smoke into the cool night air. "They can be so impersonal, don't you think?"

"What d'you want, Fooks?" Artie shifted in his chair and looked around furtively.

Fooks copied Artie's caution, glancing right and left over his shoulder. Just crickets chirping to worry about. He lowered his voice. "I want a Dakota Territory bank examiner's identity card and a letter of introduction to the Trail County Bank in Mudwater Flats. It's a territorial bank, not a national one. Name of Cornelias Watson." *Hope I can remember who I'm supposed to be.* He waited for a reaction to his request. "You still have the equipment, don't you?"

Artie rubbed his chin. "Yeah, I've still got the equipment. But I thought I made it clear to you earlier, I don't do that sort of thing anymore.

"And I told *you* earlier, this is for old time's sake."

"I came here to Dakota to get away from people like you. How did you find me?"

"Your sister let it slip to Swan one night," Fooks said, around the cigar. "Y'know how persuasive he can be when he's schmoozing the gals."

Artie closed his eyes and shook his head at the sky. "When d'you need it by?"

"Tomorrow."

"What?" Artie exclaimed, then dropped his voice. "Doesn't give me much time, Fooks."

Fooks stuffed the cigar in his mouth and put on his best innocent face. "Artie, you know you do your best work when you're under pressure."

"Not much consolation, Fooks." Artie levered up. "I'll see what I can do. Come to my room before breakfast. I might have something for you." He reached the door and turned. "You haven't got much time to smoke that. Macy locks the door at ten and she don't let in anyone later." He smirked at Fooks' expression of dismay. "Told you. This is a respectable house."

Fooks grimaced. He'd planned to take himself off to the saloon for a few beers and some poker. He ground the lit end of the cigar against the sole of his boot.

Looks like I'm getting an early night.

Fooks tapped lightly on Artie's door the next morning. The door flew open and, seeing Fooks standing there, Artie gestured for him to enter. A quick look either way up and down the hall and he closed the door.

"Have you got something for me?" Fooks asked, amused by Artie's attempts at caution.

"Yeah." Artie went to the desk in front of the window. On it, now collapsed, stood the retouching box. Fooks had seen Artie at work before and this opened up into an inclined surface. Artie used this to alter the photo negative. His tools, including gouache paint, kneaded erasers and charcoal sticks, lay scattered over the desk. An enormous book rested on one side. From this, Artie took a card. Fooks raised an eyebrow when he saw the book was a Bible. "This is the last time, Fooks. I mean it," Artie said, handing over the identification card.

Fooks wrinkled his nose. "Where did you get a photograph of me?"

"It's not of you. It's Rev. I doctored it a little. Added longer side burns, widened the nose, sharpened the jawline. Then I deliberately made it look as though it's been replicated a lot. According to ..." He reached up to a bookshelf and took down a volume. "This is the official list of Dakota Territorial Government Organizations. They renew the bank examiners every two years. If ya asked, you've been a bank examiner for ten years. You're due for renewal next year. See the expiration date?" He drew Fooks' attention to the date on the identification.

Fooks raised his chin to Artie. "Will it pass?"

"Should do, but best not to let the bank manager look too closely."

"Understood." Fooks tucked the card away in the breast pocket of his shirt.

"Here's the letter of introduction and a business card."

Fooks unfolded it and read, nodding. "This J. B. Swerling? He a real person?"

Artie nodded. "Director of Fiscal Oversight, Dakota Territory. Got his signature from a previous forgery."

"Thanks Artie. I owe you one."

He turned away, pulling on his riding gloves.

"Er, Fooks."

Artie held out his hand, palm up.

Fooks grinned. "Of course. How could I forget?" From the breast pocket of his shirt, Fooks brought out his paper money, peeled off several crisp bills, stopped for a second, before peeling off two more. Pressing them into Artie's waiting hand, he said, "Always glad to do business with you." He gave a salute and turned back once more. "See you around, Artie."

Artie raced to the door ahead of him. "No Fooks. This is the last time. I mean it. I'm done."

Fooks straightened his shoulders. *Do I really need Artie's services again? Not exactly required for a life in hardware. My life now. Oh Sheesh.*

Deciding fast, he placed a hand on Artie's shoulder and nodded. "Okay, Artie. We're done. You have my word. I won't bother you again."

Fooks walked away, preparing himself for the long journey back to Mudwater Flats and Luke. A plan of action already forming in his head.

CHAPTER SEVENTEEN

Back in Mudwater Flats, Luke started when the hotel door opened the next day and then tried not to sigh with relief too loudly when he saw who it was. Not silently enough, it seems, when Fooks gave a brief chuckle.

"Told ya," he said, turning to close the door.

"Got what ya went for?"

"Yep."

Fooks swung his saddlebags to the floor and bounced down onto the bed. He unbuckled one side, reached in, and pulled out an envelope. He held it out.

Luke sat on the opposite bed and took out the contents. A letter of authorization to begin a bank audit, a business card and identification, with a grainy photograph of one Cornelias Watson.

"Seen many of those before?"

"Some." Luke looked up in surprise. "Cornelias Watson?"

"Name's as good as any."

Fooks watched Luke, studying the documents some more. "My associate reckons they'll pass. What d'you think?" He swallowed the stab of surprise. Luke's opinion mattered.

Luke nodded and then returned the contents to the envelope. "They look okay. Supposin' the bank checks?" he asked, holding out the envelope.

Fooks nodded in agreement. "Which is why I'll have to be quick. Hegarty didn't give me any pointers where to start looking, but I reckon the biggest accounts. Easier to hide any discrepancies."

He sighed and unbuckled his gun belt, dropping it with a thud to the floor. "Now all I need do is to rent a suit." He swung his legs until he lay on his back on the bed. "Boy, am I tired." He stared at the ceiling. "Give me an hour and let's go to the saloon. You can tell me how you got on with the wife while we're having supper. Deal?"

Luke smiled and nodded. "Sounds like a deal."

Given the run-down exterior of the saloon, it came as a surprise when the smell of the food led their mouths to water. Both men enjoyed the beef, onion and gravy pie, mashed potatoes and even the green beans. Plates mopped clean with biscuits, before being shoved away with contented sighs.

"Good," Fooks said, throwing aside the napkin.

"Reminds me of my Eloise's cookin'." Luke saw Fooks' blank look. "My wife. Mary's Mama."

Fooks pressed his lips together. "Did she teach Mary how to cook?"

Luke grinned. "Sure did."

Fooks nodded. "Mary's a fine cook. Look forward to eating."

Luke smiled. "Ya know what they say, the way to a man's heart…"

Fooks sobered and threw down his napkin. "Yeah, it'll probably take more'n that." Luke waited for an explanation, but none was forthcoming. Instead, Fooks said, "You haven't told me yet what you found out about Arnold's wife. Did you find her?"

"Nope."

Fooks raised his head in interest. "Oh?"

"Yeah, seems she packed up and left not long after Arnold's funeral."

Fooks grunted. "Not surprised. Gone back to her family?"

Luke had a rueful grin on his face. "Nope."

"Okay," Fooks smacked his lips, mastering his patience. "You seem determined to drag this out. Where did she go?"

"Canada."

"Where in Canada?"

Luke shrugged. "Neighbors didn't know."

Fooks rolled his eyes. "Canada's a big place."

"Yep, so I went to the stage depot and asked where she went. She took a stage to Mayville. I rode over there, where I found she caught a train to Larimore."

"From Larimore she coulda gone anywhere," Fooks said accusingly.

Luke wrinkled his nose in apology. "Have we got the time to follow her?"

"We'll have to make time. It's the only lead we've got," Fooks agreed, looking pensive.

"And if we find her, what does it tell us?"

Fooks rose with purpose. "If you go to all the trouble of embezzling your place of work, I bet Arnie kept some of the money for himself, only giving Smedley part of his ill-gotten gains. Stands to reason. He was taking all the risks, and he has a wife and child to provide for. If we find the wife, we find the rest of the money."

"And?"

"We return it." Fooks looked across to the card tables set up for play. "Space jus' opened up. Think I might have myself a few hands of poker afore turning in." He scrapped his chair back as he stood up.

"I thought ya were tired."

"So did I. Supper perked me right up. In need of something to exercise the mind now."

Luke caught his arm when he started away. "I told ya, Joseph Crane, doesn't play poker."

Fooks' eyes blazed, and he shook off Luke's hand. "Yeah, well, I do."

Luke watched Fooks stalk towards the poker table with the empty chair. Only to stop a few feet before, hesitate, then veering off to the bar.

Fooks ordered a whiskey, downed it in one before slamming the empty glass down on the bar. Then he turned. With a scowl at Luke, he walked out with purpose, leaving the bat-wing doors swinging wildly.

Luke waited an hour before returning to the hotel. He half expected not to find Fooks there. But he was. Laying on his bed, arms behind his head, staring at the ceiling.

Luke walked in without a word and hung up his hat. He crossed to the chest of drawers, removed his gun belt, and emptied money from his pockets. Purposefully, he kept his back to Fooks and he barely heard him speak.

"You're right."

"'Bout what?"

Fooks' tongue explored his cheek, embarrassed to admit Luke was right. "About not playing poker." The bed creaked as he sat up and swung his legs over the side. "I'm not that man anymore, but right now I don't know what man I am."

Luke smiled faintly. He sat across from Fooks. "You have to learn how to be Joseph Crane again. It'll take time and this situation ain't helpin'. Right now, you need to be a little of both men." Luke considered. "One reason why I'm here. Help ya do that."

Fooks climbed back to lie prone on the bed again, linking his hands behind his head. "I don't rightly know how to do that. Let's just concentrate on the matter at hand. Maybe it'll work itself out." He saw the skeptical look Luke gave him. "How d'you think I should approach the bank tomorrow?"

Luke turned in surprise. "Ya askin' me? Thought you were the genius master criminal."

Fooks grinned smugly. "I am. Just nice to hear someone else say it for a change."

Fooks stroked the cutthroat blade delicately under his chin. Four days of stubble proved hard to shift, and he needed to look presentable for his day at bank examining. He pulled a face in the mirror, scrutinizing for any stray tufts of dark hair. Rinsing the cutthroat in the bowl of warm water, he spun. His Schofield, in his hand and cocked, when the hotel room door opened.

Luke blinked in surprise but slightly relieved when the hammer on the Schofield released.

"Forget to knock?" Fooks snapped, thrusting his gun hard into its holster.

"Mite jumpy, ain't ya?" Luke snapped back, and then gave a short laugh. "Suppose a man in your position has a right to be."

Fooks continued inspecting his face. Deciding he'd done the best he could, he wiped the remaining foam from his face with a towel. He turned to Luke when the older man came to rest in front of the closet. A suit jacket, hung over the front.

"Smart," Luke said with a smile.

Fooks false smiled back. "Thanks."

"White shirt. Stiff collar. Somber tie." Luke waved his hand at the items laid out on the bed. "Ya even got a briefcase. Reckon ya'll pass."

Fooks crossed to the bed and shrugged into the shirt. He gave Luke a glare as he did so. "Glad you approve."

"Why wouldn't I?"

"Oh, I dunno. Maybe 'cos what I'm about to do isn't exactly lawful."

"I ain't doin' it. You are." Luke stiffened with a sigh. "Look, I knew right from the get go you'd have to do thangs which weren't strictly lawful. I'm reconciled to it now."

"Must be hard."

Luke chose not to rise to the sarcasm, but offered some of his own. "It's getting' easier."

To Luke's surprise, Fooks smiled in amusement. "Must be corrupting you, huh?" he said, fumbling with his collar.

"Here. Let me do it. Turn about."

Fooks faced the mirror on the closet door and Luke fitted the back of the collar. "How are ya gonna play this?"

"First off, I'm gonna walk in and ask to see the manager. A Mr. Gustavus Brandt. Should be interesting. Hope he's not too German."

"Thought ya ma's family was German. Something musta rubbed off."

"Ma's family raised her in England. They insisted on English most of the time. Her German wasn't great. She only taught me a few words. Not enough to hold a conversation."

"There, ya done." Luke slapped Fooks on the shoulder.

Fooks squirmed his neck to find some comfort in the stiff collar.

Reminds me of Mary.

In the bank, Fooks walked up to the nearest teller. A young woman with light brown hair.

"Good morning, sir. How can I help you today?" she asked with a smile.

Fooks removed his homburg and fixed her with his most dazzling smile. "Good morning." He rested his briefcase on the counter and poked the name plate around so he could see. "Miss Amy Forest." His smile became a beam when she colored and dropped her eyes coyly. "Name's Cornelias Watson. I'd like to see the manager, please."

Amy didn't meet his eye, her hands sprung to tidy up her position. "Yes sir. I'll see if he's available. May I say what it's about?"

"A confidential matter, Miss Forest."

She nodded in understanding. "Yes, of course."

While he waited, Fooks scanned the interior layout of the bank. The two teller positions stood on the right, behind which were bank official offices, including the manager. At the far end of the banking hall was an area demarcated by a low wooden balustrade. Behind this sat several clerks, the smell of beavering away hung in the air. In the far corner stood the vault. His heart fluttered when he saw it. Miller and West 1883. *Two tumblers, five sequences each. Just have to get the tumblers and the sequence right. Piece of cake. Two hours tops.*

He tapped his fingers on the counter to an unrecognizable tune when Amy returned. "This is Mr. Brandt, the manager." She indicated a portly, middle-aged man, with thin gray hair on Fooks' side of the counter.

"Mr. Watson, how may I help you?" He offered his hand. Fooks smiled inwardly at being proved correct. Brandt was German, and his accent slight. *Second generation?*

"Mr. Brandt." Fooks reached into his top pocket and offered a business card. "This will explain why I'm here."

Brandt blanched when he read the card. "You'd better come through to my office, Mr. Watson."

Fooks smiled and snatched up his hat, preparing to follow. Not before smiling again at Amy. "Thank you, Miss Forest."

Setting off another rise of color, Amy tidied her position again.

Once in the office, Brandt closed the door. "I wasn't informed of a bank inspection, Mr. Watson," Brandt said, facing Fooks in the middle of the office.

"Well, no, Mr. Brandt. It's an unannounced inspection. Rather negates the word unannounced if you were told beforehand I was coming." Fooks smiled pleasantly. "Wouldn't you say?"

Brandt turned a sickly green. "Yes, of course." He gestured to a chair.

Once seated, Fooks rested his briefcase on his knees and unbuckled the straps. Brandt had retreated behind the safety of his desk and sat, leaning on it, rubbing his clasped hands. When Fooks said nothing but rummaged around in his briefcase, Brandt broke the uncomfortable silence.

"Is there a particular reason for this inspection?"

"Oh yes," Fooks said, smiling brightly, before dipping his head and rummaging some more. When Brandt appeared sufficiently uncomfortable, he brought out what lay on top all along. "My identification," he said, placing it carefully on the desk, his hands resting close, ready to snatch it back if Brandt attempted to pick it up.

To Fooks' relief, he didn't try. Brandt nodded, pursing his lips." Looks all in order."

"Good." Now Fooks did snatch it back and tossed it carelessly into his briefcase. He struggled with the buckles before setting the briefcase down against his leg. "Let's get down to cases. I understand there was a robbery here about three months ago?"

"Yes, that's correct. An examiner came and inspected the books a short time afterwards. Everything was in order and the bank refinanced. Which is why I don't understand why *you* are here now."

"Ah. I'm here to check on the examiner." Fooks rubbed his ear. "I'll tell you this in confidence, so you didn't hear this from me. There's a suspicion raised over the work of that examiner. Only a minor discrepancy elsewhere, but we're obliged to check all his work from the last six months. Protocol. Procedures. You know. Making sure I tick all the boxes." Fooks smiled. "I'm sure there is nothing to worry about. This is just a formality." He paused. "Now Mr. Brandt, time's a-wasting and I should get on. Sooner I start, the sooner I'm out of your hair."

He rose. "Where do I go?"

Fooks sat at the table made available to him and watched as the ledgers for the period he wanted to audit pile up in front of him. He puffed at the amount of book work they expected him to go through. He didn't want to be in the bank for more than a day. Less if he could manage it. This lot would take weeks to go through. *Hmmm, maybe I can eliminate some.*

He pulled the first towards him and looked at the spine. 'Securities, May.' *Nope, don't think Arnie would go down that route.* He could dismiss four more weighty tomes, setting them to one side. Still left an enormous pile to wade through.

After a few long minutes of sorting, he had the ledgers he wanted to check through. Satisfyingly, the pile he had dismissed, now bigger. He started with the daybooks of the two tellers, one of which had belonged to Arnold Priestly. In order to appear thorough, he checked Miss Forest's ledger first.

Hmmm, neat handwriting.

He didn't expect to find anything amiss. If he did, he resolved to ignore it. Not his business if another employee also had their hand in the till.

After a cursory inspection, he set this aside and reached for Arnold's day book. Starting with January, he scanned down the columns, making a note when he came across a considerable deposit. He repeated the same with the ledgers for February to May. He'd need to crosscheck with the depositor's record later. When he'd finished, he had a list of twelve deposits to check over the five months, January to May.

Checking the depositor's ledger proved trickier. It required him to add down the columns for each day. His mental arithmetic, always good, but this was tedious. Stopping for a few moments to sip coffee couldn't relieve the boredom. Until...

January 15. He twice added the column, yet neither time did the result equal the total at the bottom. Someone had obviously checked and initialed the entry was correct. But it wasn't. He tried again carefully. *Nope, don't add up. Why?*

On closer inspection, he found a scuff mark over a number belonging to seven thousand. He ran his sensitive forefinger over the mark, feeling the slightly raised grain. What could have caused it? *Hmmm. Why can't I find this?* A glance at the bottom of the column, compared with his own addition, showed a difference of two thousand. He ran his finger over the scuff mark again. Something had been stuck over the figure. Could that something have contained an alteration? Saying nine, perhaps? That would make sense. With a nine instead of a seven, the column would add up. He went back to the day book. The entry showed nine thousand dollars deposited.

All around him the scratch of pen nib on paper, the thump of stamp on pad and then the louder thump when they brought it down, the clack of feet on the wooden floor. Nobody took any notice of him. Except Mr. Brandt, who lurked in his office doorway. Fooks raised his hand, and the manager made his way over.

"Yes, Mr. Watson?"

"Who writes up the depositor's ledgers?"

"The tellers, of course. Don't have enough staff for a strict segregation of duties, I'm afraid."

"But someone else checks the addition?"

"Yes. One of the accountants. They initial to show they've checked all is in order." Brandt's face dropped. "Why? Have you found something?"

Fooks smiled. "No. No. Just wondering about the process is all."

Brandt walked away, regarding Fooks suspiciously. Fooks smiled at him until Brandt went back into his office. Fooks lost the smile. *Okay, now I know what to look for.*

By the end of the morning, Fooks had found fifteen thousand dollars' worth of false accounting over the five months from January to May. The books of non-local banks had proved particularly interesting. *Ah, so Arnie indulged in a little kiting, did he?* Altering a check drawn on an out-of-town bank, taking advantage of the time it would take to verify. Withdrawing the funds in the meantime. *Risky. Had to keep an eye on it. Lucrative. Very lucrative but...*

Fooks winced. *Thought I was dealing with an upright citizen here. Shame on you.* Fooks chuckled. *What's ole Jack gonna say?*

CHAPTER EIGHTEEN

Luke found Fooks sitting in the easy chair in their room. The suit jacket hung neatly on its hanger.

"Ah, ya back. That was quick," Luke said, turning to shut the door.

"Didn't take long." Fooks swirled whiskey in his glass. He downed the amber liquid, savoring the fiery feel as it slid down and leaned forward to set the glass on the table. "Arnie *was* embezzling the bank all right. Found numerous arithmetic errors in the ledgers. And some kiting. Hats off to him, Luke. His methods were ingenious. Doubt if I uncovered all his little appropriations. Expect he was at it for years. Found about fifteen thousand, but then I only went through the last five months and I guess he knew he was about to end it." He shook his head. "What is the world coming to Luke? If a bank of all places can't look after your money safe."

Luke raised his eyebrows at the irony of Fooks making that statement.

"I know. I know." Fooks levered to his feet and pulled at his collar and tie, wincing a bit at their tightness. His fingers moved to loosen the tie before throwing it off completely. "The bank had an inspection right after the robbery. I made an excuse to the manager that the examiner had made mistakes and I'd been sent to check on his work." Fooks grimaced and he reached behind his neck to unfasten the collar. He sighed in relief when it sprung free. "Seems there was a need to. A blind man coulda spotted the discrepancies I found."

"Ya think the examiner was in on it?"

Fooks shook his head, laying aside collar and tie. "Naw, think he was just incompetent. I've a good mind to let the authorities know."

Luke grinned ruefully. "Perhaps ya should."

"Not sure…" He nodded his head from side to side, considering. "Anonymous tip off maybe?" He flashed a quick grin. "If I'd known about this wheeze earlier, I mighta considered a crack at it myself."

Luke sent him a glare. Fooks looked innocent. "Just sayin'."

Luke grunted and sat on his bed. He bent to pull off his boots with a groan. "How much did Arnold get away with?"

Fooks sat on the bed opposite. Luke pummeled his pillow before laying down. "As I thought, he hit the biggest accounts. A little here, a little there. If what I found in his last five months is any indication and given his imminent departure, I reckon about thirty, forty thousand in total over the eighteen months he was there. How much he gave to Smedley is anyone's guess. Must have been a fair amount to keep Smedley interested."

Luke whistled.

"Yeah, but Arnie got cold feet. The yelling Hegarty told me about musta been Arnie telling Smedley he was done. Doubt Smedley, would like such a lucrative and easy source of money drying up. The gang hit the bank and as they were leaving, Smedley killed Arnie." Fooks pursed his lips. "Only explanation that fits."

"Jack will not be happy."

"I know. We'll just have to prove it."

"And how do we do that?"

"You said the wife went to Canada?"

"Yep. At least that's what she told the neighbors."

Fooks pulled a face. "She got family there?"

"Arnold and Jack do."

Fooks sat up, interested. "How close family?"

"Uncle, by all accounts."

"Why would she go to him?"

"All she said to the neighbors was Arnold had an uncle in Canada and she and the boy were goin' there to make a new life."

"Well then, I guess we follow her."

At Larimore the following day, they found Mrs. Priestly had boarded a train for Grand Forks. Too late in the evening to inquire further as to the lady's onward journey; they checked into a hotel. They had just returned to their room after dinner when a knock on their door sounded. Luke and Fooks looked at each other. They weren't expecting anyone. Fooks retrieved his gun from its holster, hung on the bedpost. He nodded to Luke to open the door as he moved to the other side, out of sight of anyone coming through the door.

"Howdy, Mr. Fletcher," Tobias Swan said, strolling in casual as you like, saddlebags draped over his shoulder. "Sure glad to catch up with you finally. I've been all over this territory like a rash." He noticed Fooks standing open-mouthed. "Ya can put that pop gun away. I'm here now." He motioned to the gun in Fooks' hand.

"Wha'. Tobe! What are you doing here?" Fooks' eyes were out on stalks.

Swan smiled, swung the saddlebags from his shoulder onto the nearest bed.

"I don't understand. Mary sent a telegram but you couldn't..." Fooks, overwhelmed, didn't resist when Swan held his upper arms, then pulled him into a brotherly embrace. A shuddering gasp escaped him and Swan tightened his arms. Trying to control his emotions, Fooks pulled away. Swan wouldn't let him. Fooks gave in and surrendered to his friend's embrace. He whimpered into his shoulder.

"It's okay, Flo. I couldn't come right away but came as soon as I could." Conscious of Luke's presence, Swan let Fooks go but kept him at arm's length for a moment before giving him a shake. "Sheesh, ya look ... dunno ... not like I expected."

"Saloon's still open. I'll take myself off over there for a while. Ya can join me when ya finished catching up," Luke said, reaching for his hat. With a final backward glance, he left. Neither man fully registered his going.

Fooks replaced his gun and wiped his face smartly, hoping Swan hadn't noticed. Together they sat on the bed, Swan's arm flung around Fooks' shoulder.

"Mary tells me ya don't remember being Joseph."

"Not really but..." Fooks tossed a hand towards the door, faintly surprised not to find Luke there, "Luke's helping to fill in the gaps. You've seen Mary?"

"Went there first. Then trailed ya all the way here. Good job Mr. Fletcher's been sending back regular telegrams, else I'd have the devil's own job tracking ya."

"Has he? I didn't know that."

"Figgered ya didn't. Part of the deal, apparently."

Fooks stiffened. "The deal he made with Priestly? You didn't run into him, did you?"

"Relax. No, Mary knew I was coming and Wash sent his eldest boy to head me off at the train depot when I got in." Swan pulled a face. "Not sure Priestly woulda remembered me. Certainly not all gussied up in eastern clothes."

Fooks rubbed his cheek and smiled weakly. "I'm glad you're here, Tobe. You've no idea what it's been like. All these strangers." He shook his head. "Just too much to take in."

Swan patted Fooks' shoulder. "I know, but now I'm here, we can make sense of it together." He smiled. "Your daughter's cute."

Fooks broke into a fond smile. "Yeah, isn't she? Bright as a button."

"Got me a boy now. Fact it's why I was late. Looking forward to watching him grow up."

Fooks laughed. "Oh, you wait for all the sleepless nights. All the walking up and down in your underwear trying to get a fractious baby..." Fooks sobered. "I remember," he breathed. He buried his head in his hands. "I remember holding Susan and jiggling her up and down. Only Pappy seemed to work." His eyes watered. "Sheesh, Tobe, this thing's so random. I can't stand it."

Swan put a comforting arm around Fooks' shoulder.

Fooks threw him off. He scrubbed at his eyes. "I know you've just got here, but I need to go for a walk. Clear my head."

He stumbled out of the door almost at a run.

Luke returned shortly afterwards to find Swan reclining on Fooks' bed. "I saw him walking up the street," he said, in explanation for his return. "Where is he goin'?" he asked, turning to shut the door.

"Taking a stroll. This memory thing has hit him hard. How's he really doing, Mr. Fletcher?"

Luke tossed the door key on the bureau. "Up and down, I guess. One minute he's the Joseph Crane I know. The next he's ... a whole other person I don't know." He sat down heavily on a chair. "You bein' here has to be a good thang."

"I came to help with his memory. Found out there's now this mess to sort out. I reckon I can help with that, too. What's it all about, Mr. Fletcher? Wash only gave me the highlights."

Luke told him the story so far.

"The Smedley's aren't renowned for their gentlemanly ways."

The hotel door opened. Swan's gun leaped into his hand. Two concerned faces greeted Fooks when he came back to the hotel room.

"Ya okay?" Swan asked, holstering his gun.

Fooks nodded, turning to close the door. He moved to sit on the bed next to Swan and leaned forward, idly rubbing his thumbs together. Swan kept a hand on his shoulder. Fooks reached around and patted the hand.

"I'm okay, partner. I'm okay." His hand dropped away. "Has Luke filled you in?"

Swan nodded.

From his top pocket, Fooks threw something onto the nightstand. "I picked that up while I was out."

Luke unfolded a railway timetable. He studied it for several moments. "If Mrs. Priestly's goin' to Canada, she'd have to go to Grand Forks. From there, the alternatives are Devil's Lake and Park River. Neither goes through to Canada, but there's another possibility. Here's a map." He held it up. "No alternative but to change." He indicated the line, which ran all the way to Winnipeg.

"We could shortcut the travel time if we ride across to Ardoch," Swan mused. "But then we'd lose her, Flo. We should find out what her destination is first before we make any rash decisions."

Luke shook his head. "The train stops at Neche. All passengers alight and state their destinations. Have their bags searched too." When he saw their blank faces, he added, "Customs. Although given the isolation up there, guessin' it ain't too thorough a search. Easy enough to stash cash in between layers of clothes."

Swan looked at Fooks. "What d'ya think?"

Fooks considered. "I do like the thought of not getting on anymore trains. Riding for a while has its attractions. Priestly gave us two months. It's been five weeks already." By the look on his face, Luke hoped for a more leisurely pursuit. "Save us a bit of time, Luke."

Swan slapped his thigh and stood up. "Okay, riding it is. First thing in the morning, I'll go get some horses and all the gear." He glanced down at Fooks. "But for now, I'm gonna get a room and get some shut-eye. I'm beat." He gave Fooks' shoulder a final shake. "Glad ya see the sense in us doing this, partner. These men aren't like us."

"No." Fooks looked up. "No, they're not." Fooks looked up as Swan made for the door. "Say, did something happen to me six years ago?" He kept his eyes on Swan, who sat back down. "I guess only you can tell me."

"All tied up with why we went straight."

Fooks turned to him eagerly. "What happened to make us go straight? Stop being those men?"

Swan took a moment to compose himself, flicking an anxious glance at Luke. "We was on a train we were fixing to rob. Afore we got to the spot we'd earmarked, the train screeched to a halt. Yep, someone else had the same idea as us. Nothing we could do but sit there pretending to be legitimate passengers." Swan looked thoughtful. "It shoulda been a simple heist. All went well. No one was hurt. We had to watch while this other gang robbed us of *our* money.

"But it was a setup. The Pinkertons were waiting for them. Killed some of the gang, rest are in prison. Not doing too well the last I heard."

Swan winced. "Same thing happened on another train a few weeks later. Pinkertons were there as a welcoming party."

Swan licked his lips. He noticed how intently Luke listened and directed his next words to him. "Now the thing 'bout Fooks is he don't like to be beat, Mr. Fletcher. Other gangs with the same ideas but getting caught each time. Rather dented his pride."

Fooks pressed his lips together.

Swan chuckled. "But it was the bank which proved the final straw."

"They were waiting for us when we came out. Near got caught too." Swan looked away. "Lost two good men that day," he said quietly. "The posse gave us a hard chase. Your horse got shot from under ya."

Fooks gasped. "Neddy?"

Swan knew how fond Fooks' was of his former horse and he patted his hand. "I took care of it. He didn't suffer."

"Thanks."

"But you. Apart from the fall which knocked ya out, ya weren't hurt. Got ya across my horse and we got ya back to the Wall. Didn't wake up for two days. Thought we might have to get a doc to ya. When ya did come round, ya were kinda different."

"How?" Fooks frowned.

"Quieter. Reflective. Ya got to thinking it could only be a matter of time before it was us. It was time to get out. We talked it over and we decided. We had to get out but safely." Swan twitched his head. "Well, as safely as we could.

"Heard Wash Turner was sheriff in an out of the way place called Bronze Canyon. Not a place we knew. Never figured the place was big enough for us to bother with. And we didn't know if we could trust him. We knew Wash from when we were kids after our folks..." Swan swallowed hard. "After we lost our folks. It had been a long time, and he'd changed sides."

He gave a lop-sided grin. "We decided to risk it." Swan paused. "An' we're glad we did." He looked direct at Fooks. "Aren't we?"

Fooks sat up straight. "Yeah, I guess so."

"We weren't evil men, Mr. Fletcher. Just a little misguided. Plenty of worse villains out there. Like the Smedley Gang."

"I know. And I'm not sure I want to take them on," Fooks said, glancing over at Luke, "given our limited resources." He hesitated. "Guess as we've made our decision 'bout which side of the law we're on, we don't get a choice."

Swan smiled and patted Fooks' arm, agreeing with his words. *Well done, Flo. Think ya coming around.*

Almost immediately after leaving Larimore the next morning, Fooks and co. crossed the northern branch of the Turtle River. From here on the land became gently undulating grassland, peppered by rocks and boulders, small streams, shallow lakes. Dry from the fading summer heat, negotiating this landscape wasn't difficult, but the features made it slow. They were reduced to walking in places, not willing to risk their horses. Finding a concealed pothole could pull a tendon or, worse, break a leg.

Swan pulled up once they reached the top of a low hill. Concealed behind a massive boulder, he stared back into the distance. He got down. Going to his saddlebags, he retrieved binoculars. By now, Fooks and Luke, realizing he was not with them, had turned back.

"Problem?" Fooks asked.

"Dunno," Swan said, distracted. "Thought I saw something moving back there." Looping the strap around his neck, he raised the glasses to his eyes. Adjusted them before training them on the spot of interest.

Fooks dismounted, threw the reins to Luke, and walked over. He stood, hands on hips, by the side of his partner. "Are we being followed?" His voice noticeably deeper.

"Yep."

"Let me see." Fooks snatched for the binoculars, forgetting the strap around Swan's neck. A strangled squawk emitted, resulting in swapped irritated glances. "Where?" Fooks asked when Swan had untangled himself.

"Bottom of the valley. Just coming around the bend in the creek."

Fooks scanned in the direction Swan pointed. A moment later, he lowered the binoculars sharply. "Oh."

"What's up, boys?" Luke remained on his horse. He'd already told them he was only getting on and off again unless he had to.

Swan looked up, closing one eye against the sun. "We've got ourselves a tail, Mr. Fletcher."

Fooks handed up the glasses and folded his arms tight across his chest. "Sam Hegarty and three others. My guess: the Smedley Gang."

While Luke saw for himself, Swan turned to Fooks. "Thought ya trusted Hegarty?"

Fooks shook his head. "Not what I said. He seemed to bear me no ill will about the way we kicked him outta Guardian Wall."

"The way *you* kicked him outta Guardian Wall," Swan smirked.

"All right. The way *I* kicked him out of Guardian Wall," Fooks agreed, disgruntled. He tossed a hand towards the oncoming riders. "Looks like I was mistaken."

"Someone tried to improve Hegarty's looks with their fists," Luke said matter of fact and handed down the binoculars. "Don't think they succeeded."

"How d'ya wanna play this?" Swan asked, accepting the binoculars back from Luke. He peered through them again. "Mr. Fletcher's correct. Someone did a real number on Hegarty. One eye's swollen shut, face a mass of bruises, fingers on the right hand probably broke. Way he's riding, I'd say cracked a few ribs too."

Fooks chewed his lips for a moment. "Smedley musta found out Hegarty talked to me and found out what it was all about." His eyes strayed to Swan's holster. "Have you been practicing with that thing?"

"Some." Right on cue, he stuffed the binoculars between his knees. Taking out his Colt, he spun it several times by the trigger guard around his finger and returned it to the holster.

Fooks false smiled. "Very flash, but not what I asked."

"I can still hit what I aim at, Fooks. Don't ya worry about me. It's you and that pop gun which has *me* worried." Swan's eyes fell to the gun Luke wore, and he widened his eyes.

"Not used a gun much last few years, but it ain't something ya forget, Swan," Luke said with a growl.

Swan nodded and turned back to Fooks. "We can't know their intent. We're worth a sizable amount of easy money to 'em don't forget."

"Not as much as we were, Tobe." Fooks turned away. "We got cheap." He rolled his eyes.

Luke mastered his expression while Fooks swung up onto his horse next to him.

"We let them catch up. I don't wanna be caught unawares." Fooks stared into the distance. "Let's try to control the situation our way. Do we agree?"

Luke nodded. "Makes sense."

Fooks turned to Swan, who stood running the reins of his horse through his hands, thinking. "Yep," Swan agreed. "Let's keep going and find a place where we can talk."

With that, he vaulted with some athleticism onto his horse.

CHAPTER NINETEEN

"This looks like a good place," Swan said, half an hour later.

They'd come across a rocky outcrop. Behind lay a campsite clearly used before. Fire pit, complete with ashes, rocks drawn up for sitting, a well-worn log on the other side. The trail ran off to one side. Boulders provided cover on both sides. Giving it a wide berth would add at least an hour. For those trailing them, this delay would be unacceptable. The Smedleys would have to come through here if they didn't want to lose their trail.

"Thinking the same thing." Fooks passed a leg over the high pommel of the saddle and jumped down. He dragged his horse away, heading for the group of tall and bulky boulders overlooking the trail.

Swan, now on the ground, handed the binoculars up to Luke. "Keep an eye on 'em, Mr. Fletcher. While me and Fooks get this set up." He pulled his horse around to follow Fooks before turning back. "Try not to let 'em spot ya."

Luke scowled. "What? Do ya think this is mah first rodeo?" He walked away, shaking his head.

They made their preparations with Swan insisting on checking line of sight and firing angle repeatedly. Luke scowled and muttered under his breath after the fourth run through and Fooks sat down hugging his knees.

"I'm done," he said, when Swan tried chivying him to his feet. Fooks chewed his bottom lip. "If we're not ready by now, we'll never be. You're making me nervous and I can't afford to be."

"Okay." Swan sighed reluctantly. "They'll be here soon, anyway. Still there, Mr. Fletcher?"

Luke peered through the binoculars again. "Yep. All four of 'em."

"Good." Swan sat next to Fooks and mirrored his posture. "Bit like old times this isn't it?" He threw off his hat to the ground beside him.

"Seems like yesterday," Fooks said, dryly. He swallowed hard. *Do I really want to do this? Anything can happen.*

"Sorry. Forgettin'. Swan patted his arm. "We gonna try to take 'em in?"

Fooks moved his jaw from side to side as he considered and shook his head. "Nope. Haven't got the resources right now."

"Hey! I can hold my end up," Luke protested.

"It's not that, Luke. We're in the middle of nowhere here. Like to have a few more men behind me and a nice cozy jail cell waiting nearby."

The sensible explanation didn't stop Luke from looking disgruntled.

"Sure, ya wanna do it like this?" Swan asked, bringing Fooks back to the plan and to his own reservations. "Dunno much about Smedley, but from what I hear, he's got a short fuse. And he's a killer."

Fooks let out a shuddering breath. "I know, but I don't like what he's done to Sam. Nothing for it but to go in hard and confident." Fooks nodded, before adding with a smug grin, "'Sides I have Tobias Swan looking out for me. Not to mention..." He glanced back at Luke, "all the knowledge of our U.S. Marshall retired."

Swan followed his gaze. "Must be hard having him as a father-in-law."

"Kinda hard having *any* kinda father-in-law. Dunno how to talk to him or act around him." He ran his fingers through his hair and then reached for his hat. "Enough of this. Let's get this over with."

He placed his hat on his head carefully and took a few seconds to adjust it so it sat low over his eyes. Using Swan's shoulder like a lever, he uncurled heavily.

Not long after, they were in position, Swan hidden behind a rock, gun angled down on the trail. Luke crouched on the opposite side; his gun trained at an angle behind Swan's. Neither wanted to catch the other in any crossfire, and certainly not their companion.

Fooks swallowed hard. Waiting was tough. *Well, prepared as much as we can. Just a matter of biding our time now.*

⊢———•———⊣

Not long now.

Fooks took up position in the center of the trail, awaiting the oncoming men to appear around the corner. He could hear the horses' hooves and the creak of the saddles. He stood up straight and tall, shoulders back. Confident.

"Howdy fellas. Mind telling me why you're following us?" he asked the moment Smedley in the lead appeared.

Smedley brought his group to a halt. The two others came up, either side of him. Hegarty remained on his own in the rear.

"Ya mistaken friend. Happen to be going in the same direction, that's all."

"Is that a fact? Looks like one of your number could use some doctoring. We've bandages and salve if it's a help."

Smedley cast a glance back at Hegarty. "Naw, he's good."

The four sat on their horses, waiting. Fooks didn't move. Now he had a closer view of Smedley, he didn't like what he saw. The man had a cruel mouth. The polite words up until now failed to disguise it. Smedley sat easily, but experience told Fooks he was a coiled spring. The two men on either side of him appeared nervous. The one on Smedley's left, not too subtle, dropping his right hand to hang close to his gun, the other kept his hands high, clasping the reins of his horse. Hegarty looked done in and Fooks dismissed him as a threat. He wasn't even wearing his gun. The man on the right had it tucked into his waistband.

"Ya plan on letting us pass?" Smedley asked, when the standoff became unbearable.

"Nope," Fooks said, simply. "Wanna word with you first."

Smedley laughed. "If ya mean to rob us, friend, let me tell ya we don't have more'n a few dollars between us."

"Somehow, I doubt it. Wanna get off your horse and let's talk like civilized men."

Smedley scanned up at the rocks. "Where's ya buddies?"

"Around. Don't you worry about them. They won't hurt you." Fooks grinned. "'Sides it isn't them you need to worry 'bout. It's me."

The smallest of movements, making Fooks frown. Then it happened fast.

"Easy boys." Swan stood, gun drawn and leveled at Smedley. The man on his left closed his fingers inches from the butt of his gun. The man to the right hovered his hand in midair.

Hegarty's eyes widened. Well, one eye widened, the other swollen shut, but he spoke in awe.

"Tobias Swan, mighta known ya'd not be far away from Fooks."

Smedley appeared unconcerned when he looked up at Swan. Fooks now held his gun pointing at them and Luke had also appeared with his gun drawn.

Fooks cocked his head, closing one eye against the sun. "So, you know who we are," Fooks said. He'd be surprised if Smedley said no.

Smedley tossed his head behind him. "Our man there let it slip."

"Take out ya hardware real slow and toss it over there." Swan pointed out Luke's side of the trail. Four distinct thuds followed. The two flanking riders pulled rifles and threw them, too. "Rifle too Smedley. Rest of you, get ya hands up."

Smedley rolled his eyes and laughed. "Anything ya say, Swan." He reached down and withdrew the rifle from its boot and tossed it.

Satisfied the men were now disarmed, Fooks holstered his gun and folded his arms. Luke collected the discarded hardware. Swan scrambled down the rocky incline, stones skidding out from under his feet, gun still levered at them until he reached Fooks.

"Now what?" Smedley asked.

"You." Swan gestured to the man on the left. "Get off ya horse. Slow." When he was down, Swan motioned to the other man. "Now you. Just like ya partner." Then when he moved too suddenly, he barked, "Slowly man."

The man raised his hands in apology before warily dismounting.

"That's better." Swan raised his chin. "Hegarty?"

"I don't think I can Swan," Hegarty gasped. "They beat me pretty bad."

Fooks and Swan both turned to Luke. He straightened up from making a cache of their guns behind a rock and gave a sharp nod.

Luke gave the others a wide berth to reach Hegarty. The injured man groaned loudly when Luke peeled him as gently as he could from the saddle. Reaching the ground, Hegarty nearly lost his footing. If Luke hadn't been there to hold him up, he would have toppled over. With Hegarty bent double, Luke guided him past the group and along to the camp. He tugged Hegarty's horse along behind them.

"You two follow 'em. Lead ya horses."

Fooks raised his arm to show the way. When they'd moved past him, he looked back at Smedley, still sitting on his horse. "I'm not satisfied with your answers yet, Smedley. You and me are going for a chat. Bring him, Tobe." Fooks gave Smedley a lingering look, before turning to stalk up the trail.

Their camp stood a short way along the trail off to one side. A meagre fire crackled away with a coffee pot wedged in the embers. As Fooks arrived, Luke eased Hegarty down, emitting an oomph from them both. Fooks went immediately to the coffeepot and offered it to their other guests.

"Sure," one said, with a shrug. The other nodded.

"Pull up a rock then." Fooks picked up two previously used enamel mugs, discarded the spent contents, then refilled them. "What do they call you?"

The two swapped glances before one answered. "Chronister," he said, accepting the mug.

"Pleased to meet you. Frankie, isn't it?"

Chronister gave a curt nod. "I answer to either."

Fooks smiled, tight-lipped. "Very wise." He turned to the other, holding out a mug to him. Even at arm's length, Fooks could smell the unwashed body. "So, you must be Cole, the brother."

He nodded.

"Ah, and a man of few words."

Fooks sat on a handy log opposite when Smedley arrived, followed by Swan.

"What's this all about, Fooks?" Smedley asked, accepting the offered mug. He took a seat on an opposite rock near to his two men. Swan remained standing. He'd holstered his gun and hooked his thumbs in his gun belt, ready if one of their guests should make a move. He shook his head when Fooks offered coffee.

Fooks took a long, slow, drink, regarding the three men, considering how to play this. Finally, he sniffed and set aside the now empty mug on the log beside him.

"Tell me about Arnold Priestly."

He watched Smedley closely. A brief flick of recognition before Smedley shrugged. "Who?" he asked, glancing up at Swan.

"The man ya killed in Mudwater Flats," Swan said.

"The teller in the Trail County bank," Fooks said. "Y'know, the bank you robbed?"

Smedley's face lightened. "Oh, yeah, him. Why d'ya wanna know 'bout him?"

Fooks gave back a grin guaranteed to annoy Smedley. By the scowl appearing on Smedley's face, he'd succeeded. "Cos I'm asking."

Smedley shifted his position.

Fooks continued. "I figure you don't know Arnold Priestly has a brother. Jack. Jack Priestly." Any sign of recognition on Smedley's face? *Nope, none.* "He works for the law and he's not too pleased someone killed his brother." Now Smedley was cottoning on. "Way I heard it; he's gunning for the man who done it. Pulling in all sorts of favors to find him." *Kinda true, I suppose.*

"Where d'ya hear that?" Smedley said, with a growl.

Fooks leaned forward. "Let's just say it's come to my attention." He gave Smedley a hard look for a moment before adding, "What d'you plan to do about it?"

Smedley gave it some thought. "I can't deny it's troubling news, Fooks, but here's the thing. This Jack Priestly is like any other lawman in the country." He shook his head. "Hopeless. They ain't caught me yet. Not even come close. You know what I'm saying. Ain't caught you yet either and you're..." He leered. "Smarter than most. So they tell me."

Fooks smiled. He glanced over to where Luke tended to Hegarty. Turning back to Smedley, he sobered. "That's 'cos I don't beat up my men."

Smedley's gaze went to Luke and Hegarty and he laughed. "So that's what this is all about. Never figured ya for a bleedin' heart, Fooks. Why I heard ya can be right ruthless." He chortled into his coffee.

"I can be," Fooks said, with menace, keeping his eyes locked on Smedley. "You still haven't explained why you're following us."

Smedley shook his head, drained his mug, and set it on the ground. "Like I said, we're just going the same way. It's a free country after all and..." He rose to his feet, one eye on Swan, and motioned to his men to do the same. "I'm done answering ya questions. Thanks for the coffee. We're leaving now." He took a step forward and stopped.

Swan stood in his way, gun drawn and pointed at him. "No, you ain't. Suggest ya sit back down and answer his question." When Smedley didn't move, Swan pulled back the hammer.

Smedley held up his hands. "Okay, okay. Ya're holding all the aces."

Fooks acknowledged Swan's help. As Smedley and his men retook their rocks, Fooks raised his chin in Luke's direction. Seeing he was finishing up doctoring, he asked, "How is he?"

"Done what I can. Could use a doctor."

Fooks turned his attention back to Smedley. "Now see, here's the difference between you and me. I am smart and d'ya know why I'm smart?" He didn't give Smedley time to answer before carrying on. "I don't kill men who wrong me. There's far more subtle and painful ways to take revenge. Entertaining too."

Fooks drew out his gun and turned it over in his hand, regarding it speculatively. "Can you dance?" he asked, in barely a murmur.

Smedley viewed the gun warily for a moment before going on the attack. "What d'ya mean?"

"You heard." Swan said.

"Don't ya ever sit down?" Smedley scowled up at him.

"Nope."

"I'm working on a tan. Ya blocking my sun."

"A real shame. Are you gonna answer his question or not?"

"Can I dance? Sure, I can do-Ce-do if I have to. What's ya point?"

Fooks smiled. "Like to see some of your moves." His smile faded and pointed the gun at Smedley. The click of the hammer sounded loud in the canyon. Fooks aimed at a spot between Smedley's legs. "Just about there oughta do it. The splinters from the rock will ensure you'll put on a right nice show for us. Shame we haven't got any music."

"What d'ya want, Fooks?" Smedley, plainly rattled, stiffened in place. He closed his legs, then changed his mind and opened them again wider. "I don't have anything ya want."

"Yes, you do. And I've asked you twice already. Politely. Now I'm *not* asking politely. Why are you following us?"

"An' I keep telling ya, we're not."

Fooks looked up at Swan. "Want a spot of entertainment?"

Swan shrugged. "Sure, why not? Unless ya want me to do it? Ya aim is likely to be off these days."

Fooks peered along the sight of his gun. "Naw, I'm good," he said, casually. "Okay, Robin, are you ready?" He didn't wait for an answer. His finger moved on the trigger, squeezing. "Let's dance."

CHAPTER TWENTY

"I thought ya were really gonna have to do it for a moment there," Swan said, as he stood next to Fooks watching three men ride back down the trail until it forked. They steered their horses to the left, towards Gilby, where Smedley said they were headed.

"So did I." Fooks stood with his arms folded. "Think we can trust them not to double back?"

"Nope. They'll hold back, I reckon. Spend a half hour in Gilby and then follow on. Heard Cole Smedley is a decent tracker. Doubt he'll find our trail too difficult to follow."

"Perhaps we should set a false trail?"

Swan considered for a moment, before shaking his head. "Naw. They must know Ardoch is the only other town in this vicinity and we have Sam, remember? He don't look too well, Fooks."

Smedley had agreed to leave Hegarty with them. They'd take him to a doctor. On reflection, Smedley would have agreed to anything. Fooks made his hand shake when he aimed the gun at the log near Smedley's legs. Of course,

Smedley wasn't aware this was an act, but he'd wisely decided not to chance it. Smedley had explained their journey by gabbling out a story about meeting up with an old pal. Telling them about a job worth doing. He didn't say if it was a robbery and Fooks didn't ask. Probably best not to know.

Swan turned away. "C'mon, let's get going. How far into Ardoch?"

Fooks fell into step beside him. "Luke reckons about ten miles." He glanced up at the sun. "Should be there before nightfall."

"Think Sam'll make it?" They both turned to look over to where Luke boosted Sam into the saddle.

"Hope so. Else I really will have a score to settle with Smedley."

They reached Ardoch without incident and left a very unwell Hegarty with the doctor. Tomorrow might be a different story.

The next morning, to their surprise and relief, they saw no sign of the Smedleys. Fooks and Swan went to visit Hegarty before they continued their journey. Sam was sitting up, looking much better. His right eye, still swollen shut, but the bruises on his face were darkening. He appeared more comfortable and his voice stronger when he greeted Fooks and Swan.

"Gotta thank you boys for bringing me into town. Don't reckon I woulda made it otherwise."

Fooks sat on the side of the bed and smiled. "Yeah, what we figured."

Swan drew out a chair and sat backwards on it, arms resting on the back. It creaked ominously. "We didn't want ya death on our conscience. What gave Smedley cause to beat on ya like he did?"

Sam took a deep breath before wincing and putting a hand to his chest. "He saw me talking to ya. Wanted to know who ya were and what our conversation was about.

He's a mean sonofabitch Fooks, wouldn't let it lie." Sam shook his head. "Kept pounding on me until I told him."

Fooks bit his bottom lip. "Yeah, exactly what I thought." A flicker of pain crossed his face. "I'm sorry you got hurt, Sam. I surely didn't mean for it to happen."

"I knows ya didn't. What's done is done. If there's anything I can do for you boys, just say the word. Mind," He held up his bandaged and splinted right hand. "Might havta wait a few weeks."

"The best thing ya can do for us, Sam, is stay away from Robin Smedley," Swan said. "The man's trouble."

Hegarty nodded. "Yeah, knows that now, Swan."

"You take care of yourself, Sam." Swan swung his leg over the chair and spun it around.

"Now listen. Smedley knows we brought you here, but Fletcher's gone to tell the sheriff to look out for him. Doubt if Smedley will make trouble in town. You should be okay while you're here healing up. With a bit of luck, Smedley will tire of waiting. I think he wants to get on after us. Take care when you leave here, just in case he leaves someone behind. Okay?" Fooks rose and looked hard at Hegarty.

"Sure thing Fooks. And thanks again."

They'd reached the door when Hegarty said, "Oh. This might not be important, but I'll tell ya, anyway." They came back. "One time when Arnold Priestly came out to the hideout, he brought his wife and boy with him. She's a real looker Fooks."

Fooks and Swan swapped glances. "Thought he wanted to find her to get the rest of the money," Swan said, with a frown.

"Well, I can't be sure now, but Smedley took more'n a polite interest in her. Know what I mean?"

"Ya think she's in cahoots?"

Sam shook his head. "Can't say. All I can say is, don't trust her."

Fooks turned towards the door and opened it. "Thanks for the warning." He went out frowning and chewing his lip. *One more piece in the puzzle, perhaps?*

"What d'ya think?" Swan asked.

Fooks had spent the last half an hour first slumped in a chair and then throwing himself out to pace in their hotel room in Ardoch that afternoon. Swan, trying to doze, knew not to interrupt him, but all this thudding, grunting and arm waving was distracting. Fooks came to a stop and stared out of the window down onto the main street. Luke walked across from the telegraph office.

"We'll know soon enough."

He'd sent Luke to dispatch a telegram to Priestly. Fooks wanted to know who had told Priestly about his brother's death.

Fooks turned when the door opened. "Well?"

Swan swung his legs over the side of the bed and sat up.

Luke closed the door and took off his hat. "Jack's sister-in-law told him in a telegram."

Fooks straightened and nodded. "Rather a curt way to do it."

"What does it tell us?" Luke asked.

"It tells us our Jack isn't a favorite of Arnold's wife. I also think there might be something going on between her and Smedley," Fooks said, then looked up, frowning. "What is her name, anyway?"

"Elspeth," Luke said. "Boy's name is Peter. He's eight."

"What makes ya say that, Flo?" Swan asked. "Smedley ain't exactly God's gift."

Fooks shrugged. "Some women like a bit of rough. Seems odd Arnold would take her and the boy out to visit with Smedley. Perhaps she got to making a comparison and liked what she saw."

"Ya think she was in on it?"

"'Tis a possibility. Dunno without knowing more. Guess we'll have to consider her as a hostile witness until we know."

Luke sat on the bed next to Swan. "Also asked Priestly where this uncle of his lived."

"And?"

"Gretna. Just over the border into Canada. Seems he's some kinda storekeeper."

Fooks grinned, dimples widening. "We've got ourselves a destination."

Luke grunted. "Yeah, an' we better geta move on. We don't know how far behind us Smedley is. Winter ain't far off and they come early up here, and Canadian winters are even worse than those in Wyoming. Don't think my old bones will take too kindly to be snowed in above the line."

Swan stood up and reached for his saddlebags. "Yeah, an' I got a wife an' a newborn I want to get back to afore snow piles up."

Fooks threw his hands in the air. He'd been looking forward to playing some poker in the saloon that night. The brief glimpse he'd had the previous night held the promise of some rich pickings in this town. It would appear his companions had other ideas. He made a half-hearted attempt at collecting his belongings.

"I got a train timetable here," Luke said, looking at the leaflet in his hands. "Train leaves in fifteen minutes. It'll get us into Neche by nightfall." He smiled. "Then tomorrow, it's a quick hop over the border to Gretna."

"Sounds good, Mr. Fletcher." Swan intensified his saddlebag stuffing.

Fooks stood hands on hips and watched the others hurrying.

"Sheesh, when you two boys get the bit between your teeth, you really do, don't ya?"

"Hurry up, Flo. Else we'll leave ya behind." When Fooks didn't move, Swan added, "You're the one under the time pressure. Ya wanna be running from Priestly the rest of ya life?"

With a scowl, Fooks reached for his saddlebags.

"Where is he?" Fooks, pacing again and fuming. "Can't take that long to visit with a sheriff, surely?"

They'd arrived in Neche the night before, too late to visit the sheriff's office. Luke took himself over there first thing after breakfast this morning. Fooks and Swan returned to their hotel room to wait.

Swan looked up from cleaning his gun. "Relax Fooks. Mr. Fletcher knows him. Said he did when we got in. Y'know how it is. These ole boys get to reminiscing and forget the time."

"They'll have gone through each other's entire life history by now," Fooks grumped, tossing a hand in the air. "Twice."

Swan wiped the barrel of his Colt with a soft cloth. "Ya ain't got any more patient, considering ya don't remember much."

Fooks stopped and glared at him. "I remember things." He turned and walked to the window, twitching aside the sheer curtain to view the main street.

"How's that coming along?" Swan returned his shiny gun to its holster and cleared away his cleaning materials.

"Slowly." Fooks turned from the window and gave a deep sigh. "Still lots of holes. I don't always realize there is a hole until something happens which I don't understand."

"I can't say I know what that feels like, but the fact ya remembering things must be good. Right?" Swan busied himself tucking his things away in his saddlebags. "I mean, it must be like discovering ya a whole new person each time."

"I am a whole new person. I just don't remember *why* I'm a new person. I liked the old me."

Swan shook his head. "No, ya didn't Flo. Ya got disillusioned."

"Me?" Fooks stalked towards him, jerking a thumb back at his chest. "But I'm the best. How could I get disillusioned by that?"

"The train at Imber, the next one at Sadler's Crossing, the bank at Rapid Forks. Want me to go on? Ya went into a sulk 'bout them all."

"Give me a break. I don't remember those three places." Fooks waved his hands in irritation. "And I don't sulk."

Swan rolled his eyes at the last comment. "No Fooks, ya don't."

He opened his mouth to protest when someone slid a note under their door. They exchanged glances before Fooks went to pick it up.

Swan moved swiftly to throw open the door. "Just the clerk," he said, before joining Fooks.

Fooks held the note at arm's length and puffed at the appalling penmanship. He managed to decipher it enough to read:

If you want to see the old man alive again, meet at the Catton place on the Pembina road at twelve noon. Don't be late. Smedley.

"Oh, great." Fooks handed the note to Swan.

"This puts a different spin on things. What do we do?"

Fooks stood, hands on hips, thinking. "We'll have to go out there, of course, but I don't fancy our chances."

Swan sucked in a breath. "All the feelings of a trap."

"Yep." Fooks stared at a spot on the rug and then he gave a smug grin. "So, we have to make sure things turn out in our favor, won't we?"

"How do we do that?"

Fooks took back the note and reread it. Then he nodded. "We go over to the sheriff and persuade him to back us up."

"We?" Swan rose to his feet. "We? Uh-huh." He waved a finger. "*You* can go see the sheriff."

Fooks scowled. "But my dodger'll be on his wall. This new batch is making lawmen look more closely at us again an'—"

"So's mine. It'll be right up there next to ya but," Swan stepped forward, "I'm better at breaking ya outa jail if things go wrong." He placed his hands on Fooks' shoulders. "Mr. Fletcher is bound to have told his friend, the sheriff, he's traveling with his son-in-law. Now put on ya best worried face and get on over there."

"How d'you figure?"

"Stands to reason. If they're old pals, he might justa told him what he's doing here. We're a long way from home, Fooks. We need all the help we can get from where ever we can get it."

"Yeah, and he might have told him who I am. I go waltzing in there and I'm straight into a cell." He turned away.

"Now, why would Mr. Fletcher do that?" He didn't wait for an answer. "Fooks, ya need to do this." Swan was firm.

"I know. I know. Just need to work up to it, that's all." Fooks stood, arms akimbo, and took a deep breath. "Okay." He reached for his hat and plonked it on his head, giving Swan a false smile. "Promise you'll get me out before supper?"

CHAPTER TWENTY-ONE

Fooks walked over to the sheriff's office with a scowl. When he reached the door, he stood hand on the handle for a moment. Fixing his features into the worried expression Swan prescribed, he pushed in. The sheriff stood, frowning at paperwork, but he looked up when the bell tinkled. *Sounds like a candy store. Perhaps that's what I'll turn into.*

"Help ya?" the sheriff said, his eyes fixed once again on his papers.

"Yeah." Fooks turned and closed the door, resisting the urge to be on the other side of it. "Name's Joseph Crane. Understand you know my father-in-law, Luke Fletcher?" He hooked his thumbs into his gun belt and pulled back his shoulders.

"Yeah, I know Luke. He told me 'bout you. Going up to Canada to look over a prize bull, I hear." He held out his hand. "Dave Garvey."

So same story as before. Okay, I'll play along. Fooks gave a tight-lipped smile and shook the offered hand. "Pleased to make your acquaintance."

He rubbed his cheek as he considered how to proceed. "That's right. On our way up to Canada. Perfectly legitimate business, which is why I was surprised by this." Fooks stepped forward and took the note from the breast pocket of his shirt. He handed the note over. "Slipped under my door, not ten minutes ago."

"What's this?" Garvey took it with suspicion. He stiffened as he read it. "D'ya know this Smedley?"

"Yeah."

"And?"

Fooks took a step forward. "Luke may not have been entirely open with you, sheriff." He chewed his lips.

Garvey motioned to a chair behind him and Fooks shook his head. *Last thing I wanna do is sit.*

"Suit yourself." Garvey took the seat at his desk, waiting for an explanation.

"Luke is working undercover. Brought me along 'cos he thought I might have some insight into the fellas we're tracking." *Close enough.*

"Who're you tracking?"

"Robin Smedley and the Smedley Gang." He waved a hand at the note Garvey held. "Looks like they found us instead."

"I've heard of the Smedley Gang. They can cut up kinda rough."

"Yeah, and now they're killers, too. I don't think they know who Luke is, but if they do, then he's in a lotta trouble."

"You planning on making this meeting?"

"Yep. Can't do anything else. Gotta play along. Be obliged if you would bring a few of your deputies along. Secure the area. Y'know that sorta thing."

Garvey picked up a paperweight and slammed it down on top of the note. "How many men has Smedley got?"

"Last time we caught sight of them, just Smedley and two others. Can't rule out he's acquired extra local help though."

"I can only muster two regular deputies. Think the four of us'll be enough?"

Fooks twitched his head. "Gotta partner over at the hotel. He's a pretty reasonable shot. Five of us should be plenty if we're organized."

Fooks sat. "What's the lie of the land around the Catton place? And how far outta town is it?" Now in his element, talking about planning.

Fooks and Swan approached the deserted farmstead cautiously. Tumbleweeds blew across the approach. A loose shutter creaked in the wind. This far north, noticeably colder. Both wished they wore coats, instead of just shirt sleeves.

Garvey and his two deputies had scouted out suitable places to hide and watch.

Swan looked across to Fooks when two men came out of the house onto the rotten porch. Both carried rifles.

"I shoulda hid with the others," Swan said, out of the corner of his mouth.

"Smedley will expect us both. If you aren't with me, it'll make him nervous. I don't want him any more nervous than he already is."

"He don't strike me as the nervous type."

Fooks grunted. "We'll see, won't we?"

They brought their horses to a halt.

"Howdy, boys. Pull ya horses over there," Chronister said, pointing to the well a few feet away. "Then get on down." He and Cole Smedley walked out to meet them.

Once on the ground, Fooks and Swan waited for further instruction. Behind them, Robin Smedley had come out of the house with Luke. The latter, with his arms tied behind his back and mouth gagged. Smedley hustled him into a chair on the porch, back to the wall.

"Lose the hardware, shall we?" It was Chronister who spoke. "Slow now. Left hand. Thumb and forefinger only. Put 'em in here." He indicated the well bucket.

Two guns clanked into the metal bucket and Cole turned the handle, which lowered the bucket.

Chronister motioned with the rifle that Fooks and Swan should approach the house.

Smedley sat on a chair, gun in hand, resting between his legs. He grinned as they walked up, stopping just before the porch. "Well, now Fooks. Looks like the tables have turned somewhat."

Fooks inspected Luke for signs of mistreatment. Although he appeared to be in pain, Fooks couldn't determine the location. After what happened to Hegarty, he'd imagined all sorts. Luke nodded slightly at Fooks' silent inquiry.

"What d'ya want Smedley?" Swan asked.

"Why have you brought us way out here at this time of day?" Fooks asked. "I was planning a siesta this afternoon."

Smedley laughed. "What I like about you, Fooks. Ya've got a sense of humor." He paused. "Ya here 'cos last time we met ya didn't answer my question."

"Don't recall ya asking a question," Swan drawled.

"That's 'cos I didn't get the chance. You had the drop on us." Smedley stood. "Ya gave me an idea last time. The only difference is I'll act on it." He rose and turned to Luke. "Lean forward, old man."

Luke swallowed and lent forward slowly. Fooks stared, openmouthed. *Sheesh, Smedley is gonna shoot the wall behind him.*

Fooks went to take a step up onto the porch.

"Why the heck would you do this? He's done nothing--"

He broke off when Smedley pulled back the hammer and leveled the gun at arm's length at Fooks' head.

"Now I want an answer from ya Fooks. You know where Elspeth Priestly is, don't ya?"

"Might but if—"
Smedley pulled the trigger.

CHAPTER TWENTY-TWO

Sheesh, that was close.

The bullet whistled past Fooks' right ear. A little behind him, someone poked a gun between Swan's shoulder blades, stopping him from lunging at Smedley. From the smell emanating from the body, it could only be Cole Smedley.

Fooks winced and shut his eyes. He raised his hands.

Smedley cocked the gun again. "Now that I've got ya attention. Where is she?"

Fooks glanced at Swan. "We don't know for sure—"

Another bullet flew. This time spinning Fooks' hat away. Fooks gasped. *Far too close.*

"Let him tell ya," Swan yelled.

Fooks took a ragged breath, thinking fast. *Gotta lie. Play for time.* "Altona. We think she's over the border in Altona."

"Where in Altona?" Smedley cocked the trigger again.

"Don't know."

Smedley leveled his aim at Fooks' head.

"All right. All right." Fooks swallowed hard. "She's gone to Priestly's uncle. Don't know his name, but he's a storekeeper." Fooks raised his hands higher, and hated himself when next he spoke. His voice sounded more of a squeak. "Don't know what kind." He hoped Smedley believed him.

It took a moment. Fooks and Swan were on tenterhooks until Smedley released the trigger and nodded. "See, that wasn't so hard, was it? Now this gives me a dilemma. Can't really go a-visiting an' leave you two boys alive. 'Sides, ya worth fourteen thousand dollars. Dead or alive."

Ten. Not the time to tell him we're cheaper, Fooks.

Smedley grinned. "I like the dead part. Easier to transport. An' that's a tidy sum to start a new life. So—"

"There's a force out here. Get ya hands up," yelled a voice from a distance.

"Who's that?" Smedley demanded.

Fooks looked innocent.

"Shots fired. Sounds like the local law to me," Swan said.

"Ya went to the law?" Smedley cuffed Fooks to the ground and then aimed a kick at his stomach. Fooks groaned and curled up, anticipating further attacks.

Swan turned abruptly, sweeping the gun in his back aside, hoping to knock it out of Cole Smedley's hand. But no, he still held it and now he leveled it at Swan.

"Gotta go, Rob." Chronister came at a run, firing off shots towards the distant voice.

Answering shots had Swan diving for the ground beside Fooks.

"'Nother time fellas."

The Smedley Gang ran to the side of the house, where their horses waited. Garvey and his men advanced on their position. The Gang took off before Garvey could get close, the lawmen retreated swiftly to fetch theirs.

Swan laid a hand on Fooks' arm, who nodded. "I'm all right. Go."

Swan was up and running to the well. Eager to retrieve his gun and horse. In that order.

Fooks' first instinct was to go with him, but then a strangled moan from Luke reminded him he had other priorities. He rose to his feet painfully, with a hand over his stomach, he staggered onto the porch and tore away the gag. "Oh, Sheesh. Are ya hurt Luke?"

"Naw, just kept me tied up tight. Playing devil with my shoulders."

Fooks fumbled to untie Luke's hands. Luke had tried slipping his bounds, only succeeding in cutting into his wrists. The knots were tight and the rope slippery with blood. Pulling made Luke grunt in pain. "Hold on." Fooks reached into his right boot and brought out a slim blade. He sawed away at the rope until Luke could pull his arms free.

"Thanks."

By now Swan had retrieved his gun and mounted up. "Here." He tossed Fooks his Schofield. "I'll go after them. You get Mr. Fletcher into town."

No time to argue. He'd turned his horse's head around and galloped after the others.

Four horses galloped after the fleeing three. The latter had a head start and their horses, fleet of foot. The land, flat and featureless, except for a dotted line of trees way up ahead. Neither Garvey nor his deputies bothered firing as they raced in pursuit. But confident of his ability, Swan did. Yet, his bullets went wide. He cursed. *Out of practice.*

After several miles, Garvey and his men pulled up. Swan streaked ahead before realizing he was alone. He neck reined hard around and brought his horse alongside Garvey.

"Why'd ya stop?" Swan fought to control his prancing horse.

Garvey pointed to the line of wind wavering trees up ahead. "Border is past those trees. I can't pursue."

"What? They're gettin' away, man." Swan stared after the men, disappearing into the distance.

Garvey shook his head. "I'm sorry, I can't. I'll notify the Canadian authorities when I get back."

"What about Luke? Ya friend. They hurt him."

Garvey's face took on a pained look. "If I go across the border, I could set off a diplomatic incident. The Canadians are a mite touchy about their territory being violated. I can't risk it."

"Ya worried about paperwork?" Swan's eyes widened, incredulous.

"No," Garvey said. "Listen, I have to live here. I don't agree with it, but I've gotta work within the rules." He took a deep breath. "You can go across. You're a private citizen. I can't stop you." He saw Swan's indecision. "But I ask you this: what can one man do alone?"

Swan chewed his bottom lip as he considered. Ahead, the Smedleys had skirted the trees and were far on the other side. Looking back at Garvey, he shook his head in frustration.

"Ya right." He turned his horse around. "I'll join up with my partner and then decide what we'll do."

On the surface, Luke appeared fine apart from his wrists. Fooks didn't want to take any chances. And if he would admit it, feeling a mite woozy from Smedley's treatment of him.

In town, Fooks roused the doctor from his post lunchtime snooze and demanded he treat Luke right away. The inebriated man needed some persuasion. Fooks held him at gunpoint before he would rise. Waiting outside the consulting room, Fooks idly flicked through a magazine before carelessly tossed it aside.

He stood staring out of the window when the door of the consulting room opened. He turned.

"Ya can see him now," the tired doctor said, tossing his head behind him.

"Will he be all right?"

"Yeah, 'Xpect. Now if there's nothing else?"

Before Fooks could answer, he was already gone.

With a sigh, Fooks entered the consulting room. Luke lay in his henley on his back on the bench, his head turned towards the wall. Bandages wrapped around both wrists. Fooks walked over cautiously. He placed a hand over his stomach as he took a seat. *Perhaps I shoulda let the doc take a look at me, too.*

"He patch you up?"

"Yeah," came the taciturn reply.

Fooks looked guilty. "I'm sorry Luke."

Luke turned his head. "What for?"

Fooks waved vaguely in Luke's direction. "Getting you hurt. You're my responsibility. I shoulda looked out for you better."

"No, ya not responsible for me."

"Yes, I am," Fooks insisted. "I have to explain this to Mary. She trusted me to keep you safe and…. I let her down."

Luke shifted about until he could see Fooks' face. "Listen to me, son. I'm responsible for myself. I walked away from spendin' time with m'old friend Garvey an' I wasn't payin' attention. It was my fault those fellas jumped me. You've nothin' to be guilty about. D'ya understand? Nothing."

"But still…" Fooks huffed, deciding it wasn't worth it. "Okay. What did the doc say?"

"Apart from grousin, y'mean? Awh, says he expects me to live, but I'll have a permanent limp."

"I didn't think your legs…" Fooks broke off and closed his eyes. *You're joking.*

Luke chuckled. "I'm okay Fooks. Shook up is all," he said, patting his arm. "I'll be fine in a day or two." When Fooks opened his eyes, he added, "I've had worse done to me."

When the outside door opened, it was Swan. "Hallo?"

"Back here, Tobe."

As Swan walked in, Luke struggled to his elbows. "Owh. D'you get 'em?"

"Naw, they made it over the border. Sheriff couldn't pursue. Didn't make sense to carry on alone." Swan aimed a kick at an innocent chair. "Dammit Fooks. They were in sight and we were gaining."

"Easy Tobe."

Luke pushed himself up, forgetting his wrists hurt. "Owh." He gingerly swung around to sit on the edge of the bench.

Anger forgotten; Swan looked at Luke in concern. "How are you?"

"I'm fine," Luke said with a growl. "We need to get after 'em. I've gotta score to settle with Mr. Robin Smedley. Now help me find m'shirt."

"You're not going anywhere, old man," Fooks said.

"We'll see 'bout that. And less of the old man. I ain't that old." Luke dropped one foot to the floor, intent on standing up.

Swan stood ready to intervene when Fooks drew himself up to protest. "Look, we don't have time for you two to butt heads. I'm sorry Mr. Fletcher, we need to get after 'em quick. Me an' Fooks'll take care of it."

"D'ya know where they're goin'?" Luke said in a growl. "'Cos--"

"Sure, Fooks told 'em Altona. We're going to Gretna."

"Where in Gretna?" Luke said, pushing away from the bench to stand unsteadily.

Fooks sniffed. "Don't reckon Gretna's a big place. Priestly's uncle is a storekeeper." He shrugged. "Can't be hard to find him."

"Unless a'course Priestly ain't his name," Swan mused.

Fooks grimaced. "That's right Tobe, think of a negative."

Swan beamed. "It's what I do."

"Ah ha, ya didn't thank of that, did ya?" Luke grinned, triumphant and dropped a steadying hand to the bench. "Ya need my help."

"Could be a maternal uncle," Swan suggested, ignoring him.

"Gretna's only a couple of miles away, less by train." Luke looked eager.

Perhaps he's hoping that's enough to persuade me to let him come along. Wrong. Fooks shook his head. "No Luke, you're staying here and healing up." He took out his pocket watch. "Train goes once a day at 3.30." He opened the watch, looked at it with a sigh, and closed it with a snap. "We've missed it. Can't afford to waste time, Tobe. Let's get going."

"Now wait a minute. If ya will help me get m'shirt--"

"Sorry Mr. Fletcher, we ain't got time to chat now." Swan chivvied Fooks out, leaving Luke protesting.

In the street, they both puffed.

"That was close. Thought he was really gonna come with us."

Fooks widened his eyes. "Never be able to square it with Mary if I get her pa killed. As it is, I've got a lot of explaining to do, despite what he says."

"How are you? Smedley hit ya pretty hard."

Fooks winced. "I'll do."

"Okay. Let's stop at the sheriff's office first. Garvey may have heard back from the Canadian authorities by now." Swan smiled. "Never know. Might have some good news."

After nearly caught out at the Catton place, the Smedleys rode hard and fast. The pursuing posse fired no shots except for one of them. His shots came far too close. Smedley risked a look behind as he zigged and zagged. *Yeah, had to be Swan.*

The posse trailed the Smedleys for several miles. It took a while to realize the posse was no longer behind them. Smedley yelled to the others to pull up. Horses blowing hard, they pulled into a ragged half circle.

"Why'd they stop?" Chronister asked, breathless.

"Dunno," Smedley looked back. All he could see, a line of trees, nothing beyond. "Must be outta that sheriff's jurisdiction." Smedley neck reined around. "C'mon. Fooks said Elspeth is in Altona. Let's go find it." He started his horse forward at a trot.

"D'ya know where it is?" Chronister asked after the retreating back.

"No." Smedley turned. "Looks like we're gonna get snow. I don't wanna be out in it if it does. Now c'mon."

Chronister and Cole looked at each other before following.

At first the countryside, flat and featureless. After a while, this gave way to farmland. The odd tree appeared, quickly followed by lines of them, most of recent planting. In time they would grow into sturdy windbreaks, but for now nothing to stop the biting wind slicing through them. None of the three had warm enough clothes on for prolonged exposure. Unfurling wet weather slickers kept out most of the elements.

All were grateful for the first signs of human habitation. A rough sign proclaimed the place as Edenburg. Two rows of houses built of logs and roofed by thatch, faced onto a broad street. As the Smedleys rode down the street, they were conscious of eyes on them, although where from they couldn't tell. They could see men and women at work in the fields behind the houses, but none were looking their way.

"Where's the saloon?" Chronister wanted to know. "Sure could use a drink."

"And a warm." Cole Smedley hunched down further into the neck of his slicker. His was old and worn. Too many holes in the seams to keep out much of the elements.

"Hush ya moaning," Smedley said with a grunt. Riding through the village made him nervous. Not a feeling he was used to. Nor did he like it. "We'll get there."

However, they didn't. Having ridden the entire length of the village, they saw no stores of any kind.

"What sorta place is this?" Cole asked.

"What's that over there?"

Chronister pointed to a more substantial building a short way off. The others followed his finger and turned their horses towards the direction. They didn't have to get all the way before Smedley realized what it was.

"It's a church, dummy." He necked reined back. "Let's keep on going. Must be a town nearby."

When they came to a junction, they stopped. There were no signposts to show where they should go.

CHAPTER TWENTY-THREE

In the sheriff's office, Garvey greeted Fooks and Swan like long-lost friends. "Ah, there ya are. How's Luke?"

Fooks tossed his head, hands on hips. "Feisty. You'll have to watch him. He's likely to follow us."

Garvey chuckled. "Yep, that's the Luke I know. He still over at the docs?"

Fooks nodded.

Garvey rubbed his chin. "I'll go over there in a while and see he gets back to the hotel. I'll station a deputy outside his door. Make sure he stays there."

"Good." Fooks gave a tight-lipped smile and nodded to Swan. *You know this man better'n me. You ask.*

Swan sighed, understanding what the look meant. "Any news?" he asked, coming to stand next to his partner. "From Canada?"

Garvey rummaged around on his desk for a moment, before coming up with a rumbled telegram. He straightened before reading. "From Chief Elliot himself. *Will alert town constable. Stop. Also border guard. Stop.*"

"How many men we talking?" Swan asked.

"Two," said Garvey. He held up two fingers and struggled to keep a straight face.

Both Swan and Fooks stared open-mouthed. "Just two?" Fooks queried when his jaw closed.

Garvey dropped the telegram on his desk. "Yep. And one of 'em is part time." He glanced at the loud ticking clock on the wall. "Border post is closed now. Won't open again until eight on Monday. They don't work on a Sunday up there."

Fooks turned aside. "Sheesh."

"Ya have to understand the law works differently in Canada. The Chief of Police, Chief Elliot, works outa Winnipeg. He only has a direct staff of ten to police the whole of Manitoba. Most of those are based in the larger towns. It's about 250,000 square miles and it's pretty sparsely populated up there. Most smaller towns have a constable, who notionally reports to him, but they pretty much do as they please."

"So, what do we do?" Swan asked. "We don't know where these men are. They're killers, and they hurt Mr. Fletcher."

"Like I told ya on the trail, I can't go after them. My hands are tied, fellas. I'm sorry. I have sent a message up to Smith in Gretna and Spanier in Altona to be on the lookout for the Smedleys." He held his hands up. "Best I can do."

"Yeah," Fooks said, with a resigned nod.

"Listen. The town constable in Gretna is Henslow Smith. He's a decent enough fella. Make yaself known to him and tell him ya business. He might help ya out. Or at least not arrest you." Garvey smiled briefly. "If ya can get the Smedley Gang back over the border, let me know and I'll be there to meet ya and arrest 'em."

Fooks sighed and then rallied. "Okay. If the border crossing is closed. How do we get across?"

"It's only a little hut. Ya just ride around the outside."

"Doesn't that rather make having an official border crossing, I dunno," Fooks widened his eyes, "Superfluous?"

"We're doing our best up here in the middle of nowhere, y'know," Garvey replied crossly. "We don't get a lot of traffic. Freight mainly crosses between Pembina and Emerson."

Swan crossed to the door. "We'll let ya know how we get on," he said, with a jerk of his head towards Fooks.

Garvey joined them at the door. "You two got coats?" He glanced skyward. "Getting colder. It's a mite early, but I wouldn't be surprised if we don't get snow overnight."

"Yeah, we have coats," Swan said.

"If I were you, I'd get moving. Gretna has a fine hotel, the Anglo-American."

Fooks offered a tight-lipped smile. "Thanks sheriff. We'll look it up."

Outside, Swan shivered. "Garvey's right. It does feel colder. Might make things more difficult if it snows."

"Boy, you're just a fountain of happiness, ain't ya?" Fooks said with a scowl and stalked away.

"Which way now, brother?" Cole Smedley asked when the trio reached a crossroads. The afternoon wore on and they had ridden miles since they'd lost the posse. Crossing landscape, mainly agricultural, set out in fields. The crops, all but harvested. Just a few workers toiled away. None near the road. All too far off to hail, and none noticed their passing.

Smedley scanned both ways and nodded. "This way is the more traveled." He pointed off to the right and made an executive decision.

"Sure this is the right way?" Cole asked.

"I don't like this. Can't we go back to Neche?"

"Shut up Frankie. That sheriff was from Neche. Ya wanna get thrown in jail?"

Chronister slumped. "Least it'd be warm," he mumbled.

Smedley turned to his brother with a scowl. "Of course, we're going in the right direction. We're going north, ain't we? Fooks said Altona was north of the border.
"

Out among the fields once more, less and less people tending to them. The countryside remained flat and featureless. More houses stood off in the distance, but even so, another couple of miles of riding before they came upon them.

This village declared itself to be Silberfeld, smaller than the village earlier. No people here either, until one old man came to the door of his house and called to them.

"*Guten Tag. Hast du dich verlaufen?*"

Smedley steered over to him.

"Good day, friend. Looking for Altona. Is it near here?"

The old man grunted. "Altona?"

Smedley nodded. "Yes. Which direction?"

The old man pointed to the left and then indicated they should go right further on. He closed his door, shutting off any further questions.

"C'mon boys, think we're nearly there," Smedley said, as they set off.

Another junction, this time three ways, presented them with options.

"The old man gestured right," said Cole.

"He also pointed straight on," said Chronister.

Smedley reached into his pocket. "Tossing a coin, boys." He flipped the coin on to the back of his hand, covering it with the other. "Heads for right, tails for straight." When he took away his hand, the coin showed heads. "We have us a direction."

It didn't take Fooks and Swan long to ride the mile and a half road to Gretna. Giving the closed border post a wide berth made them chuckle. Nothing more than an oversized shed with a nearby flag pole, although today it was devoid of flag. Someone had made an effort to plant a tiny garden leading up to the door. Outside stood a bench and a hitching rail.

"Welcome to Canada," Swan murmured.

"Don't get too attached to the place, Tobe. We'll be heading back as soon as we can."

Swan false smiled at Fooks' stiff back. He knew why Fooks was snippy. Keeping his anger in tight check and not a good sign. Meant when they caught up with the Smedley Gang, he, Swan, might have a hard time holding Fooks back. The sooner they resolved this, the sooner they could get back further south. Where it was warmer. In emphasis, Swan pulled the collar up on his coat.

Gretna wasn't big. One main street and precious little commerce on either side, except for the tall grain elevators at one end. The largest building, and the only one of more than one story, proclaimed itself as the Anglo-American Hotel. Right next to a building with all the trappings of a trading post. The sign for police, almost obscured.

"Looks like the place," Swan said, stating the obvious to Fooks' disgust. "What was the name of the sheriff?"

"Henslow Smith." Fooks dismounted and stood frowning on the boardwalk before looping his horse's reins over the hitch rail. "And I don't think lawmen are called sheriffs here."

"Then what are they called?" Swan joined him by the hitch rail.

"Constables, I think," Fooks said, moving towards the building.

Swan rolled his eyes. "How quaint."

Inside, they gazed around. *Almost as cluttered as Fooks' hardware store.* Except this store sold things his didn't. Animal furs, native leather work and beads, and animal traps. Lots of traps. The smell, a mixture of leather, metal and tobacco.

"Help you, gents?"

A beaver skin hat with tail popped up from under the counter. Below said hat, a round ruddy face, puffing on a pipe, surrounded by white and luxuriant facial hair.

"Afternoon. We're looking for Henslow Smith."

"Then ye found him." He spoke with a curious accent, English with a twist of French? No, not quite. Something else in the mix, but nothing Fooks could immediately determine.

"Joseph Crane." Fooks stuck out his hand.

"Sam Martin." Swan did the same.

Smith grunted and nodded. He eyed the hands and offered a slight wave instead. "Dave told me ye be coming. Telegram from Chief Elliot too." He scratched his chin through his whiskers. "Suppose ye in a hurry to look for these fellas ye hunting?"

"Er…" Fooks began.

"Kinda. They're evil men, Mr. Smith. Shouldn't leave 'em roaming," Swan finished. "And we don't know where they are exactly. We trailed them to the border, but they could be anywhere now."

Smith nodded, with more chin scratching. "Yes, 'tis a worry all right, but see here's the thing. Can't close up right now. Expecting a rush."

Fooks and Swan tried to resist looking around. The store was empty except for the three of them, and no one appeared to be beating a path to the door outside.

Smith cackled. "May not look like it right now. Trappers come in 'bout this time every Saturday, wanting to sell their pelts, get cleaned up for the Sabbath tomorrow." Smith sucked hard on his pipe. "Tell me more about these fellas. If they haven't shown up before, I'll get right on it Monday morning."

"Ya mean ya can't do anything until then?" Swan barely kept his tone civil.

Smith shook his head. "No working on the Sabbath."

Fooks and Swan swapped glances, frustration clear on both their faces. Nothing for it but to give the man descriptions of the Smedley Gang.

"And there's something else," Fooks added, almost as an afterthought. "We know they're looking for a woman and a boy who we've reason to believe are here in Gretna. Have there been any new folks in town recently?"

"Hmm." Smith considered. "A boy, ye say? How old?"

"Eight. We think his name is Peter."

Smith turned aside. "One moment." He went to the back of the store to a door half hidden by boxes. "Chartres, come into the store for a moment, will ye, honey?"

"Oh, Pa Paa, I've gotta finish my homework in time for the Sabbath," a female child's voice protested. She had the same curious accent as her father.

Fooks and Swan smiled.

"Never ye mind 'bout ye homework. This won't take more'n a few moments."

A girl of about ten, with long black hair in two braids framing her face, stomped into the store.

"Chartres, tell these gentlemen about Peter."

Chartres rolled her eyes at Smith. "He's new in school. Came up from the south two months ago. Staying with Mr. Beauchemin."

"He here with his ma?" Swan asked, leaning an elbow on the counter.

"Yes, sir."

Smith smiled and put his hands on his daughter's shoulders. "Thank ye honey. Ye can finish ye homework now."

Fooks scratched his cheek. "We need to speak to them. Warn them--"

"Yeah. Where are they at?" Swan interrupted.

"Hmm." Smith tapped his fingers on the counter. "Here's the thing. I don't know ye. I can't be giving out the whereabouts of residents of this town to just anyone."

"But ya've got the messages from Garvey and ya Chief... Chief..." Swan turned to Fooks.

"Elliot."

"Yeah, Chief Elliot."

"I know." Smith sucked on his pipe as he considered. "Here's what I can do for ye. Looks like ye be staying in town a bit, regardless. Go next door to the hotel. Get yeself a room. When I finish up here, I'll pay a visit to these folks an' ask if they want to see ye. How's that?"

Swan and Fooks held a silent conversation.

"Better make up ye minds quickly. I'm about to get the rush I told ye about."

Both turned to the door. Outside, a group of trappers congregated. They carried a selection of animal hides, broken traps, both modern and ancient rifles and scary looking huge knives. Although laughing and pounding each other on the back in friendly camaraderie, these frontier men were an insular lot. They viewed strangers with suspicion. And Fooks and Swan were strangers in a strange country.

Fooks smiled and nodded at Smith. "We'll sit tight Constable Smith. Wait to hear from you."

Smith gave them a salute. "Ye do that. Hope ye like our hospitality while ye waiting."

Fooks and Swan had to battle their way out of the store. At one point Swan felt himself pushed back inside. Eventually, he popped out of the door like a cork from a champagne bottle. He joined Fooks on the boardwalk and brushed himself down.

"Don't think I like Canada. Let's not stay."

"I agree, but we have to see this through first. And I don't like not knowing where the Smedleys are. We need to be on hand when they show up."

"Ya reckon they will? Might jus' forget the whole idea." Swan looked hopeful.

Fooks shook his head. "Naw, Smedley's on a mission. He wants the rest of the money. And Elspeth too, by all accounts." He tossed his head at the hotel. "Let's see what they can offer us. Could use a rest before supper." He put a hand to his stomach.

"Hurt where Smedley punched ya?" Swan asked.

"Yeah, it's a mite tender."

"The doc see to ya after Mr. Fletcher?"

Fooks shook his head. "I'm okay, Tobe. Had worse."

Swan chewed his lip as he watched Fooks walk away. *Mmmm, I'll keep an eye on ya all the same.*

Hospitality at the Anglo-American Hotel proved basic, but nothing worse than they were used to. Fooks stood by the hotel room window and watched the goings on next door. The crowd of happy trappers returned to the street, counting bills, handing some over repaying debts, laughing and clapping each other on the back. Fooks could hear their voices, but couldn't understand their speech.

"Think they must speak some kinda dialect up here," he said, in a mutter.

Swan looked up from cleaning his gun. "Oh yeah, what's that?"

Fooks shook his head. "Dunno." He walked away from the window and watched Swan for a moment. "Smith spoke English with a peculiar twang."

Swan rubbed the barrel of his Colt, peering at a spot intently before giving it an extra harder rub. "French, weren't it?"

Fooks grunted. "Yeah, possibly, but I think something else is in there. Couldn't get a handle on it."

"The daughter had a look of native 'bout her."

"Who knows? Those trappers are all swarthy." Fooks rolled his eyes. "And hairy."

"And smelly." Swan raised his arm and sniffed. "D'ya think they have baths here?"

Fooks chuckled. "You've got soft in ..." He sobered and turned away. "Where is it you live again?" he asked, with a frown.

"Boston." Swan collected up his cleaning gear. With a glance at Fooks' stiff back, he stuffed it away. "Ya all right?"

When no answer came, he walked over and put his hand on Fooks' shoulder. "Flo?"

"Can't get used to it," Fooks said, his voice breaking. "You living in Boston, of all places." He shook his head.

"I'm happy there. With m'wife and now my boy."

Fooks gave him a weak smile. "You never told me what he's called."

Swan walked away. "Oh, we named him after you." He spun back to see Fooks' look of horror and laughed. "Joseph. We named him Joseph." When Fooks relaxed, Swan slapped his shoulder. "I wouldn't do that to ya, would I?"

Fooks let out a relieved sigh and his face lightened.

"How long d'ya think we'll have to wait before we hear from Smith?"

Fooks returned to the window. "All the trappers are done. Oh." Fooks straighten and grinned at Swan. "The sign just got turned to closed." Swan joined him at the window again. "And there goes Smith."

"Do we follow him?"

Fooks considered. "No. He told us to wait here. This is a foreign country, Tobe. Let's do as we were told."

"Supposin' he tells Mrs. Priestly about the Smedleys being around? She could run out and we never find her." Before Fooks could reply, Swan rushed on. "Or worse. The Smedleys find her. Ya sure ya want a woman in the hands of those fellas?"

Fooks stood, hands on hips for a moment, considering, wriggling his jaw back and forth. "She came here for a reason, Tobe. Must feel safe here."

Fooks rubbed his cheek. "We don't understand the situation. I'll watch for Smith coming back and if he don't come see us immediately, we'll pay him another call."

He moved back to the window and continued his vigil. Unconsciously, a hand went to his stomach.

CHAPTER TWENTY-FOUR

The Smedley Gang rode for miles across the increasingly cold, flat countryside. Snow flurries swirled around them as they plodded up a slight incline. At the top, they could make out another village some distance off. This one bigger than the two encountered before with signs of commerce. One store at least. While they rode down the road towards it, their eyes scanned for a saloon, or hotel, or anything where they could eat and drink. More importantly get warm. They were to be disappointed.

"What sorta place is this?" Chronister said, hawked up and spat on the ground.

"Not one that's hospitable, that's for sure." Cole flexed his fingers, trying to spark some warmth into them.

Smedley led them to the hitching rail outside the general store. He dismounted stiffly and turned to the others. "We don't all have to go in. Wait here."

"The heck ya say." Chronister dismounted, then Cole. If one of them would be warm for a few moments then they all were going.

Seeing there was no dissuading them, Smedley led the way.

The store, orderly but full, largely containing farm implements and basic agricultural equipment, rakes, hoes and whatnot. A blond, blue-eyed man met them in the main aisle.

"*Guten tag. Wie kann ich dir helfen*?"

"Howdy. Looking for directions," Smedley said, ignoring the foreign question.

The man looked at him blankly. "*Entschuldigung, ich verstehen sie nicht.*"

"Directions? Altona?"

"*Ach Altona ja. Am Ende der Straße biegen sie links ab, und dann rechts. So kommen sie direkt hin.*"

"English?"

The man shook his head, then held up a finger. He turned and walked back behind the counter. Chronister's hand moved to his gun as the man rummaged for something underneath. Smedley stretched out his hand to stop Chronister from going for his gun.

"Careful friend. My partner gets a mite jumpy in cold weather."

The man eyed the strangers warily for a second before bringing out a sheet of paper and a pencil. "Altona," he said and began to draw a map.

They crowded around while he drew. "*Hier, Gnadenfeld,*" the man said, tapping where he'd drawn a village. A few lines indicated roads culminating in another village. "Altona."

"How far?"

Smedley tapped on the map where they were now and then, Altona. "How long?"

"Is there a hotel?" Chronister asked, eager to know. The man gave them a blank expression. "A saloon?" Chronister thought for a moment. "A tavern?"

The man nodded. *"Taverne ja."*

"How far?" Smedley tapped the map Altona again.

The man shrugged and held his hands open.

Smedley groaned. "Thank ya." He snatched up the map. "C'mon boys."

"Auf Wiedersehen." The cheerful call came behind them.

Outside, foot in a stirrup, Cole asked, "What lingo was that? Thought they spoke English in Canada."

"Dunno." Smedley sat astride. "Must be some sorta dialect we ain't come across before. Least we've got a map now," he said, patting the pocket where he'd put it. "Can't be much further. Fooks said the place wasn't far from the border."

"Ya sure this woman's worth it Rob?" Chronister asked, swinging his leg over and plunking down into the saddle.

"If she's got the rest of the money, then yeah, she's worth it." Smedley leered, widening his eyes. "And now her husband is outta the picture, she might be worth it for more'n just the money."

"What about Fooks and Swan?" Chronister asked.

"What about 'em?" Smedley said, with a snarl.

"They want the money too. Doubt if they'll give up easy."

"They're a long way behind us."

Smedley neck reined away, leaving Cole and Chronister to swap glances before kicking their horses into motion.

"They know where Altona is," Chronister said.

"Yeah, well so do we." Smedley scowled at Chronister when he came alongside. "Now.

Fooks dropped away from the window. "Here he comes." He checked Swan was ready. Swan sat on the bed facing the door. His Colt drawn and on his lap. Swan nodded.

A few moments later, Fooks threw open the door to Henslow Smith.

"Constable." He gestured for him to come in, his eyes sliding to the man's middle. Partially hidden behind his dark brown buckskin coat hung a wide, hand-woven belt wrapped several times around his waist before knotted tightly. This allowed the fringed ends to fall loose down his right thigh. Predominately red, an intricate design of blue, white, green and black ran down the center.

"Looks like ye were expecting me." Smith took in the room, noting the Colt, which Swan reached to put away in its holster hanging from the bedpost. "I've spoken to Maxime Beauchemin," he said, gesturing with his pipe. "He thanks ye for the warning about the Smedleys and their purpose. He says he can deal with them. Ye said ye sent them to Altona?" Fooks nodded and Smith paced, puffing on his pipe. He sent clouds of noxious smoke into the air and Swan waved a hand in front of his face. "Then ye have time. I've sent a note up to the Constable there. Asked him to watch for them."

Fooks and Swan swapped glances.

"Thanks, er ... Constable. How far's Altona?"

Smith considered. "About seven, eight miles, I suppose."

Swan made a grab for his saddlebags. "Best get going, Joe."

Fooks held out a hand, stopping him. "Hold on. Who's this Maxime Beauchemin?"

"He's ..." Smith winced and shook his head. "I suppose ye could say he runs the general market."

Fooks rubbed his chin thoughtfully. "D'you know him well? What sorta man is he?"

Smith sniffed. "Came to Gretna with me and a few others at the end of '70 after the reign of terror in Red River. We'd had enough of politics. Just looking for somewhere quiet to settle."

"So, you're Métis?" Fooks asked cautiously. He pronounced Métis like may tee.

"Canadian, Mr. Crane. That's what I be."

Fooks held up his hand. "I meant no offense, sir."

Smith chuckled. "None taken. We're a mixed lot up here. Ye'll have seen the grain elevators across the street?" When Fooks nodded, Smith continued, "Most folks settling here now are farmers escaping persecution in their old countries. German speaking Russians. Mennonite church. Particular about their religion. Those of us who aren't, respect their traditions. No work on a Sunday." He puffed once more on his pipe. "I won't keep ye. Stay here tonight but feed up at the cafe. Ye won't find it open tomorrow. Speak to Gabrielle. She has some sway with Maxime Beauchemin. Might be able to help ye."

He made for the door. Swan stood up in his way, clearing his throat of pipe smoke. "Like to see Beauchemin. Can we talk to him?"

Smith considered. About to suck on his pipe once more when Swan stopped him by a hand on his arm. "This is urgent Sh… Constable." He looked to Fooks for support, but he was pacing. Lost in thought.

"I'm aware." This time, Smith sucked on his pipe. "But what can I do?"

Swan mastered his patience with difficulty. "Ya can tell us where the Priestlys are so we can protect 'em. Smedley won't stop 'cos it's a Sunday."

Smith shook his head. "No, can't do that. Maxime said no, and he will deal with anything which comes up."

"What does that mean?" Swan asked, with a frown. Another glance at Fooks. Still lost.

Smith's smile was enigmatic, and he waved his pipe at Swan. "Nothing for ye to worry about. Now I'll be on m'way." He left with a nod.

Swan aimed a kick at the bed leg when Smith had gone. "Dammit, Flo, what are we supposed to do now? Apart from die of suffocation. Sheesh, what does he pack that thing with? Horse—"

"I'll open the window. Prefer to die of the cold." Fooks pulled aside the sheer curtain and threw open the window.

He stared down at the street, taking deep breaths of clean air. Swan stomped over and did the same.

"Did ya hear what Smith said? He won't do anything until Monday. Could be too late."

"I heard." Fooks glanced out of the window again before letting the curtain drop. "Almost dark. Businesses all closing up."

"Who or what are Métis? Ya asked Smith if he was one."

"Not exactly sure. Think they're mixed European-native folks. French mainly, but Smith doesn't sound French. Not entirely." He shook his head. "Can't place his accent at all."

Then he turned to Swan. He smiled smugly, causing Swan to growl. "You hungry?"

Swan swallowed his impatience. "What ya got, Fooks?"

"Didn't it strike you as odd Smith steered us to eat at the cafe tonight? When the hotel has a perfectly good restaurant." Fooks waited for Swan to catch up. "And he gave us a name. Gabrielle."

Fooks tapped Swan on the stomach with the back of his hand. "C'mon. Let's go eat."

Somewhere along the line and even with the aid of the map, the Smedleys missed a turning. They rode for hours until darkness fell.

"This can't be right," Chronister said, for the umpteenth time.

"We oughta turn back," said Cole.

"It's miles. No, we go on." Smedley said, taking out the map once more. Difficult to see clearly in the fading light. "Can't be much further to Altona."

"Ya keep saying that an' here we are. In the middle of this god forsaking freezing country. If I don't get warm soon, parts of me are gonna start dropping off. An' there are parts of me I don't want dropping off if ya get m'meaning."

"All right Frankie, I get it. Ya cold. What would ya have me do?"

"Let's find shelter. There must be a barn or something around here."

"Where?" Smedley cast a hand wide.

"I dunno," Chronister said with a shrug. "These folks are farmers, ain't they? Farmers have barns, don't they?"

"Back in the villages we came through, the barns were attached to their houses," Cole said. "No chance of sneaking into one of them." He'd already concluded they were spending the night outside.

"Let's go on for a while longer." Smedley kicked on. *Can't be much further.*

On the street, two cafes faced each other. Smith hadn't said in which they might find Gabrielle. Fooks stood on the boardwalk, hands on hips, in front of the nearest to the hotel. It was called *Das Leben ist Schon*. With a sigh, he turned away. "Ah," He said, and pointed at the cafe opposite, *The Petite Auberge*. He set off across the street, leaving Swan wondering what was wrong with this one.

Swan soon forgot his query. When they entered, a young girl smiled a greeting and gestured to a table. A name badge pinned to the top of her apron told them they had found Gabrielle. The café, nearly full, but their table just where they were comfortable sitting. Backs to the wall, facing the street.

"How we gonna play this?" Swan asked, in a low voice.

Fooks studied the menu. It wasn't in any language he recognized. Then he stuffed it back in its holder. "I'm gonna order supper," he said, with a nod. "I think," he added, in a murmur. He turned on his dazzling smile when the girl approached. Only to lose it when she spoke.

"Boon swayr."

"Er." Fooks took out the menu again. *Perhaps if I point.... And take pot luck.*

"D'ya speak English, ma'am?" Swan asked, seizing the advantage.

She smiled. "Yes. Of course." Her accent had a different twang than Smith's. Hers even more French, but again, something else there. "You are American?"

"Yes, ma'am." Swan said, with a smile. "Visiting from the South. What's good today?"

A brief flicker of insult crossed her face before her smile returned. "Everything," she said. "Do you require help with the menu?"

Fooks smiled his best smile. "Yes, please ma'am. What language is this?"

"It is in Michif but it is an approximation. An *aide-mémoire* for me. But if you have some French..." She broke off, seeing their faces blank. "I will translate."

Sometime later, Gabrielle brought them large plates of a rich stew of meat and winter vegetables, with something she called *La Galet*. It resembled a flat baked biscuit and the perfect accompaniment. She said the meat was moose. Leaner, gamier and tougher than beef. Neither of them recalled eating it before, but both gave it a go. Swan cleaned his plate in double quick time. Fooks had made a valiant effort but a substantial portion still remained when he pushed the plate aside.

"It was delicious, ma'am," Swan said, passing over his plate. Fooks nodded his thanks with a watery smile.

"Ye didn't like?" Gabrielle asked.

"It was delicious, ma'am. Just not as hungry as my partner here. He can eat for America."

Gabrielle rolled her eyes. "Would ye like dessert?"

The partners glanced at each other, having a silent conversation.

"No ma'am," Swan said, with a smile.

"We'd like some information, though," Fooks said.

Gabrielle tightened her hold on the plates. "What would ye like to know?"

Fooks scanned around the cafe first. A handful of diners remained but they were some distance away. Nevertheless, he didn't want to be overheard and dropped his voice. Choosing his words carefully, he said, "We've reason to believe there are three dangerous men in the vicinity. They're looking for some folks here in town. We think you know where they are. Now we need to find these folks and warn them. Protect them. Can you help us?"

"How do I know *you* are not two of these dangerous men?" Gabrielle set the plates down on the table with a thud. Her tone demanded a clear answer.

Swan pursed his lips. "Fair point, Joe."

Fooks lifted his head and smiled. "Because Henslow Smith can vouch for us. In fact, he sent us to you." He wrinkled his nose. "I think."

Gabrielle stared at him for a long moment, before picking up the plates once more. "He had no right to do that. Pa Paa said no. He has taken precautions to guard against these dangerous men. Should they show up, they will be taken care of."

"How?" Swan queried.

"I have said too much." She marched away, calling out. "*Deu Puchinn kaa kakwaatakitaak.*" They concluded they were getting dessert whether or not they wanted it.

"What does she mean?"

Fooks shrugged. "I think we'll find out when we get our dessert." He stared at a spot on the table, thoughtfully. "She said Pa Paa," he mused and looked at Swan. "Gotta feeling she's Maxime Beauchemin's daughter. Wouldn't you say?"

Dessert came in bowls with a jug of thick cream. Both regarded it suspiciously. Swan spied raisins, not his favorite, but he picked up his spoon to try.

"It will not poison ye," Gabrielle said, seeing their hesitation. "Try with cream." She pointed at the jug. At the slight dip in her stance, she whispered. "I finish in half an hour. As ye are so concerned, I will talk to Pa Paa then. Go back to the hotel and I will contact ye tomorrow." To stall their protests, she added, "It's the best I can do." She offered a slight smile. "Don't worry. All will be well." She walked away smartly.

"The Smedleys are still out there, Fooks," Swan said, quietly.

"I know, and that's a worry."

Swan dipped his spoon into his dessert. "Do we follow her?" Swan crammed a full spoonful of pudding into his mouth. He gave Fooks a broad, creamy smile. "Ooh, it's nice."

Fooks shook his head. "I'm getting the impression Mr. Beauchemin is a big man in these parts. If he says he can handle something, I'm guessing he can." Fooks dipped his spoon into his dessert. "We're just gonna have to trust that's he's right."

They'd made a fire, brewed some coffee, and ate the remaining sticks of beef jerky. The notorious Smedley Gang, shadows of their former selves, sat cold and hungry.

"Are you sure this woman has the rest of the money?" Cole asked again. "If I'm gonna freeze to death, I'd like it to be worth it."

His brother poked a stick at the pathetic fire. "Yes. Stands to reason."

"How d'ya figger?"

"'Cos I'm telling ya, ain't I? Now quit ya whining. Ya're as bad as he is." Smedley nodded his head when Chronister joined them.

"Got us a rabbit," he said, holding up said animal.

"Jus' the one?" Cole said with a scowl. "Could eat that all to myself."

"Ain't exactly a high-class diner out here, y'know." Chronister sat on the other side of the fire.

"Just for the one night, boys. When we get to Altona, we'll have a right good meal, I promise," Smedley said, looking from one to the other. These two had locked horns before. He found himself in an unusual position. Peacemaker. Now was no time for them to go at it again.

"Fooks and Swan will have gotten to her by now. Bet they're not eating a stringy ole rabbit in the cold, in the middle of nowhere."

"Cole, I don't wanna hear another word 'bout it again tonight. We're going the right way, I tell ya." Smedley made a patting motion. "Jus' trust me, will ya? Get the rabbit skinned and let's get eating."

"And if we don't find the woman or Altona tomorrow, we cut our losses and head back to the U.S." Chronister said it as a statement of fact. Cole nodded his agreement.

Smedley looked from one to the other will a scowl.

"Yeah, okay," he said reluctantly. *Fine Saturday night this is turning out to be. With these two old women.* "We'll head back tomorrow. *The hell we will. I'm not giving up on Elspeth and the money.*

CHAPTER TWENTY-FIVE

Sunday morning saw Luke Fletcher and a sheepish deputy in tow enter the sheriff's office in Neche. "What are you doing here?" Garvey said, seeing Luke walking in.

"Sorry Sheriff. He wouldn't take no for an answer," the deputy blurted out first.

Garvey sighed. "All right, deputy. Get off home now."

"Wasn't his fault, Dave. I pulled rank," Luke said as the door closed.

"You haven't got any rank," Garvey told him, throwing down a pencil in disgust. "Not anymore."

"Maybe not, but nice to know I still got a reputation." Luke chuckled, then sobered. "I'm goin' after them. What do I need to know?"

"The hell ya are. I told Crane I'd keep ya here. Safe. Ya ain't healed up yet."

"I'm fine Dave. Stiff is all. Loosen up when I get movin'."

"You ain't moving." Garvey rose to his feet. "D'ya want me to lock ya up? 'Cos I can, ya know." He pointed at the cell. "Vacant possession. Three squares a day. Have my wife bring ya a nice cozy comforter and some extra pillows if ya need 'em."

"Appreciate ya consideration, Dave. But I gotta go look out for my son-in-law. Mary would never forgive me if I let anything happen to him."

Garvey drew himself up. "He can take care of himself, Luke." He strode to the noticeboard and stare at it. "He go by another name sometimes?" he asked, without looking around.

Luke shifted uncomfortably and licked his lips. Garvey stood in front of two wanted posters: Florian Fooks and Tobias Swan. When Luke didn't answer, Garvey looked back and raised an eyebrow.

Seeing Luke wasn't about to confirm or deny, Garvey turned back to the noticeboard. "His partner is a real fine shot. Don't think he hit any of those Smedleys, but he came close. Had 'em zigging and zagging all the way to the border. Sight to behold."

He gave the two wanted posters one more glance, before twitching his head. "When I saw these new fliers, I thought, why are the authorities bothering? Must be dead by now." He turned back to Luke. "Or in another country, perhaps?" When there was no reaction from Luke, he sighed. "Guess it don't matter none."

"What do I need to know, Dave?" Luke asked, bringing the conversation back to the matter in hand.

"Don't look as though I can persuade ya to stay." Garvey clasped his hands in front of him on the desk. "Things north of the border are a mite confused. Hardly any recognizable law. Racial tensions spark off at a moment's notice. Not just amongst the white folks. Religion is at the heart of it. Métis don't like the settlers. Settlers tolerate the Métis. Gretna is a melting pot. All makes for an uneasy way of life. Spills over the border sometimes, but I can deal with it."

Luke pulled out a chair and sat down. "Tell me what ya know."

Garvey told him what he told Fooks and Swan about Henslow Smith. "Ya won't find him at work today. He ain't a Mennonite, but he respects their way of life. Guess ya boys will have found that out for themselves by now." He opened his desk drawer. "If ya set on going, this may help."

He brought out a miniature case, balked a little before deciding quickly, and pushed it forward. "If Crane is who I think he is," he said, meaningfully, "then I wouldn't be surprised if he knows how to use this. Have him send me a message when ya've got the Smedleys. I'll be waiting for him."

Luke kept his head down. *Who does Dave mean? Smedley or Fooks? Or both?* He opened the case to reveal a telegraph pocket relay and line clamp. With a nod, he shut the case with a snap and looked up. Garvey's face revealed nothing.

"I dunno if *Joseph* knows Morse code, but I'll give it to him, anyway." Luke pocketed it and stood. He held out his hand, suddenly eager to get away from Garvey's suspicions. *Must be how Fooks feels.*

"How long should we wait for Gabrielle to come?" Swan asked, joining Fooks at the window of their hotel room on Sunday morning. Their room had a view of Gretna's main street, dusted with overnight snow, just as Sheriff Garvey had predicted.

"Breakfast won't be over yet. Be awhile I guess," Fooks said, distracted. He felt better today after a good night's sleep. Less bruised. While he watched out for Gabrielle, he mulled over events which had led them here. *Why the delay in letting us see Mrs. Priestly? Is she really here? Or—*

Swan interrupted his thoughts. "Great. And there's snow. I can't *stand* all this waiting around, Fooks. I gotta *do* something." He stomped away. "Sooner we get this over with, the sooner we can get back on our side of the border."

"I don't like it any more than you. She said she'd come with her pa's answer and I'm sure she will." Fooks turned away to look out of the window again. "You can go at any time. It's me who has to see this through."

Swan growled. "Awh, I can't leave ya here alone. Ya know that."

Fooks smiled at Swan's concern, but then his face fell. "Uh-ho."

"What?" Swan joined him once more. "Oh."

Riding along the street came Luke Fletcher. As they watched, he turned up the collar of his dark canvas coat and hunched his shoulders.

"What's he doing here? I told him to stay."

"He's not a dog, Fooks."

"What does he think he's come here to accomplish?"

With that, Fooks threw open the window and hollered Luke's name. On the third yell, he succeeded in getting the man's attention. Luke rode over.

"Why are you here?" He didn't wait for an answer. "Coming down." Fooks shut and latched the window. He turned away, scowling. "Great," he said, in a mutter. "As if we haven't got enough to cope with."

"Mr. Fletcher isn't the only one we need to worry about," Swan said, continuing to look out of the window.

"What d'you mean?" Fooks asked with a snap and plonked his hat on. Hands on hips, he demanded an answer.

Swan inclined his head outside. "Fellas keeping watch on the hotel. When ya yelled, they broke cover."

"Smedleys?"

Swan shook his head. "No. If I was a betting man, Beauchemin's men, I'd say. Keeping an eye on us."

Fooks started for the door. "What do they look like?"

"Dangerous."

Fooks chewed his lips, thinking. "Grab your coat and things. We'll be leaving right after I've chewed the old man out."

He shrugged into his coat and pulled his saddlebags over his shoulder before turning towards the door.

As Fooks and Swan descended the stairs into the Hotel lobby, Luke came through the entrance.

"What the hell are you doing here?" Fooks asked.

"Listen, somethin's been botherin' me 'bout this whole business," Luke said straight away when they met in the middle of the lobby. "Which is why I had to come here. Ya ought to know my thinkin'."

"What's that?" Fooks asked, shifting his saddlebags to a more comfortable position. He folded his arms. Always difficult in his thick Mackinaw coat. *This'll better be good.*

"Jack Priestly thinks his brother was killed in the robbery. Hegarty gave ya the same impression. Yet when I spoke to Sheriff Gomez in Mudwater Flats, he said Arnold Priestly was shot." Luke shifted, seeing he'd got their attention. "Gomez showed me the report he'd written for the insurance claim. Didn't say nothing 'bout Arnold bein' killed." The two younger men swapped glances. "So, I'm wonderin'--"

"*Boon Matayn, Messieurs Crane pi Martin?*"

Both Fooks and Swan frowned at the new arrival, who addressed them. Although smartly dressed, he had an air of alertness about him which looked out of place in his formal attire. And a formidable, dangerous look about his mysterious face.

"Yeah? Who--"

"*Taanishi Etienne dishinihkaashoon.*" At their blank looks, he shook his head and took a deep breath. "Je suis Etienne." He paused, then continued in French. "*Je travaille pour Monsieur Beauchemin. Vous venez avec moi. Ici.*" He made a beckoning motion.

"Think he wants us to go with him," Luke said.

Fooks twitched his head. "Guess we'd better do as he says." Then he turned to Luke. "I'll deal with you later," he said, strolling away after the strange little man.

Luke rolled his eyes at Swan, who grinned. "Ya get used to it," he said, with sympathy.

The man Etienne conducted them into a comfortable parlor on arrival at the Beauchemin house. A middle-aged man kneeled before a fire, feeding it kindling. He wore a white shirt and paisley vest. Around his middle a sash of similar design to Smith's and worn in the same way. He straightened up when they came in and turned. He was tall and dark; flecks of gray sprinkled his wavy hair. His face barely concealed annoyance.

"Crane and Martin. Hen told me about ye," he said, without preamble. His accent, thick with French overtones. "And who is this?" He gestured to Luke.

Fooks stepped forward and held out his hand. "Yes sir. Joseph Crane." Fooks smiled pleasantly. "And this is my father-in-law, Luke Fletcher. Who won't do as he's told and stay in Neche." He leveled a stare at Luke. "Where it's safe."

"Now just—"

A grunt of acknowledgment, hand ignore. Swan came to stand by Fooks, not bothering to offer his hand. "Samuel Martin."

"My name is Maxime Beauchemin, as ye already know. Henslow and my daughter have chosen to disregard my instructions regarding your presence in Gretna."

"We're concerned about the safety of your guests, sir. The men searching for them are ruthless. Not to be messed with," Swan said.

Maxime winced. "There is no need. I am aware of what they are capable. My nephew found that out to his cost."

"Your nephew being Arnold Priestly?" Fooks asked, with a frown.

"Yes. Arnaud. Elspeth has told me his misfortune and these men's part in it." Maxime turned to rest a hand on the mantle shelf. "I do not doubt for one moment they are capable of great harm to her and her son." He made a fist and thumped it on the shelf. "However, they are my family. They have come here for my protection and I will give it gladly. Kinship is everything for the Métis."

Fooks rubbed his cheek. "I appreciate you want to protect your family but—"

"No buts Crane. I *can* protect my family. And I will. I have the resources to do so."

As the conversation unfolded, Swan had scanned the room. He stepped forward. "This room, this house, is a mite too grand for a general store owner. What resources are ya talking about?"

Maxime gave a bitter laugh. "How very perceptive of ye, Martin, but it is none of your business." He threw himself into a chair by the fire. Maxime did not extend an offer to his visitors. "I rarely work in the general store, but this respectable occupation allows me to stay here and live unmolested."

"Unmolested? Why should--" Swan stopped when Fooks put out a hand.

"Are you wanted, sir?" Fooks asked.

"No. At least not the way *you* mean." Maxime raised his chin defiantly. "I am no criminal. I am a victim of kinship."

Fooks and Swan swapped confused looks, and Maxime laughed. "Ye are ignorant of Canadian politics, I see."

When Fooks winced, Maxime sprung to his feet. "Very well. I will tell you who I am and the reason I can protect my family with no help from you. Then you will leave this place and return to the United States of America. Where ye belong."

Fooks and Swan were under no illusions. The information Maxime was about to impart wasn't common knowledge, even here in Canada.

"Have ye heard of the Red River Resistance in 1870?" At shaking of heads, Maxime continued, "The Métis attempted to set up their own land and government under the direction of Louis Riel. He was a firebrand and driven. My half-brother, Andre, was a member of the provisional government Louis Riel set up. Although he was more conservative than Louis. Their endeavors were only a partial success. Manitoba became a province and accepted into the Canadian Federation as they wished. But the Canadian government has reneged on most of the conditions negotiated. After the resistance, there followed …", Maxime bit his lip, "my wife was killed during the reign of terror. Many of my people migrated to new lands, some further West, some to the North, some to the United States. A few of us chose to remain in Manitoba. I settled here in Gretna with a few friends, including Henslow Smith. We wanted to be close to the border. In case of trouble.

"Trouble has come once more. The North West has erupted again. More fighting. More deaths. There is much tensions between the Canadian government and the Métis people. Because of my brother's involvement in the provisional government of 1870, I am possibly of value to both sides. Andre lives now in obscurity and seeing him is dangerous. Yet he was not as influential as many believe. For myself, I want nothing to do with politics, but it doesn't mean anything to those who might try to use me to get to Andre. If they try, I have men sworn to protect me. And my daughter. Loyal men. Métis warriors. Living unsuspecting lives like I do. Here in Gretna, I am safe. I insist Arnaud… Arnaud's family are safe here also."

Maxime turned to Fooks and Swan. "If these men … this Smedley Gang. If they come here, I will deal with them."

Fooks nodded. "I understand you believe you can protect your family, but it's not just about their safety. Arnold stole money. We believe his wife has some of it with her."

"Ah, now we get to the nub of it. Ye want the money."

Fooks and Swan swapped glances. "No. Arnold's brother, Jack, sent us to bring back the man who killed his brother. That man is Robin Smedley, and he's looking for Elspeth right now because *he* wants the money."

"Jacques, yes, I remember him. The brothers do not get on. They are very different."

Fooks frowned at Maxime's choice of words. Then dismissed them as the choice of a non-English speaker. "Can we speak to Elspeth, sir? It should be her decision. Not yours."

Maxime checked the clock on the mantle shelf. "She knows ye are here. It is near time for church and she can see ye for a few moments only."

Maxime marched to the door and threw it open. "Etienne!" A brief muffled conversation, in a language none of them understood, ensued.

Elspeth Priestly appeared a few minutes later behind Etienne. A slim woman of middle years with black hair, pulled back in a neat chignon, covered by a thin net. She let out a gasp upon seeing the visitors. She groped for a nearby chair.

"Mama!" The small boy at her side looked up in alarm.

"Elspeth, what is it?" Maxime went to her, full of concern.

Elspeth dropped a shaking hand away from her face. "That's the man..." She pointed at Swan and let out a sob. "Who shot Arnold. Get out! Get away from my family!" She pulled her son close and dissolved into wracking sobs. The boy tried his best to comfort her.

Maxime's head snapped around and fixed Swan with a stony gaze. "Is this true?"

"No," Swan denied. "We had nothing to do with the robbery. Or the shooting."

Elspeth raised her head, tears running down her cheeks. "You liar!"

With a nod, Maxime directed Etienne to take up position behind the Americans. Fooks snapped his head behind. He hadn't heard them come in, but he wasn't too surprised to see more Métis standing there beside Etienne. Two he recognized had been on watch outside the hotel.

"No. Sir, I've never set eyes—"

"It was you. I saw it happen." Elspeth sobbed into her hands.

Swan and Fooks looked at each other in confusion.

"Three dangerous men," Maxime mused. "*Haen, deu, trwaa.*" He nodded to his men. Silently, more men congregating in the rear.

"Sheesh." Swan let out a hiss, acknowledging for the first time their presence. When they pinned his arms behind his back, he knew they were in real trouble.

"No, we're not them," Fooks shouted, when he too had his hands restrained. Luke found himself in similar restraint. He winced as the position put strain on his shoulders, barely recovered from Smedley's treatment the day before.

"But I only have your word when..." Maxime waved a hand towards the Priestly family. "When they say different. And I do not believe ye." He barked out an order in rapid Michif. The three were hustled away.

"Wait. What are ya gonna do with us?" Swan struggled against his bounds. The man holding him attempted to turn him.

Maxime smiled. "I told ye I would protect my family. My men will make sure ye are no longer a threat to them."

"Ya've got it all wrong," Luke cried.

Maxime shrugged nonchalantly

"We're not the ones—"

A cuff behind his ear stopped Fooks, knocking his hat off, and he groaned when a canvas sack descended over his head. He felt himself bundled out of the room, firmly held on both sides. Aware of Swan and Luke, stumbling along behind him.

This can't be happening.

CHAPTER TWENTY-SIX

Sunday morning, the Smedleys peeled themselves out of their makeshift beds. Shaking their slickers clear of the light dusting of snow, which had frozen.

"Sheesh. It was cold last night," Chronister said, blowing on his hands. "We'd better reach Altona today, Rob."

Smedley poked at the embers of last night's fire, hoping to spark it back into life. "We'll have some hot coffee and get going."

"No. Let's go now," said Cole, moving to the horses. They'd camped the night on the edge of a small wood, hitching the horses well inside to give them some protection from the elements.

"Yeah. I'm for that too. Sooner we get outta this damn cold, the better."

Chronister stamped after Cole, leaving Smedley alone by the feeble fire.

"It's like riding with a pair of old biddies." Smedley muttered as he too got up.

Fortunately, at the next road intersection, a signpost showed them the way to Altona. A short way along the road, they rode into the village, much like the ones they'd encountered the day before. Agricultural with no stores. They found this village deserted today.

"Why would ya woman want to live here?" Chronister asked, when they stopped at the end of the short street.

In truth, Smedley had wondered that himself. Nothing he'd seen so far in this god-forsaken country chimed with the woman he knew. She always craved the latest fashions, gadgets and innovations.

Spotting a man appearing from the back of a house, Smedley pointed. "There's someone." He kicked his horse forward.

"Howdy, friend."

The man, clearly in a hurry, stopped. *"Guten Tag,"* he said.

"Is this Altona?"

"Altona, ja." He nodded in confirmation.

"D'ya speak English, friend?"

"A little."

"Is there a hotel near here? A bar? A cafe?"

The man shook his head. "New Altona." Now he pointed to the right, wanting to continue his hurrying.

Smedley grunted. Not more riding. "How far?"

The man shrugged. "Quarter mile."

Now Smedley tipped his hat. "Thank ya kindly." With a jerk of his head, he urged the others forward. Hopefully, the end, now in sight.

"This is more like it, Rob," Chronister said, when they rode down the main street of New Altona a short while later. "A hotel. A bar. Stores. Even a train depot." His eyes grew round and big, like a kid in a candy store.

"People," Smedley breathed, spotting the few about, all hurrying in one direction. Following their progress, he realized it led to a church.

"Hate to say this, but everywhere is closed," Cole said with a growl.

"What?" Chronister almost snapped his neck, looking around so fast. "He's right. All the stores have a closed sign up."

"Except for one," Smedley said, bitterly. He squared his shoulders. He dismounted in front of the store with the police sign prominent. "Okay. I'll go in and ask. You two wait out here in case."

"In case of what?" Chronister asked.

Smedley scowled. "I dunno. Just in case." He turned, paused for a beat, then marched with determination up to the door.

Sunday morning found Constable Spanier, notionally part of the Manitoba Provincial Police, standing at the window of his office watching Altona's main street. Nearly time for church, which stood further down the street from his office. Families of all sizes hurried along, kids sliding in the slush. Like most people of his ethnic origin, blond and blue eyed. His straw like hair, cropped close and recently barbered. He was tidy and smart as befitting his position in town. Can't command respect for the law if the officer is slovenly. The sole concession to individuality, the thick handlebar mustache he sported.

This twitched when he lifted his head with interest. Riding down the main street came three disheveled men. They appeared as though they had spent an uncomfortable night out in the open. Probably come into town for a bite to eat and get warm. *Good luck with that here.* He held the telegram from Constable Smith of Gretna. He studied it again, this time checking the descriptions given.

"*Ja, das sind sie.*"

He raised his head to yell. "Henning, *Schnell.*"

A young man appeared, hurriedly buttoning up his fly, suspenders down around his waist.

"*Ja, Vater.*" He joined his father at the window.

"Siehst du diese drei Männer? Finden sie Dietrich und beschatten Sie sie. Ich möchte wissen, wo sie sind, mit wem sie sprechen und wohin sie gehen. Verstanden?"

"Warum? Wer sind sie?"

"Gefährliche Männer laut Konstabler Smith in Gretna. Springen du jetzt dorthin."

Spanier watched his son run to comply, struggling to pull up his suspenders as he went.

"Hold on! I'm coming." Henslow Smith answering the bang on the door of his store, slid back the top bolt, then bent for the bottom one. A bang on the door came again. "All right, will ye." He threw open the door to the telegraph messenger boy. "Georgie? What's the—"

Georgie thrust a note at him. "From Constable Spanier in Altona. Urgent."

Smith mumbled a thanks as Georgie skipped away. He closed the door, frowning at the note. For a brief moment, he considered not reading it. 'Twas Sunday after all. Then he remembered the telegram he'd sent to Altona yesterday about the three desperadoes in the vicinity. With a sigh, he unfolded the note.

> *Three men you described in Altona now. Will*
> *watch them. Send word if they leave town*
> *heading your way. Spanier.*

Smith's brow wrinkled in confusion. Maxime had caught the three men. Hadn't he? He'd sent word he would take care of them. Smith rubbed his cheek, puzzling over the note. Another three? Two men saw him yesterday. Neither looked like desperadoes. Far from it, in fact. And they'd checked out with what Garvey in Neche had told him.

Thinking hard, Smith took his pipe from the top pocket of his shirt and tapped out the remains from earlier against a bucket he kept for the purpose. He repacked the bowl and spent several minutes lighting it. Only after he'd taken a couple of satisfying puffs and filled the store with a heady smog did he decide what to do. A quick glance at the big clock behind the counter told him Maxime would be in church by now.

Chartres appeared in the doorway leading to their living quarters.

"Pa Paa, breakfast is ready."

Smith glanced once more at the telegram from Spanier. "Nothing I can do until Maxime gets back from church," he murmured. *Time enough to break me fast.*

Fooks, Swan and Luke, crammed together, jolted along in the back of the covered wagon for miles. Their predicament, grim. Outside, ear-splitting shrieks. A new sound for all of them. A frightening sound. Impossible to figure out what could be the cause. Sacks covering their heads didn't help.

Fooks sensed they were alone. No guard. *That's something. Opens up possibilities.* He tested the latigo, the rawhide straps, which bound his hands behind his back. Seeing how tightly bound they were. Very. *Can I still do this?*

The jolting of the wagon made keeping their balance difficult. Luke fell sideways after a short while. He'd cried out at the impact on his shoulders. Then cursed. After several attempts to right himself, he found he couldn't.

"Best ya stay there, Mr. Fletcher," said Swan, his voice muffled by the sack.

"Easy for you to say," Luke said with a mutter, struggling to find a more comfortable position.

Fooks and Swan remained upright with difficulty, riding the bumps and jolts as best as they could.

"What d'ya think they're plannin' on doin' with us?" Luke raised his voice so they could hear him over the shrieking.

"Don't wanna think about it," Fooks said with a grunt. He'd spent the time worrying the latigo binding his hands. Nearly there with loosening. Swan apparently trying to do the same, based on his squirming and grunting.

"Why did the woman say she recognized Martin?" Luke mused.

"And why did she say I shot Arnold? I wasn't even there."

"All important questions," Fooks said, straining at his bounds. "Ah, finally," he said, with a gasp, bringing his arms slowly around in front of him.

"Ya done it?" Swan asked.

"Yep. You?"

"Nearly."

Fooks pushed up his sack so he could peer underneath. He could clearly see the driver through the slit of the front flaps. If they were quiet and careful.... With one eye on the driver's back, Fooks pushed off the sack. Leaving the latigo dangling from his wrists, he went to Luke and relieved him of his sack. A pile of their hats lay crumpled beneath him. Luke had landed on them when he fell over.

"Thanks. Dunno what used to be in there, but it sure stank."

"Shhh," Fooks warned.

With a puff, Swan pulled off his sack, latigo trailing from his wrists.

"What is that infernal noise?" Luke winced when Fooks untied his wrists, still bandaged and sore from yesterday. Now bleeding again.

"Dunno. Just be grateful it's there. It's hiding our voices."

Swan, nearest to the back flaps, ventured a peek outside. "Can see about two men on horseback. Fully armed." He peered around as far as he dared. "And others in strange carts with two enormous wheels. Think it's those carts making the noise. Sheesh." When he'd seen enough, he dropped back. He shook his head. "Guess they forgot to oil 'em before starting out."

"How many altogether?" Fooks asked.

"'Bout nine. They could be the trappers we met yesterday in Smith's store."

"Plus, the driver up front," Fooks said.

"Don't fancy our chances, Fooks," Luke said.

"What's the plan?" Swan asked.

"No chance of jumping out the back?"

Swan shook his head. "No, not without being seen. They'd cut us down before we got more'n a few feet, I reckon. Don't like the look of 'em Fooks. These are wild men."

"Then we'll wait until we stop. Something may come up."

"It's snowing by the way," Swan said, matter of fact. "Our bodies won't be discovered for months if it keeps up all winter."

"Ya're a ray of sunshine, aren't ya?" Luke said with a scowl.

Fooks put his hand out to stop Luke from unwrapping the latigo around his wrists. "Leave it. And keep this handy." He dropped a sack into Luke's hands.

"Can ya set me up at least?"

"No. Best not."

Luke growled. "Real uncomfortable down here like this."

"This ride ain't supposed to be comfortable, Mr. Fletcher."

"You haven't got shoulders giving ya gip, Swan," Luke replied, in irritation.

"I told you to stay in Gretna," Fooks said.

Luke scowled. "Yeah, ya did. I shoulda heeded ya."

Fooks put a hand on Luke's arm. "You're here now. We'll have to make the best of it."

"Yeah, for the little time we have left." Luke said, in a mutter.

The wagon slowed. Swan scuffled around to his previous position before he'd untied himself.

"This could be it, fellas. We're pulling off the road."

CHAPTER TWENTY-SEVEN

Spanier dropped away from the window when he saw the man approach, sitting behind the desk as the bell tinkled, trying not to look as though he expected a visitor.

"Howdy, sheriff." Smedley tipped his hat in greeting. Always paid to be polite to the law.

"*Guten Tag.*"

Smedley's face dropped at the German but pressed on in English, nonetheless. "Is there any place open in this town?"

Spanier thrust out his chin, implying he didn't understand.

"Does anyone speak a proper language in this place?" Smedley, now annoyed, added, "like English?"

"I speak English," Spanier said, deliberately making his accent thicker than it truly was. "You won't find anywhere open in this town today." When Smedley's face demanded further explanation, he added, "Sunday."

Smedley cursed under his breath.

Spanier made his decision. He didn't have a reason to lock up this man or his friends outside. Nor did he have the manpower right now to force the issue.

"Seven, eight miles to the U.S. border. Neche is the first town after the line you'll come to. Most places there'll be open."

"Which way?"

Spanier pointed back along the main street. "You will first come to Gretna. It won't be open either, but the border is just on the other side."

Spanier watched Smedley mount up and ride away. He reached for paper and pencil. "Henning." He scribbled out another note to Henslow Smith in Gretna. Out back, Henning only just returned from sending the previous note, stopped to finish dressing himself, appeared at a run, his face flushed with exertion.

"*Lass Eric das schicken. Dringend.*"

Another banging on the door of his store interrupted Smith's breakfast. This time, expecting it. Sure enough, when he threw open the door, there stood Georgie, the messenger boy again.

"You sure are popular today, Constable Smith."

Smith pressed a dime into the boy's hand and watched him run off as he closed the door. Puffing on his ubiquitous pipe, he regarded this new telegram. *Could be bad news.* He opened it and read:

Men heading your way. Will follow. Spanier.

Smith checked the time on the big clock. Ten o'clock. Maxime should be back from church right about now. Finishing his breakfast would have to wait. Time to get over there and tell him he'd captured the wrong men.

Smith hammered on the door of the Beauchemin residence. Just back from church, Gabrielle was about to unpin her hat and still had on her coat. She answered the door in a fluster. "Hen-----"

"Need to see ye, Pa," Smith said, pushing past her into the hall.

"Yes, of course." Gabrielle closed the door and called after him. "They're all in the parlor."

Waving a hand signaling he'd heard, Smith dashed down the hall.

Smith burst into the parlor.

"Maxime, the men ye're holding aren't the ones." He switched to Michif to explain further. Better to get Maxime's attention.

Maxime came to his feet and rattled out questions.

"English, Pa Paa." Gabrielle stood in the doorway and nodded to the Priestlys.

Maxime gave a sigh of acknowledgment, then repeated the questions in English.

"Spanier's following them from Altona." Smith waved the telegram before Maxime snatched it from him.

Maxime read quickly, then looked sharply at Elspeth. "The three men here earlier. *Are* they the ones who shot Arnaud?"

Elspeth stiffened. "I..." She swallowed hard. "It was Robin Smedley who shot him. He leads the Smedley Gang."

Maxime stalked across the room. He loomed over her. "And are those men the Smedley Gang?"

Elspeth shook her head. "I don't know."

"Do not lie to me, Elspeth. You told me ye knew the Smedleys. Arnaud had dealings with them before."

"I know. I know. I—"

"Tell me the truth," Maxime barked. "If the men who were here earlier are not the ones, then who are they? "

Elspeth put a hand to her face. "I wanted to protect Arnold." She swallowed hard. "I recognized the stockier man."

When Maxime turned to her, she licked her lips. "But from another time." She shook her head. "I was on a train once which they robbed. I think the dark-haired one was there too. I don't know about the older man." She looked up at Maxime, imploring. "But regardless Maxime. They're still crooks. Evil men. They deserve everything they get."

"So, they are not the ones who shot Arnaud?"

Elspeth fixed her eyes on her hands resting in her lap. She shook her head. "No. They didn't rob Arnold's bank." Her eyes glistened. "But they've robbed others, I'm sure of it."

"Enough."

Maxime crumpled the telegram. "Etienne!"

As the wagon slowed, Fooks hastily looped the latigo once around Luke's wrist, balled the remaining length into Luke's palm. "Hold on to that."

Swan picked up the sack and pushed it over Luke's head. "Sorry 'bout this Mr. Fletcher."

By the time they'd stopped completely and the Métis came to the back, both Swan and Fooks looked as though they hadn't moved. When the Métis pulled the sacks off, both Swan and Fooks blinked hard, pretending they hadn't seen daylight for a while.

There were no words either could understand, but they understood the gestures. Difficult to get down from the wagon with their hands behind their backs. Fooks had a hat clapped on his head, not his hat, Swan's. Too big for him and it slipped forward over his eyes, making it doubly difficult to negotiate the steps. Not to mention, snow flew into their faces, the wind cutting through them. *Glad we have our coats.*

Two of the Métis helped Luke when he slipped on the steps, and steady him once he reached the ground.

Sure enough, they were in a woodland clearing just off the road. Fooks and Swan scanned around, sizing up options for escape.

"What are ya gonna do with us?" Luke asked.

"We're not the men ya boss thinks. We came to help," Swan said.

The guards either didn't understand English or weren't authorized to negotiate. Rifles prodded the three towards a track between the trees. A silent conversation took place between Fooks and Swan. They'd been in similar situations like this before. They knew what to do.

A short way up the track, Fooks made his move. Pretending to trip over a tree root, he threw out a hand free of latigo, as if to grab the nearest man for support. Instead, his right fist connected with the man's chin, cannoning him into two of the others. Taking advantage of their distraction, Swan seized the rifle from the man nearest to him. When rifles trained on him, he cranked the lever on the stolen rifle and pointed it at the nearest Métis.

"If ya don't want him dead, suggest ya back off."

Fooks saw this as an opportunity not to be missed. Not pausing, he grabbed Luke's arm and hurried him away, further into the woods. Leaving Swan to hold the men at bay.

"Run. Dunno how long I can hold 'em," Swan yelled.

Fooks and Luke crashed and stumbled through the trees. An animal track made it easier to keep on their feet. Yet last night's snow hid tree roots and other obstacles in the exposed areas. Further where the snow hadn't and couldn't reach, it was clearer but more overgrown. Here, their progress slowed. Rifle shots echoed. Bullets thwacked into trunks as they passed. Any minute now, one of them expected an impact in the back.

Fooks led them deeper into the woods, where the trees were more densely packed. The snow was wet and heavy. The trees, not yet finished their annual leaf drop, and this early snow clung to leaves, limbs and branches. This additional weight caused several trees to snap, and the toppled trunks hampered their progress.

The shots became less frequent. Too difficult to aim with accuracy in these conditions. Swan soon caught up. Helping Fooks with Luke, who was feeling his age and aching from cramping in the wagon. Together, they dragged him along.

Sounds behind them stilled. No movement at all.

"Have they given up?" Luke gasped as he stumbled along.

"Naw, still there," Swan replied. "Gone quiet is all."

CHAPTER TWENTY-EIGHT

Outside the parlor, Smith conferred with Maxime. He spoke in English. Whilst he spoke everyday Michif, the situation right now, too urgent. He wanted no misunderstanding. Maxime's English was better than his Michif.

"Do ye know where your men have taken them?"

Maxime shrugged on his coat and took the hat Gabrielle handed him.

"Yes. I hope so." Maxime walked away, but Smith's hand on his arm stopped him.

"Not good enough, Maxime. These men's lives are at stake."

"I know that."

Etienne appeared at the front door. "*Lii zhvoo parii.*"

"Maxime—"

"We do not have time, Hen. Now let us ride."

The remaining Métis retainers, appearing ghost-like in the now falling snow, had already mounted up outside. Maxime had a brief conversation with one, then turned to Smith.

"My men took them to West Moon Woods."

"Off the Altona Road?" Smith asked, advancing towards a horse. Etienne handed him the reins.

"Yes," Maxime confirmed, already aboard.

"All right. I'll let Spanier know and I'll catch ye up."

Smith rode away, further into town. Maxime and the others took off at a fast lope for the Altona road.

In town, the light snow settled on everything. Outside on the prairie, where the land was flat and cultivated, the wind blew stronger and the snow swirled. The earth road, clear of snow as it blew around, accumulating just in the side gulley. The brief break of sunshine earlier in the day had turned the overnight snow into slush. Now refreezing, the road proved treacherous. The going, of necessity slow. Smith took his time catching up, pushing his horse as fast as he dared.

"This is crazy," he said, breathless when he joined them.

"If those Smedleys are out in it, then so are we," Maxime said, gritting his teeth.

"Who's ye best rider, Maxime?" Smith asked. "Send them ahead. I told Spanier we'd be coming up the road. He'll be looking out for help."

Maxime, his shoulders hunched against the cold, shook his head. "I cannot, Hen. It is too risky to push on too fast. I will not have any of my men risk their lives."

"We need to get there in time."

"I know that." He looked across at Smith, concern etched over his features. "What would ye have me do? I cannot change the weather."

Right after he spoke, the wind whipped up, and the snow fell more heavily. Maxime glanced back at his party. All still there. With steely determination, he pressed on.

Smith rode at his side, trying to estimate where they were likely to meet the three men, Spanier and his force. Would this be before or after they reached West Moon Woods?

Constable Spanier followed the Smedleys out of town, but he kept back. The road between Altona and Gretna ran long and straight over flat country. A man could see for miles and a group of three horsemen equals a sizeable target.

However, Spanier hadn't counted on the weather. No sooner were he and his two sons out of the town limits, the snow came down. Although the snow shower wasn't heavy, at least at first, the wind swirled all around. Visibility came down to a few feet.

Spanier didn't want to press on too fast in case he came up behind them. The last thing he wanted was a fast pursuit in these conditions. The slush on the road clearly showed three iron-shod sets of hooves moving toward Gretna. Had to be them. Being Sunday, there were unlikely any other travelers on the road today.

As they rode, Spanier chewed the ends of his mustache, wondering about the three men. The one he'd spoken to, in his mind at least, typically American. Brash, and clearly felt he was entitled. The other two just looked defeated. He'd seen the telegram from Chief Elliot out of Winnipeg. Spanier was under no illusions: these were the same three men. What had they done so wrong Smith should warn him to be careful?

Cole Smedley kept to the rear, looking behind them now and then. After some time on the road, with the snow coming down, he trotted his horse forward to come alongside his brother and Chronister.

"We're being followed, brother."

"Yeah, I figured we might be," came the reply. "That sheriff was a mite too suspicious for my liking."

"What makes ya think it's the sheriff?" Chronister asked. "Could be someone going in the same way as us is all?"

Smedley scowled. "Ya see anyone else on this road?" To press his point, he added, "In weather like this. Only a fool would be out if they didn't have to be. Get real, Frankie."

Chastised, Chronister rode in silence for a while until his curiosity got the better of him.

"Are we gonna do anything about it?" he asked.

Smedley chewed his bottom lip, then glanced behind. He couldn't make out anything, but he trusted his brother's instincts.

"Not much we can do." He tossed his head at his brother. "Drop back again. See if ya can get a look at 'em."

Another few miles of riding and out of the snow in front of them loomed movement.

"What's this up ahead?" Chronister asked, pointing.

"Some of those day-trippers ya said were out here."

Chronister turned a worried look in Smedley's direction. Cole rode up beside them to get a closer view. They now rode three abreast.

"I say it's a considerable force."

"Yeah, that's what I was thinking," Smedley said, in a mutter more to himself than his companions. "Those behind us still there?"

"I reckon."

Smedley cursed. He scanned either side of the road. Not that he had much visibility. The weather had closed in around them. By the little he could see, all open farmland. Nowhere to pull off the road to and hide. Until Cole pointed off to their left.

"There brother. Trees."

"Maybe we can hide there and wait until whoever these two groups are, pass us?" Chronister suggested, already feeling more hopeful.

Smedley nodded. "Yeah, let's do it."

Almost as soon as they pulled off into the trees, a rifle cracked.

"Did ye hear that?" Smith said to Maxime, on hearing the rifle crack.

Before Maxime could answer, one of his men, the one scouting out in front, turned and rode back. He spoke in rapid Michif. Maxime nodded and cast an anxious look at Smith. "I am sorry," he murmured.

Smith reached out a hand to cover his friend's. "We don't know for sure," he said.

More rifle shots reached their ears. Maxime and Smith exchanged glances. Not a pattern which told them there was an execution taking place.

"Perhaps they get away." Maxime looked hopeful. He turned to his men when the woods came into view on their right. Their destination. He gave them instructions and two cantered off, leaving the remaining two with Maxime and Smith. They too kicked up a gear.

"Let's hope we're in time," Smith said to himself.

The rifle shots had slowed when they met up with Spanier.

He nodded to Smith and Maxime. "The men went into the woods," Spanier said, reining to a stop. "Who else is in there?"

"My men," Maxime growled. "They brought three others here, who I thought..." He broke off and hung his head.

"We don't know, Maxime," Smith said. "Spanier, we'll need to go in careful. You follow your three. We'll find the Métis. And hopefully, we can do this with no bloodshed."

They split up and entered the woods separately.

CHAPTER TWENTY-NINE

"This ain't good, Flo," Swan gasped, as they took refuge behind a fallen tree. Scant cover, but it would have to do.

"I know." All Fooks could respond. He swept off the substitute hat so he could watch their back trail. Usually, he would expect to hear sounds of movement of men creeping through the trees. Twigs breaking underfoot, that sorta thing. Even the natural sounds were silent. He found it unnerving and he ran his trembling fingers through his hair. Seeing his own hat perched on top of Swan's head would be funny if the circumstances were different.

"Who are these guys?" Luke whispered.

"Métis, I think. Shhh."

"They're all around us Fooks," Swan said, his superior hearing picking out sounds Fooks couldn't.

Fooks swallowed. "If we surrender, they'll kill us."

"Rather go out fighting."

"Yeah, me too." Fooks turned to Luke. "Any ideas?"

"One of ya could climb a tree," he suggested.

"And have 'em pick us off like a roosting hen?" Swan was incredulous.

Luke looked up. "Still lots of foliage up there. One of us might get away."

Fooks considered the merits of Luke's suggestion. Who could climb? Best Swan held the rifle. Luke was… well out of the question for Luke to climb the tree. That left… "He's right. I'll go. Cover me."

He took off. A rifle cracked, but in the confines of the trees, aiming proved difficult. The shot missed, but not by much. Worried that his weight might cause the trunk to snap, what with snow laying heavy on the branches above, he started to climb. He'd done this often as a boy. Today, he hadn't lost the knack, and he soon disappeared into the canopy. The leaves kept him concealed from the ground, yet the shower of snow he'd dislodged gave away his location.

"Now what?" Luke asked.

"We make a stand," Swan said, and levered a round into the breech. "There." He'd spotted a Métis creeping up on them, took aim and hit the bark of the tree near the man's head.

"I hope ya can understand me. No one comes any closer. Let's talk," Swan yelled to the wild.

To their left came a familiar voice. "That you Swan?"

Luke looked at Swan. "Is that Frankie Chronister?"

Swan nodded, then called out, "Yeah?"

"There's three behind ya. We've got 'em covered."

"Thanks."

"Don't thank us yet, Swan." This time the voice of Robin Smedley. "Three on ya right. 'Nother three on ya left, but further away."

"We've got ourselves a stalemate, then."

Luke frowned. Swan made the obvious statement for a reason. *Why?*

"Sure, looks like it."

Now Luke understood. *Talking tells us where the Smedleys were. Useful to know in a gunfight.*

"They all accounted for?"

"Reckon so." Smedley's words were punctuated by a pistol shot and a yelp of pain. "Winged one. Don't think I put him out of action, though."

"Pity. Ya need to practice more."

"Yeah, but likely I might be getting some in the next little while."

For now, the Smedley's appeared to be on their side. Luke rubbed his chin pensively. *Guess we'll find out later how they come to be here in this precise spot just 'bout now. If there is a later.*

Hearing Fooks tell Swan they were Métis gave Luke an idea. *I wonder.* "Think they speak French," he murmured. He moved closer to Swan and whispered in his ear. "I wanna try somethin'. Go with me."

Swan nodded. "Whatever ya got, Mr. Fletcher."

Luke rose, hands in the air. *"Cessez le feu."*

Luke swallowed hard. Now he had their attention, what to say now? *Okay, here goes.* He took a deep breath. *"On parle s'il te plait?"* Luke shook his head in disgust. *Idiot, that wasn't the right form.*

Two of the Métis crept into the open, one of them eying the rifle Swan aimed over the log at them. The leader of the two spoke in accented French, *"Nous ne sommes pas ici pour parler. Vite. Qu'est-ce que tu veux dire?"*

Luke frowned, translating in his mind. *French is a tad rusty. Think he said, not here to talk. Hurry up and speak. Or somethin' like that. Now how to answer?*

Watching from his eerie, Fooks pursed his lips. *That's a surprise, old man. You speak French.*

Before he could ponder anymore, Fooks saw a band of men creeping up from the left. Hard to tell through the leaves, but one could be Maxime Beauchemin. Had he come to help or watch? Then he caught the scent of Smith's noxious pipe smoke and knew for sure. Unlikely, Smith would be involved in killing them. A commanding shout in Michif and the Métis surrounding them stepped warily into the open, hands and rifles held high.

Behind came confusion. Scuffling, a gunshot, and shouting in a multitude of different languages. Fooks peered around, holding onto the branch for dear life. A party of men had snuck up behind the Smedleys and had them.

Or did they? The Smedleys showed no sign of surrendering to this unknown force. *Am I gonna witness a massacre here?*

The three Smedleys stood their ground while the Métis and others he couldn't yet identify advanced on them.

"Put ye guns down," Smith advised. "There's no good way out of here for ye."

"Back off, old man," Smedley snarled back. "We're not ya concern."

Smith took a long puff on his pipe and let an enormous cloud of smoke escape towards Smedley. "Reckon ye are."

Smedley coughed once. "That's where ya wrong," he said with effort, turning purple from suppressing further coughs.

Cole and Chronister crept closer to each other, eying the Métis warily. Chronister jabbed his rifle at one who came too close.

"We've got ourselves a stand-off, Constable Smith." Swan said. "Or whatever ya call it in Canada."

Smith nodded, thoughtfully. "Yes, that's about right." He said something in Michif to Maxime by his side.

Maxime's face hardened. He swept round to point at Robin Smedley. "You! Who did it? Which one of ye?"

Smedley took a step back, bringing him closer to the tree where Fooks hid. "One who did what?" Although he'd stopped coughing, there was still a noticeable tremor in his voice.

Maxime levered a cartridge into the breech. "The one who killed my nephew." He raised the rifle to eye level, pointing it at Smedley. "Ye'll do."

All three Smedleys took a step back, closer once again to the tree. Up top, Fooks scrambled into position trying to be as quiet as he could. *Just a little more.* He didn't want to alert Smedley to his presence there, although Smith raised his head, frowning in Fooks' direction.

"Maxime, if he's the one, let the law handle it," Smith said, casually.

"No. I protect my own, Hen. Ye know this." Maxime tightened his hold on the rifle.

Fooks cast around, identifying where everyone was. Swan and Luke stood some way off, Métis behind them and to their right. Smith and Maxime in front of them. A big blond fella and two others stood watching from behind. Fooks wasn't sure who they were, but they seemed to know Smith at least. He'd seen them exchange a few words earlier.

"I don't like this, Rob," Chronister said, taking a step nearer to his leader. "Who are these fellas?"

"Does it matter? They've got us surrounded," Cole said. "Don't like the odds, brother. Perhaps we oughta do like they say and give up."

"Yes, he's right, ye know," Smith said, nodding in agreement. "Best for all of us if ye drop your weapons now."

Smedley's face creased into a snarl. "Naw, ain't doing that."

Fooks gathered himself. His heart raced. Smedley stood directly underneath him. If he dropped, what would happen? Too many men with guns out there. *Not sure of all their intentions. Swan and Luke know I'm here, though. And I think Smith does too. Perhaps I'll live.*

He moved into position. Then once he was certain, he launched into space, praying Smedley wouldn't move. That he'd still be there to land on.

"Brother, look out!" Cole cried.

Smedley took a step to the side. He flicked a glance up. Too close. Couldn't bring his rifle around in time.

Fooks' foot caught Smedley's shoulder. Instead of falling forward onto Smedley, he fell backwards away from him. Legs went up in the air and he landed on his back. The fallen leaf litter cushioned his fall somewhat, but not by much. "Oomph."

The impact with Fooks knocked Smedley forward. The rifle spun from his hand. Quickly on his feet and facing Fooks.

Fooks hopped up smartly. A sliver of sun concentrated on the wet leaves made them slippery. Despite being out of balance, he swung a fist. Connecting with Smedley's chin. Pitching him backwards. Momentum tumbled Fooks on top of him. He staggered upright, fists ready if Smedley came at him.

And come at him, he did. From the ground, Smedley launched himself at Fooks' legs. They swept from underneath him.

Uneven ground hampered Fooks' struggle to get to his feet. Smedley wasn't having it. Upon him again. Fooks, on his knees, took the punch to his side. Wind hissed out of him. Went to ground, gasping for breath. Smedley slammed into him. Turned Fooks onto his back. Smedley's hands gripped his throat. Fooks forced Smedley's head back. He scuffled around. Tried to lever the man off. The ground churned up. Too soft. Couldn't get any purchase.

Fooks shook Smedley right and left. Find the advantage. Too strong. Succeeded once. Smedley pulled them back. Change of position, enough. Fooks raised his knee. Connected. Smedley grunted. Hands loosened briefly. Returned to choke harder on Fooks' throat. Face inches from Fooks.

Fooks clawed at the hands. Blacking out. Flashes of light pin-pricked his vision. Strength fading. Losing. Going to die. *Help!*

CHAPTER THIRTY

A crack sounded right above his head. The fingers at his throat swept away. Smedley lurched sideways. His weight left Fooks.

"That's for tyin' me up and callin' me old man."

A panting Luke came into view. Fooks gasped not understanding what just happened. Luke dropped the branch and held out his hand to Fooks.

"Ya all right?"

Fooks only dimly aware of Chronister surrendering his rifle. Cole Smedley considered using his before flipping it around and handing it over to a waiting hand. His gaze went to his fallen brother, prevented from going to him by the end of a rifle in his ribs.

Fooks took the offered hand. The pull wasn't strong enough. In danger of falling back. Then Smith was there to help. Fooks rocked to his feet. He staggered about for a moment.

"What happened?" His fingers flew to his throat. His eyes skimmed around until they found Swan, grinning at them from some distance away.

The blond fellas moved in to secure the Smedleys, two of them hauling Robin up between them.

"We got 'em, son." Luke almost whooped.

Fooks swayed. Guns leveled at him from all nationalities. Automatically, he raised his hands.

Swan pushed aside an enthusiastic young Métis aiming his rifle at Fooks. "Put ya gun down. He's with us," he commanded. With his other hand, he held out Fooks' hat to him.

Maxime shouted in rapid Michif. The leader of the rear party, the ones who had the Smedleys, repeated in ... *what language? German?*

"Well timed Constable Spanier," Smith said.

"Ja. Wer ist wer?"

"Ye got the three men I wired ye about. Good work."

The trees were alive with languages. *A regular Tower of Babel. Sheesh.* Someone needs to take charge here. Fooks slapped his hat against his thigh to dislodge the snow accumulated on it. Disgusted, he plonked the sartorial disaster on his head. *Reckon that's me.*

"Gentlemen!" Fooks yelled and felt his throat. He swallowed with difficulty. *Owh, that hurt.*

When the talking stopped and everyone paid attention to him, Fooks cleared his throat and continued, "Can we *please* have a common language?" He fixed them with a hard stare. To avoid doubt, he spelled it out. "That'll be English."

The Métis looked at each other and then at Maxime, who nodded. The man Fooks now knew to be Constable Spanier shrugged. Henslow Smith sucked on his pipe. Robin Smedley, still hanging floppy but beginning to come around, moaned. His two men were downright disgruntled. Luke had a pleased smile. Swan handed the rifle over to its rightful owner and nodded knowingly. Fooks now in charge.

Fooks rubbed his cheek when he had all their attention. Then, hands on hips, he addressed them. In English.

"Let me say once and for all. We..." He gestured to Swan and Luke. "... are *not* the men who shot Arnold Priestly. *I* was sent here by Arnold's brother Jack to find who did." He pointed at the Smedleys. "And we have found them. They are Robin Smedley, Cole Smedley and Frankie Chronister. Collectively known as The Smedley Gang. Wanted in the U.S. for armed robbery and murder." He raised his chin towards the Métis surrounding them. "Hold on to them tight."

"Which one of ye shot my nephew?" Maxime barked, standing in front of the three.

"They'll not be fool enough to admit it here, Mr. Beauchemin," Swan said, going to his side. "Time enough for this later."

Maxime swung around. "Stay out of this. I need to know." He nodded to his men. Spanier and Smith moved to intervene.

"Maxime, let the law handle this." Smith switched to Michif, which had the desired effect. Maxime shifted uneasily next to Spanier, who seemed to loom over the proceedings. With obvious reluctance, Maxime agreed.

Fooks tilted his head. The snow shower, at last slowing. Was that the sun threatening to peep out? *Might make things a little more pleasant.*

"Gentlemen, we need to talk. Over here is best, I think." Fooks said and stalked away. He didn't want the Smedleys overhearing their conversation.

"Now."

Once all assembled in a semi-circle around Fooks, Swan voiced the question on all their minds. "What do we do now?"

"Can't arrest them. They've done nothing wrong in Canada," Smith said, and sucked deep on his pipe.

As one Swan and Fooks crabbed sideways. Luke frowned at them, wondered why. He found out when Smith's noxious smoke enveloped him.

"They're wanted for murder back in the States," Swan said. He turned to Maxime. "Not jus' for Arnold."

Maxime flattened his lips into a tight line.

"Er," Luke said with difficulty. His face took on a pained expression as he tried not to cough. His hand reached out to grab Fooks' arm, wanting to say something.

With a frown of irritation, Fooks ignored him. "So, what do we do with them?" Fooks tossed his head in the direction of the Smedleys.

"Haven't really got the facilities to hold them more'n a few days," Smith said.

Maxime rattled off something in Michif, then shook his head when he saw three blank looks. With a sigh, he switched to English. "I do not want them hanging around close to my family."

Smith sucked on his pipe some more, thoughtfully. "Ye know." He took the pipe out of his mouth and waved it. "This part of the borderlands did used to be called Smuggler's Point..."

Luke clawed at Fooks' arm. "Joseph..."

Fooks shook him off. "Not now Luke."

Maxime grinned. "And the Métis *are* good at smuggling. One advantage of living in Gretna. It's only a hop to the medicine line."

"What's the medicine line?" Swan asked.

"The border. The Métis call it the medicine line because of the change of jurisdiction," Maxime said smugly.

Smith gave him a hard frown. "Don't tell me Maxime."

Maxime nodded, but couldn't wipe the smug expression from his face.

"Is the border well marked?" Fooks asked, determined to bring the conversation back to the matter at hand.

"Away from the official crossing points, it becomes more of a chalk line," Smith said with a chuckle. "There are a few stone cairns. Most have fallen or grassed over. Can't see them except if ye know where to look."

Fooks took a few steps away, rubbing his chin. Then he about turned, grinning. "So, if you don't know for certain where the border is, it's possible you could cross over without knowing it." He glanced across meaningfully at the Métis and the Smedley Gang in particular.

Smith sucked on his pipe again before taking it out of his mouth and releasing a cloud of smoke into the air. "Surveyors stuck to the 49th parallel rigidly. Took no account of natural geography. Surveyed straight through boulders and mountains, even trees. That's what we've got here. An arbitrary line."

"Robin's too dazed right now to be thinking straight, and I doubt if the other two will know about this," Fooks said. "Is there somewhere which *looks* like a border but isn't? On the U.S. side?"

"I know a place. My men and I will accompany ye." Maxime looked smug. "Or a little beyond, just to be sure."

"Garvey said he would meet us at the border if we can let him know we're coming," Swan said.

"I will have one of my men ride ahead," Maxime said. The group broke up.

"Hold up." Swan held up his hand. "If ya can't arrest them, what do we tell them? So, they don't cotton on."

The group came together again, each pondering. Fooks turned to Luke. "As far as I understand it, there are only certain crimes which a person in Canada can be extradited back to the U.S. for." Fooks turned to Luke. "Is that right?"

Luke swallowed hard. "Yeah." He spoke with difficulty, his voice husky. "A treaty back in 1842 spelled out the specific offenses, and robbery and murder are most definitely on the list." Luke looked at Smith, who nodded.

Fooks pressed his fingertips to his lips, clearly thinking. A moment later, he smiled broadly. "Okay, then here's the plan." With a glance at the Smedleys, he lowered his voice, causing the group to lean in to hear. "They're gonna ask what you intend to do with them."

Fooks addressed Spanier. "We'll tell them you're taking them to Gretna to sort out the paperwork for them to claim asylum in Canada."

Now he turned to Smith. "They're not gonna know it don't apply to murder." He looked thoughtful. "We'll escort them to Gretna. Only Gretna isn't where they think it is." He grinned the full double dimple. "It's in the good old U. S. of A."

Grins rewarded him all round.

"Better be smart about it," Swan said, with an eye skywards. "Might snow again."

"Can only be to our advantage," Fooks said. "But he's right. We'd best get going."

CHAPTER THIRTY-ONE

They chivvied the Smedley Gang along to the wagon which Fooks and company had showed up in. In a bizarre swap, Fooks, Swan and Luke planned to ride their horses.

"Where are ya taking us?" Robin Smedley asked, while the Métis helped him in. He blinked hard, eyes still unfocused. His brother and Chronister, already seated inside. Neither needed much encouragement, both wanting to get out of the weather. At least the covered wagon would be out of the wind and warmer.

"Gretna," Fooks said.

"What's at Gretna?" Chronister asked, peering out from the back. In the absence of Robin Smedley's leadership, he had stepped up.

"Closest town to the border," Fooks told him with a grin. "There Constable Smith, will process your application for asylum."

"Asylum?" The three hostages held a silent conversation. "What's asylum?" Chronister wanted to know.

"If the authorities catch you this side of the border, they have to send you back to the U.S. That's called extradition." Fooks resisted a smug grin at the look of horror on the faces of all three men. "If you claim asylum, you get immunity from prosecution. Means the authorities here can't send you back."

"Don't like this Rob," Cole said. He glanced at his brother, who sat slapping his cheeks and blinking hard.

"Oh, it's perfectly legitimate," Fooks said cheerfully.

"Ya wanted below the line," Swan stated. "Ya claim immunity from prosecution here in Canada and ya're free men." Swan paused for effect. "'Course ya have to stay in Canada for the rest of ya lives. But hey, it's not so bad, is it? All this fresh air and wide-open spaces." He held his hands out and then gave the brim of his hat a tug, shaking loose the snow settled on it.

Cole Smedley sat hugging himself. "Can think of warmer places to hole up," he grumped

"Beggars can't be choosers, Cole. Neither can wanted men." Fooks shrugged. "Your choice."

"How does it work? This asylum," Smedley asked. He put a hand to his head. A gesture Fooks recognized as a sign of a headache.

"You make an application saying you fear arrest in the U.S. and you sign it saying it's true. We'll," Fooks flicked a hand between him and Swan, "Sign it too, confirming your account and you're done. Safe in Canada. With all their lawful protection." Fooks waved a hand at Smith and Spanier, who stood a short distance away. "They'll be obligated."

"If this is so easy, why haven't you gone for it?" Smedley asked, not entirely convinced. He closed his eyes.

Fooks gave a tight-lipped smile. "Prefer somewhere warmer."

"So, what's the catch?" Chronister asked.

"Catch?" Fooks widened his eyes in surprise. "What makes you think there's a catch?"

"'Cos there always is with you, Fooks. Ya not exactly the most straightforward of men." Chronister said, with a grin.

"I think you're doing me a disservice—"

"Leave it Frankie." A tired Smedley made a half-hearted attempt to intervene. "What will be will be."

Chronister ignored him and shook his head. "You—"

He broke off when the wagon jerked forward.

Fooks gave a friendly wave. "See you in Gretna." He turned away, chuckling.

The wagon rattled out of the clearing. Spanier and his men and two of the Métis followed.

Luke put out a hand to stop Maxime from giving the order to one of his men to ride ahead. "Don't send ya man. Ridin' fast in this weather is suicidal," he said. "'Sides they might see him and smell a rat."

He pointed upwards at the telegraph wire overhead. "I've a better idea and it'll be quicker." Luke rummaged in his pocket. "Garvey gave me this." He handed the rubber case to Fooks. "D'ya know how to use it?"

Fooks opened the case and sucked in his cheeks. "Been a while. Not sure I can remember my morse code."

"'Course ya can," said Swan. "Cattleman's pass is more'n six years ago so ya should remember."

Fooks glared at him. *Yeah, I do. Didn't go too well.* He looked down at the pocket relay again, then up and finally behind them. "That one." He nodded to the pole with climbing spurs. "Let's wait until they're gone so they don't spot me climbing." He turned to Smith. "Where shall I say we'll meet Garvey?"

"The Pembina river meanders about north of Neche. I would suggest one of the northern curves. It'll look like a border." Smith waved his pipe in emphasis. A plume of smoke drifted in Fooks' direction.

Fooks stopped himself from waving a hand in front of his face. Contenting himself with disguising a cough instead.

"How about Houlette La Barre?" said Maxime. "Garvey knows the place. Seen him there a time or two." Maxime gave an innocent shrug at Smith's silent question and answered in Michif. Judging by Smith's returning hiss, Maxime referred to unlawful activity.

Fooks and Swan shared their own silent conversation. It would appear, Maxime Beauchemin, for all his outward respectability, wasn't quite on the level.

"Houlette La Barre. Got it."

About to walk away, Maxime stopped Fooks with a hand on his arm. "What about my nephew?"

"Your nephew? I don't understand. He's--"

"Nope, I've been tryin' to tell ya," Luke said, with a rueful grin. "He's not, is he, Monsieur Beauchemin?"

Maxime looked guilty. "No. Not exactly."

"What does that mean?" Swan asked, frowning hard. "Either he's dead or he isn't."

"That's what I came after ya to tell ya. Arnold didn't die in the robbery," Luke said. "Did he, Monsieur Beauchemin?" He looked straight at Maxime.

Maxime looked down and shuffled his feet. "He might as well have. My nephew is unlikely to survive the winter."

"Why didn't you tell us when we came to see you?" Fooks asked.

"I thought if ye knew he still lived, ye'd try to take him back. I want him to spend his last days in peace."

"So, Arnold's a boodler." Luke spoke calmly.

"A what?" Swan turned to Fooks, looking to see if he knew what it meant.

"A boodler," Luke confirmed. "A fugitive who crosses the international border, where U.S. law can't touch 'em."

"I told ye. Arnaud is not fit to go anywhere. Let alone--"

"Monsieur Beauchemin, Arnold can't be extradited," Luke said. "The extradition treaty between Canada and the

U.S. right now is a muddle. Sure, Canada will honor extradition for murderers, arsonists, robbers and forgers, but Arnold's crime is embezzlement. The treaty don't apply."

"So, he can live here Scott free and there's nothing anyone can do about it?" Swan pulled off his hat and puffed. "Sheesh. The law sure is an ass."

"It would appear so. I hear the politicians are trying to do somethin' about it but nothings firmed up yet. Seems our government is draggin' its feet over one particular clause Great Britain wants included."

"How d'ya know this stuff, Mr. Fletcher?" Swan asked. "Don't doubt ya, but it feels like we should be on solid ground here."

"As a U.S. Marshall, it was my job to be aware of all the dodges a felon could take and their consequences." Luke grinned. "Kept up to date since I retired for personal interest."

Fooks frowned. "I thought Canada was independent."

"It's a Dominion," Smith said. "Independent in all but name. Great Britain still controls foreign policy."

"Sheesh." Swan clapped his hat back on. "So, we hogtie Arnold, get the money, and take him back. Dying or not."

"Nope. Previous attempts to do just what ya suggest have floundered in our courts." Luke turned to Smith. "And the Canadians take a dim view of kidnappin' in their territory. Isn't that right, Constable Smith?"

Smith nodded sagely, sucking deep on his pipe. "That's about the size of it."

"So Arnaud is safe?" Maxime looked from Smith to Fooks.

Fooks stood, hands on hips considering. "Mr. Beauchemin, if Arnold is as ill as you're suggesting then I think he ought to live out the rest of his life in peace. Don't you?"

Maxime beamed. "Yes, I do, Mr. Crane."

Fooks slapped Swan in the stomach with the back of his hand. "Let's get this message sent before we all freeze solid. C'mon, need a boost."

At the base of the pole, Fooks emptied all his pockets of anything metal, patting his Mackinaw jacket hard to be sure. With a flourish, he pulled out riding gloves. "Hate doing this," he said, in a mutter as he pulled them on. Then he removed his boots, scowling when the wet immediately soaked into his stockinged feet.

When he signaled, he was ready, Swan made a step with his hands. The boost Fooks received just high enough for him to grab the lowest rung of the metal spurs driven into the side of the pole.

At first, easy to climb, just like a ladder. Fooks always had a head for heights. And a fear of falling. He concentrated harder the higher he climbed. *Keep three anchors connected at all times,* he chanted in his head. The state of the spurs alarmed him. They couldn't be more than a couple of years old, but some of them wobbled when he transferred his weight to them. He found himself having to work out strategies to avoid suspect ones. Made his climb harder. He reached the top section and stopped. He wasn't sure about the next four spurs, two metal, two wooden.

"You all right Fooks?"

"Yeah." Fooks looked up. So near. If he could just reach the cross piece, he could haul himself all the way. He made sure of his grip on the pole and tested the first dodgy looking spur gingerly, gradually increasing the amount of weight he pulled down. Then with a sigh, he transferred all his weight and stepped up.

He rested his forehead against the pole for a moment before tackling the next. This one rusty and loose in its socket. He tried jamming it in further, hoping he could find a more secure biting point. The angle proved difficult and he couldn't get enough impetus behind it. Deciding he'd done the best he could without a hammer, he gave it a tug. It held, but he wasn't convinced. His eyes sought the next spur. The first wooden one. It appeared in better shape. Not crumbly, but not brilliant either.

"Swan, there's a couple of dodgy spurs up here. Might be coming down fast."

"Okay. Lots of leaf fall here. I'll see if I can pile up some for ya."

"Thanks," Fooks said, sarcastically.

He took a deep breath and reached for the rusty spur. Making sure of his other holds, he tentatively transferred his weight. It moved, but soon resettled itself. Fooks quickly pulled himself up. Now he had just the two secure anchors. After the next one, he would just have the one. If it held, he could reach the cross piece.

"Here goes."

"Careful Flo."

"I intend to be." And then to himself. "Don't you worry about that."

This first wooden spur felt more secure than the previous two, but he hadn't tested it. Which was a mistake. This one crossed a deep cleft in the pole. When he pulled up, it moved. Pulled outwards. Suddenly.

Fast.

"Yeow!"

CHAPTER THIRTY-TWO

"Flo!"

His feet lost their purchase. Fooks dangled from the loose, rusty spur. This too moved under all his weight.

"Sheesh!"

He scrambled for the lower spurs, found one. Then the other. His foot slipped. He cast around before finding another foothold. Now secure, he clung to the pole itself, gasping. Concentrating on the spurs cutting into his stocking feet, gave him reassurance he was still alive.

"Are ya okay?" Swan shouted up.

"Yeah, I think so."

"Can ya move?"

"Dunno."

Fooks turned his head. Keeping his cheek pressed against the smooth wood, he looked up.

"If I can push myself up a bit more…. Think I can reach the crosspiece."

Slowly, Fooks edged his way up. The loose, rusty spur appeared to have settled into a more secure place. Trying not to put all his weight on it, Fooks used it like a spring to launch himself at the crosspiece. His fingers curled around the wood. Not secure yet. He inched them further up and over. First one foot on tiptoe, then the other until his body stretched up. Tentatively he moved up to the next spur, the first wooden one. Enough to get his hands fully over the crosspiece. With a firm hold, he pushed up. Other foot found the one which had dropped. It held.

He was there.

Fooks balanced precariously on the top of the pole, straddling the wood designed for the purpose. Feeling secure enough to start his business. Providing he didn't look down. The activities down below were a distraction. The Métis looked to be setting up camp. *Hardly the weather for a picnic but these Canadians are a funny lot.*

He shook his head at the ridiculousness of it. Right now, he needed to concentrate and remember how to do this. He'd only done it once before. *No wait, I've done this twice. Yes, that's right. Cattleman's Pass musta been the first time.* Judging by what happened afterwards, he wasn't sure it was successful, but hey ho. *Second time was...* He frowned. He remembered a second occasion, but not where it was.

"Fooks ya okay?"

The shout from below startled him, nearly unseating him.

"Yeah. Just trying to remember how to do this."

"Can ya think faster? Starting to snow again."

"You think I don't know this? I'm closer to it than you are." Fooks settled back. "Leave me be. I've got this."

He took a deep breath to calm himself. He ran his gloved hands down his pant legs, trying to dry the moisture from them. *Okay. Let's give this another go. Practice makes perfect and all that.*

He wavered for a moment before placing his fingers on the top of the screw above the glass insulator, the dome like cap which held the wires. It didn't show much sign of corrosion. As it proved after an initial grunt of effort, the wing nut moved. Once free, he could tease out the two lines separated from one another by the screw of the wing nut.

Now he brought out the rubber case and took out the clamp. This comprised four thumb screws, two on each side, one above each other. The top two were spaced apart, the bottom two connected by the frame. Freeing his right hand from its glove, he clenched and flexed his fingers. Cold, damp fingers weren't going to make this easy. Glove dangling from his mouth by the thumb, he inserted the free lines from the top of the insulator into the top two screws. Making sure he had input and output the correct way round. Then he tightened the connections.

The other item he removed from the case was the pocket relay, the telegraph key. The two terminals already had wire threaded through them and tightened. He took the free ends and connected them to the two lower thumb screws of the clamp. Checking all the connections were secure, his hand hovered over the sending key. Then, irritated by the glove dangling from his mouth, he tore it free and stuffed it into his pocket.

He nodded. *Right. Let's hope I can remember my Morse code.* He began tap, tap, tapping out a message to Garvey in Neche, knew he made a mistake, tapped a correction, and signed off as Crane.

"How'd it go?" Swan asked, ten minutes later when Fooks had slithered safely to the ground once more. Thankfully, his journey down fast but uneventful.

"Might have sent Garvey my Omi Klassen's *apfelstrudel* recipe," he said with a lopsided grin.

"Well, let's hope he appreciates a good pastry," Swan said with a grin before slapping Fooks on the shoulder. "C'mon let's get back to the others."

After breaking camp, they soon caught up with the slower wagon containing the Smedleys.

"Ya all right in there?" Swan rode alongside the back of the wagon. Fooks came up on the other side.

Chronister poked his head out between the flaps. "Yeah, we're all right. How much longer?"

Swan turned to Smith who rode beside him to answer. "Ye not far now," he said, puffing smoke perhaps deliberately, perhaps not at Chronister. Swan ducked away to hide the grin when Chronister coughed violently. The foul air had penetrated the wagon. This prompted Cole to pound him hard on the back.

Trying not to cough, his face turning red, Smedley yelled out, "What's that god-awful noise? Sheesh, my head."

"Think it's coming from these." Swan waved a hand at the two shrieking wooden carts with the enormous wheels, trundling along behind, full of Métis. He spoke to Smith. "Don't ya have oil in Canada?"

Smith chuckled. "No metal to oil. All wood. They're called Red River carts. Traditional." He sobered into regret. "Dying out now. Like the buffalo."

"There's the river," Chronister yelled, pointing off to their right. Smedley pushed him out of the way.

"Not as wide as the Rio Grande, is it?" Chronister pulled the flap open some more. He flipped it back, exposing Cole to the elements. He looked decidedly uncomfortable, shoulders hunched and hugging himself.

"Neither is the Rio in some places." Smedley wiggled his jaw back and forth.

Fooks kept an eye on him. *Don't think you're fully convinced yet.*

"Is this Gretna?" Chronister asked, pointing to the town appearing out of the gloom.

Smith turned in his saddle and pointed his pipe in the town's direction. "Home, sweet, home."

"Can't come soon enough for me," Cole said, pulling his collar closer to his neck.

"Who's this?" The wagon slowed to a halt. Chronister stood and pointed to a group of men standing on a deep beach where the river curved. He peered closer and saw the badge pinned to the jacket of the lead man. Now he realized. "Fooks! Ya—" He made to get out of the wagon, but the click of Smith's gun stopped him.

"We're well met," said Dave Garvey, when the Canadian party came to a complete stop. "Not the weather for a lengthy pursuit." He nodded to Smith and Spanier and cast an uneasy eye over the Métis. "So." His gaze now rested on the three captives. "So, this is the famous Smedley Gang, is it?"

Swan made the introductions. "Gentlemen, meet Sheriff Dave Garvey of Neche." He paused for effect. "Dakota Territory, United States of America."

"What? That's the border." Chronister pointed at the river. "And we're this side of it. On the Canadian side."

Smith chuckled. "Pleasure to tell ye this, but the river isn't the border. Ye've been in America for about, oh, quarter of a mile, I'd say."

"If ya arresting us, ya better arrest these two." Smedley gestured at Fooks and Swan. "They're Florian Fooks and Tobias Swan."

Swan shot Fooks a worried look. Fooks held his breath.

Garvey sat looking pensive while his horse shifted position underneath him. For Fooks and Swan, the moments felt like hours. "Nope," Garvey said finally, gathering the reins and pulling his horse's head around. "That isn't who they are." Then he turned to the others. "Ya all right to bring 'em, Constable Smith?"

"I'll help ye out if ye'll forgive the intrusion?" Smith stuffed his pipe gleefully into his mouth. "I shouldn't really be here. It is Sunday after all. My day off."

Swan looked to Fooks after they'd watched Garvey and Smith lead the Smedleys away. He asked the silent question. Garvey knew who they were! Fooks shrugged in reply.

Swan rolled his eyes. "What happens now?" he asked, instead.

"We accomplished what we set out to do," Fooks replied and looked to Luke for any further comment.

Luke hunched his shoulders when the snow started again. "There's the little matter of the money Arnold embezzled."

Fooks turned to Maxime. "Does Arnold have the money with him?"

Maxime didn't answer. Fooks added, "A lot of money. More money than a small-town bank teller should have?"

Maxime kicked his horse forward. "It's not my decision, Crane. Ye'd better come ask him yeself."

Swan widened his eyes as he necked reined after him. "Back to Canada then."

Back at the Beauchemin house, Arnold sat in a wheeled chair. His complexion, pale and gray, mute testimony to the state of his health. Maxime made the introductions and left them reluctantly, when Arnold nodded.

"I might have known someone would come after me," Arnold said, when the door shut. His voice, tremulous and reedy. "You've found me. What now?"

Arnold regarded them cautiously and made no offer for them to sit. Luke sat anyway.

Fooks licked his lips. "Mr. Priestly, Jack sent me."

Arnold stared at the window. "Jack, I didn't think..." When he turned back, he asked, "Elspeth told him I died in the robbery. We thought it best."

"I know you were embezzling the bank, Mr. Priestly," Fooks said. "I checked the books. I figure you got away with at least fifteen thousand, and that's just this current year."

Arnold forced a wan smile. "You've found out more than I give you credit for."

Fooks acknowledged the compliment. "You should return it."

Arnold rubbed his eyes. "You can't take me back." He shook his head furiously. "I won't *go* back."

"No one said anything about you going back." This man was far too ill to make the journey, let alone stand trial. "You've been punished enough, Mr. Priestly. We just want to know what happened so we can let Jack know." Fooks nodded. "He thinks you're dead and he's interested in seeing the men responsible punished."

Arnold let out a hollow laugh. "Jack?" He shook his head. "Jack only thinks about himself."

Fooks pressed his lips into a thin line. "Seemed pretty cut up to me. Why else would he send me to find the men who 'killed' you?"

"And he put up most of the reward for their capture," Luke added.

Arnold gasped. "He did that?"

Fooks nodded. "Tell us what happened. How did you meet Robin Smedley?"

Arnold looked from one to the other. Fooks now perched on the edge of a chair, Swan remained standing, arms crossed over his chest.

"I met Robin Smedley in Grand Forks, when I worked for the First National there. Already had a new job lined up in Mudwater Flats. Thought it would be better for Peter. He's my son. He doesn't do well in big, crowded places. And that's what Grand Forks is becoming."

He exhaled. "Robin knew my wife. From... before we were married. S-she worked in a saloon. She was his girl when he came to town. Peter is..." He left it hanging, but the meaning obvious. Robin Smedley could be Peter's father. "I brought him up. He's my son."

Arnold swallowed hard before continuing. "Elspeth is an attractive woman. Robin threatened to tell the town what she was. I... wanted to keep my family, Mr. Crane." Arnold appealed to Fooks, who nodded.

"I understand. I'd do anything to keep mine," he said, surprising himself. He pressed his lips together.

"The Trail County Bank's books were not in great shape. Easy to appropriate a little here, a little there. It soon mounts up. I gave Robin all of it at first until Elspeth said I ought to get something for the risk I was taking. She said, if we took enough, we could cut Robin out altogether. Go away somewhere. Start afresh. So, I began reducing the amount I gave Robin, keeping the rest. Until I figured I had enough to take Elspeth and Peter away. I told Robin I was done. There'd be no more. We argued." He laughed bitterly. "Robin wasn't happy. I didn't expect him to be, I suppose." He sniffed. "It all went quiet, and I foolishly thought he'd let it lie. Chalk it up to water under the bridge.

"Until the Smedley Gang robbed my bank. All I could do was watch and do as I was told. Just as they were leaving, Robin turned and..."

Arnold put his head down and gestured at his legs. His face twisted. "That man shot me! Paralyzed me! Left me like this." He spat out the words. "You know the rest."

"Whose idea was it to have a fake funeral?" Luke asked.

"Elspeth. She said it would ensure Smedley believed I died."

Fooks chewed his lips, nodding slightly.

Arnold looked from one to the other. "So, what happens now? I told you I'm not going back."

Swan and Luke looked to Fooks, who sat forward, rubbing his thumbs. "We're not gonna take you back, Mr. Priestly. But we will take back the money."

"How do I know you won't keep the money for yourselves?"

"'Cos..." Fooks swallowed hard. *Can't believe I'm about to say this.* "It doesn't belong to us. That would be stealing." He locked eyes with Swan. "We're honest citizens. Luke here used to be a U.S. Marshall."

"Used to be?"

"Retired," Luke smiled, puffing up with pride.

"If you'll give me your word, nothing will happen to me, I'll arrange for a cashier's check for fifteen thousand," Arnold said, with a weak smile. "Will that satisfy you?"

CHAPTER THIRTY-THREE

The journey back involved a lot of changing trains and waiting around for connections. In Minneapolis a week later, Swan procured a private compartment, which meant they could talk undisturbed. Here Swan declared they would part company when they reached Omaha. It didn't make sense for him to go all the way to Bronze Canyon, when he was halfway to Boston already. Fooks had expected the conversation, but it was still hard to part from his friend.

Back in Bronze Canyon three days later, Luke and Fooks shouldered their saddlebags and trudged wearily along to the sheriff's office before it closed. Both thought it best to check in there first before going home. *Wonder what reception I'm gonna get.*

To their surprise, Wash sat behind the desk, Priestly nowhere in sight.

"Hey, you're back. Was expecting ya yesterday." Wash greeted them with a grin.

"Yeah, we got delayed in Omaha," Luke said.

"Didn't you get our telegram?" Fooks asked, letting his saddlebags slide from his shoulder.

"I sent it to Mary," Luke said, then winced. "Guess she didn't pass the message on."

"No." Wash pushed to his feet. Using a cane for support, he limped over to shake their hands. "Doc looked me over last week and gave me his blessing to resume my duties. Priestly headed out soon as I got the all clear." He pointed to the chairs in front of the desk. "Come and tell me everything."

"First, where's Priestly gone?" Fooks hesitated. "Is he gonna say anything 'bout me being here?"

"Ya don't need to worry 'bout him, Fooks. He has other things on his mind right now. He's gone to Neche. Hopes to arrive before heavy snow and the Smedley Gang's departure. Then he's gonna travel to Gretna and see his brother."

Fooks nodded sagely. "Should be an interesting conversation."

Wash nodded in agreement. "Think he wants to clear the air while there's still time." Wash opened his desk drawer. "He left ya this."

Wash tossed a white envelope on the desk in front of Fooks. He regarded it with suspicion before slowly reaching forward to pick it up. Flickers of irritation crossed his face as he read.

"D'you know what's in this?" he asked Wash.

Wash nodded, with a rueful smirk. "Yep."

"Can he do this?" For Luke's benefit, he added, "Talk to the Governor about canceling the warrants for my arrest."

Wash grinned. "Not only can he, he did." From the drawer, he brought out an altogether more official-looking envelope. "This came this morning."

Both Fooks and Luke leaned forward, eager to hear what the envelope contained. Wash made a great show of unfolding the document within, straightening it, holding it out at arm's length. Then decided he needed his glasses. Fooks nearly snatched it away but felt Luke deliberately moved so his toe connected with Fooks'. He rolled his eyes, sighed, and mastered his patience.

"Who is the Governor right now?" Fooks couldn't quite keep his impatience from his voice.

"George Baxter."

"He still gonna be around next week?" Recently, Wyoming had four governors in as many years, replaced almost on a whim by the President. Becoming a joke.

"D'ya wanna hear what he's written or not?"

Fooks waved his hand. "Yes, of course. Go ahead."

Wash cleared his throat. "I'll just read the salient bits. Considered carefully. Under the circumstances. Given the individual's present occupation and status. Length of time since last recorded criminal activity. Prepared to wave all warrants for arrest. Provisionally for five years on the following conditions. One, the individual known as Florian Joseph Fooks, shall remain at liberty only within the limits of Albany County, Territory of Wyoming. Permission to leave on submission to this office or via sheriff of Bronze Canyon. Second, Florian Joseph Fooks is prohibited from meeting or having any contact with anyone currently wanted for criminal activities in the territory of Wyoming. Three, failure to comply with these conditions could lead to immediate arrest and commitment to the Wyoming Territorial Prison in Laramie for seven years. If the conditions above are accomplished to the satisfaction of this office on the testimony of the sheriff of Bronze Canyon, after five years, the penalty for the criminal acts accredited to Florian Joseph Fooks will be deemed fully discharged. All citizen rights and liabilities will then be restored."

Fooks didn't speak. Not often that happened. Wash and Luke shared smiles at the unusual occurrence.

"You mean…" Fooks shifted his position. "You mean I-I'll be free?" The last word came out as a squeak. He cleared his throat.

Wash dropped the document on the desk. "Yes, that's what it means."

"Sheesh." Fooks leaned forward, hands over his eyes. "Oh, Sheesh! I'll be free."

"All ya have to do is sign both copies agreeing to the terms, and I'll send one back to the Capitol for the official record."

Luke put a reassuring hand on Fooks' arm. "Well done, son."

Fooks scrubbed at his eyes. "What about Swan?"

"Priestly didn't know about Swan's involvement. It's just for you Fooks."

"But we're partners, Wash." Fooks shook his head, sadly. "I can't accept this without him getting the same deal."

"Ya can't give up a chance like this, Fooks," Luke cried.

"No." Fooks was firm. With that, he levered up and shouldered his saddlebags. "It's both of us or neither of us."

He unbuckled his gun belt and dropped it with a thud on the desk. "I need to go home now."

He stalked out, leaving Wash and Luke in stunned silence.

"Didn't expect that," Wash said, after his office door slammed shut.

"Man's a fool," Luke said with a growl.

Wash sighed. "Fooks and Swan are tight, Luke. Have been since childhood."

"He can't give up a chance like this. What can we do?"

Wash looked again at the papers, biting his bottom lip. Then he folded the papers and returned them to their envelope. He pressed down firmly. "There's no time limit.

I'll just hang on to these. He'll come around when he's given it some more thought."

Luke scowled. "We've gotta hope so. When my Mary learns—"

"You can't tell her." Wash paused. "Fooks is a proud man. Any decision on this has to be his and his alone."

"For how long, though? What's this George Baxter like?"

Wash shrugged. "Took office November 11. All I know is he's a military man. Seems to know the cattle business, though. Democrat." He pulled a face. "Heard there's some controversy going on at the Capitol. Fencing of public land."

"Did he?"

"Dunno."

"In my experience, Wash. Mud sticks. Would a future governor honor this agreement?"

"Depends how long he stays, I guess."

"Then Fooks needs to sign this now. Afore, it's all change again."

Wash bit his lip. "I'm sure when he gets to thinking about it, he'll change his mind. It'll be here when he's ready."

He opened the desk drawer and swept the envelope into it.

EPILOGUE

"Mary."

Fooks walked into the living room and stopped dead. His saddlebags hit the floor with a thud. Mary stood behind the wing-backed chair, fingers gripping the back.

Fooks stripped off his gloves and removed his hat slowly. Swallowing hard, he dropped the gloves into the upturned crown before setting it aside on a bureau.

Susan sat on the floor, bangs falling over her face. The rest of her hair parted in the middle and bunched up on either side of her head. A joyous grin spread over her face when she saw him.

"Pappy!"

Susan rushed over to her father; favorite cloth rabbit clutched tightly by its long ears.

Glad he'd left his gun belt behind, Fooks hurried to catch the little girl, swinging her up. "Hey, sweetheart. How are you?"

Delighted, he kissed her, savoring the feel of her warm body next to his, then looked concerned when she pulled a face.

"You're spikey," she said, in protest.

Fooks stroked the three days' growth on his chin. "Oh, yeah. Sorry about that. I'll shave soon. Have you been a good girl for Mama?"

Susan shook her head furiously. "No."

Fooks blinked in surprise. "No? Why not?"

"Mama doesn't understand me."

Fooks laughed. He sobered when he found himself on the receiving end of a broad, dimpled grin, reminiscent of his own. *Yeah, you're gonna give me headaches, sweetheart.*

"Dr. Albright says Susan's language skills are far more advanced than they should be for her age," Mary said. "She's turning into a proper little madam."

"Am not."

Fooks laughed again when he looked back at Susan, contentment on his face. Then he noticed what the little girl wore. He turned to Mary for an explanation.

"Overalls, Mary? For a girl?"

"She's into everything." Mary rolled her eyes and shuddered. "It's just easier."

Susan's legs swung out. "Put Susan down now, Pappy. Things to do."

Fooks chuckled. "Why, yes ma'am. Of course, ma'am."

He set her down and watched her run off to where she played with her dolls, arranged in a semi-circle in front of the unlit fire. Once he saw she'd settled and he had been forgotten, he shifted his focus back to Mary. He noticed how tightly she gripped the back of the wing-backed chair. He walked forward. *She's as anxious as I am.*

"When you left, I wasn't sure you'd come back," Mary said softly, when he stopped in front of her.

"When I left, I didn't know *if* I'd come back," he said, just as quietly.

"I'm glad you did."

Fooks licked his lips. "Yeah, I, er..." He looked at Susan with her head down, chatting away to a doll on her lap. "I missed the little girl."

"What about the big girl?"

Fooks' eyes strayed to the typewriter sitting on his desk. Now his past memories were sharper, he had plenty of relevant stories to tell. He found he was eager to start before they faded again. *First things first, Fooks.*

He turned back to Mary and bit his bottom lip. "There's something I want to say." He held out his hand. "Come an' sit down."

Mary moved around the chair and took his hand. He let out a breath when he saw her pregnancy. "I'd forgotten about that," he said, softly.

She smiled and ran a hand over her bump. "Coming along nicely."

Fooks felt his eyes moisten. He sat and pulled her gently onto his lap. *This is nice. Wanna do more of this.*

He smiled, tight-lipped. "There's something I have to tell you. Confess." He rushed on before he lost his nerve. "While I was away, I couldn't be Joseph Crane," he started, slowly. "He wasn't needed. The other fella was." He paused. "Hear me out before you say anything. Okay?" Mary nodded, and he took a deep breath. "Ran into a woman I knew." He hesitated. "Before," he added, and then quickly, "I didn't cheat on you." He rubbed his cheek. "I thought I wanted her, but I couldn't go through with it. Didn't ... want to."

He didn't flinch when he met her intense gaze.

"What happened?"

"There was a lot of kissing. And some pawing. Nothing..." He shook his head. "Nothing. I stopped before there was something." He looked at her anxiously. "Do you believe me?"

To his surprise, Mary kissed him lightly on the lips. "Thank you for telling me."

"I don't want secrets between us. I'm keeping enough secrets from myself as it is." He tried a weak smile.

"What made you stop?"

"You did. I know I love you. I could feel I loved you..." He shook his head in disgust. "Pawing at another woman wasn't right." He swallowed hard. "Mary, I want to remember loving you."

"You told me once you're not a man who gives his heart easily. Yet you also told me when you met me, it slipped out of your grasp as easily as a bar of wet soap." She smiled. "I'm not sure I'm flattered by the comparison, but I understand the sentiment."

Fooks smiled, beginning to relax. "Yeah, sounds like me. I don't know how easy it'll be picking up my life with you, but I want to try. If you'll let me."

Mary nodded. "Oh." She pressed his hand to her bump. "Do you feel it?"

Fooks nodded, not trusting himself to speak. He stared in wonder and then glanced over at Susan. *This house is gonna be much too small for the four of us.*

"I think they'll be two people calling you that soon."

Slowly, he raised his eyes to meet Mary's. "Calling me what?"

"Pappy."

If you enjoyed *The Embezzlement Ledger*, please share your thoughts by leaving a review here from the link here

HISTORICAL NOTE

In retrograde amnesia the ability to form new memories is left intact and the individual can learn new skills.
However, the most recent memories prior to the injury are affected first. The extent of retrograde amnesia can vary. Some individuals may only lose memories for a few years prior to the injury, others may lose decades.

The symptoms include:

- Not remembering events that happened immediately before the injury
- Forgetting names, people, faces, places and facts learned during the period of memory loss
- Remembering skills learned during the period of memory loss
- Retaining older memories from childhood and adolescence

Retrograde amnesia results from damage to parts of the brain responsible for controlling emotions and memories.

Depending on the severity of the damage, the amnesia can be temporary or permanent, or anywhere in between. The amnesia might get better, worse of remain fixed.

Recovery can be progressive and/or spontaneous.

Inspiration for this part of the story came from the excellent academic paper by Katherine Unterman – citation below.

There are many meanings for the word boodler but in the context of this story, it means someone who is corrupt and has fled justice. Thought to derive from the Dutch word *boedle* meaning property or goods, by 19th century it had become American slang for ill-gotten gains.

Embezzlement from one's place of work, usually banking, and fleeing over an international border became rife in the U.S. in the later 19th century. Newspapers regularly reported on the whereabouts of alleged embezzlers and their carefree lifestyles in their new homes. Canada was the ideal destination. It was easy to get to. American railroads linked with Canadian lines. English was readily spoken and integration easier. Always a plus point for the fleeing criminal. Above all, the crime of embezzlement, was not on the list of crimes where extradition was possible. Embezzlement was only added to the treaty between the U.S. and Canada when the long running negotiations finally enabled the treaty to be ratified in 1890. Within a year, with no other convenient destination available, stories of boodlers disappeared from the newspapers.

Boodle over the Border: Embezzlement and the Crisis of International Mobility, 1880—1890

Source: The Journal of the Gilded Age and Progressive Era, April 2012, Vol. 11, No. 2 (April 2012), pp. 151-189

Published by: Society for Historians of the Gilded Age & Progressive Era

Stable URL: https://www.jstor.org/stable/23249072

Canada became known as the Dominion of Canada under the British North America Act, 1867. However, Britain still maintained control of Canada's foreign affairs. Canada did not become fully independent until 1931.

In French, the word Métis is often used to describe someone of mixed Indigenous and European ancestry. Métis have a distinct cultural identity, with their own customs and traditions. The red Voyageur sash, worn by both Henslow Smith and Maxime Beauchemin in this story is part of this distinct culture. It has many uses including as a washcloth, bridle or saddle blanket.

There are communities of people identifying as Métis across Canada and parts of the northern United States. Their language is called Michif and is a mixture of Indigenous and European languages, leading to various dialects depending on the Indigenous language. In this story the dialect is a mixture of French nouns, retaining gender and adjective agreement and Cree verbs.

Maxime Beauchemin describes life in his homeland of Red River. He is referring to the land which is around present-day Winnipeg and, in the 18th and 19th centuries was predominately settled by French speaking Métis, like himself and English-speaking Métis like Henslow. When the British wanted to transfer this land to Canada, Métis leaders rejected the notion that this transfer should happen without the consent of the people who lived there. Resistance at several public meetings in 1869, lead to an armed conflict which became known as the Red River Rebellion or Resistance, depending on the point of view.

When government surveyors tried to map the Red River area without regard for the existing residents' holdings, this led to the establishment of a Métis National Committee and a provisional government in 1870. This was led by Louis Riel and the government set out a list of acceptable terms for union with Canada. After negotiations the agreement became the Manitoba Act, which allowed the province of Manitoba to become part of the Canadian Confederation. The agreement allowed for a large reserve of land for the Métis.

Confusion abounded when the federal government sent a military force to Red River ostensibly to support the new Lieutenant-Governor of the province. However, this had not been part of the negotiations and the Métis provisional government had not consented to its arrival. It soon became clear that this was a plot to capture Louis Riel, who was considered a firebrand. He had no choice but for flee with his family to the United States.

One of the delegates of the provisional government was Andre Beauchemin, who represented the parish of St Vital, now a part of Winnipeg. Not much is known about him but he did appear to have several half siblings. Maxime of course is entirely fictitious.

These are two-wheeled carts, made entirely of wood and animal hide. The carts were developed by the Métis for use in the fur trade, specifically around Red River and were largely responsible for explosion of large-scale buffalo hunting. Although essentially farmers, in summer the Métis would leave their farms and hunt buffalo. More than 1000 carts could be involved in a hunt at any one time, lines often stretching for miles across the Plains. They sold the buffalo products to the fur trading companies, along with hauling the furs many miles in their carts. Until 1870, this was the mainstay of the Métis economy. After that date, the buffalo had all but disappeared from the Great Plains.

No metal is used in the construction of the Red River carts. They are distinguished from other wooden carts of the period by the large wheels, about five feet in diameter and flare out to give a wider stance. The axles are ungreased as this would mix with trail dust and act like sandpaper and eventually immobilize the cart. Consequently, when the cart was in motion, it let out a loud squeal, reminiscent of a untuned violin, and could be heard for miles. Imagine a 1000 of these carts moving together, like a thousand fingernails drawn over a thousand blackboards.

First produced by the Caton Instrument Company in 1872, they were widely used by telegraph companies and railroads. Their small size made them ideal for use by telegraph linesmen in the field either by testing for voltage on the lines or if they knew Morse Code by sending messages direct to the wire chief.

It was Catherine the Great of Russia who first encouraged a German speaking Anabaptist group to settle in the newly conquered lands of Crimea. The main tenet of their religion is pacifism and they were exempt from military service. However, by the 1870's the then Tzar, Alexander the Second, had removed this military exemption and was beginning to exert control over Mennonite schools and institutions. Time to look for a new home.

At this time the Canadian Government was offering inducements to settlers. Given their large numbers, the Mennonites were granted two large reserves in southern Manitoba, one east of the Red River and a little later the West Reserve. However, this was also the land the Métis consider theirs and promised to them by the Canadian government. Conflict was mainly around Winnipeg and the Red River areas.

Unlike other settlers, Mennonites liked to live in communal settlements, rather than in dispersed, isolated single dwellings. This gave rise to the traditional village pattern. One long street, about half a mile long, with houses joined to barns along one side. Gradually a more accepted pattern of settlement emerged and these long villages disappeared. Only a few remain today.

While today we might think of photo editing as a modern practice, the first acknowledged example was in 1846 by Calvin Richard Jones. He took a photograph of four Capuchin monks in a group, with a fifth standing some way behind. On the negative, Jones painted over the fifth monk with Indian ink. When printed, the place where the monk stood only showed as a patch of blank sky.

Image retouching used a special table. It had a variable incline plane as a working surface. A frame held the photo negative and a light, either natural or artificial, shone through from the back. Manipulations were carried out on the negative side. Among the tools used was a blade similar to a surgeon's scalpel, hard graphite pencils, ink and watercolors. The surface of the negative could be scrapped away using a hardened rubber. The portrait photographer would retouch negatives to remove blemishes and soften wrinkles.

Dead man's hand to the hand Wild Bill Hitchcock held when he was gunned down during a 5card stud poker game in Deadwood, Dakota in 1876. The hand allegedly contained the two black aces and two black eights with an unknown card, possibly the Queen of diamonds, making up the fifth. However, at the time speculation had an alternative hand: the ace of diamonds, ace of clubs, the two black eights and the Queen of hearts.

However, the Grand Forks Daily Herald newspaper in July 1886, ran an article describing a dead man's hand as three jacks and a pair of tens. It refers to a game some 47 years before, so c.1839, when a player fell dead, clutching this hand. This citation tends to undermine whatever Wild Bill derivation.

I have chosen to go with accepted as two pair is a lower hand than this version and it would be more believable for Fooks to fold with that.

ACKNOWLEDGEMENTS

I would like to thank my usual beta readers Fliss, Sue and Gin for wading through this text even though this is not their genre. This year they were joined by Jo.

My editor, Kristina Stanley, for being patient with a still learning newbie writer.

Thanks also to Regina for help with German and Heather with French. Google Translate only got me so far. Michif translating with the help of the excellent online dictionary on the Gabriel Dumont Institute website. Any mistakes are entirely my own and no offence intended.

Most of all I would like to thank my husband Murray for NOT reading any of my drafts and keeping our relationship sane.

ABOUT ME

Shirley Arnham always enjoyed writing and flirted with fan fiction over the years. Once retired from a career in accountancy, she thought what now? With plenty of stories in her head, why not try her hand at writing a book. Shirley lives in Norfolk, England and is looking forward to traveling the world with her husband.

The Embezzlement Ledger is her third published novel and the second in the Outlaw Detective series.

Discover more at: shirleyarnham.com

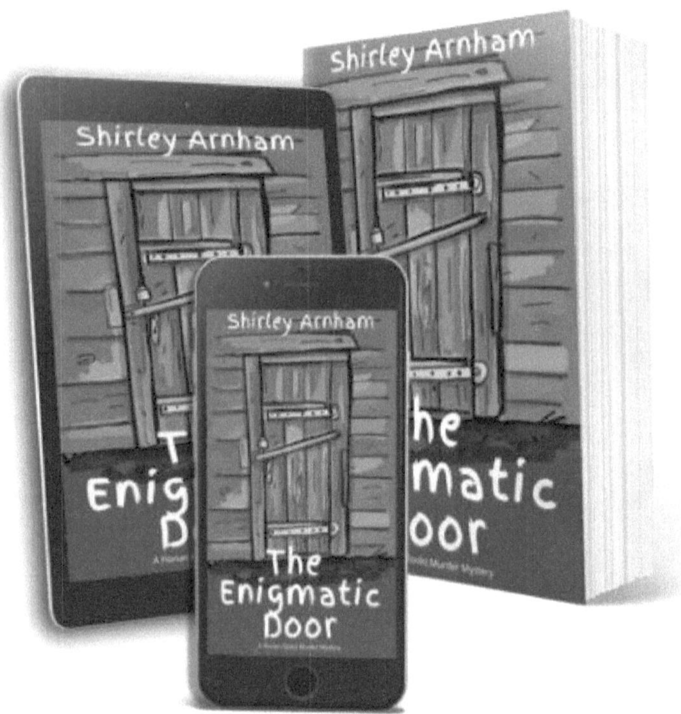
Shirley Arnham
The Enigmatic Door

The Enigmatic Door

Joseph Crane lives a quiet life in a small town in 1880's Wyoming. A genial young man with a successful business, a wife, and a baby due. Yet all is not as it seems. Previously, he was Florian Fooks, charismatic leader of the Guardian Wall Gang but that wasn't as long ago as he would like.

The shadow of his past looms large when two former associates arrive unexpectedly. Accused of murdering a prominent lawyer, they come seeking his help and Joseph doubts their guilt. Murder was never their game. If he sets out to learn more, he risks recognition and capture. But his wife needs him here. If he sends them away, chances are his former associates will hang before reaching trial. He can't have that on his conscience.

Torn between loyalty, self-preservation and a sense of justice, can he uncover the truth   behind the lawyer's murder in time without putting himself in danger?

The Enigmatic Door is the first in the Florian Fooks murder mystery series.

The Elusive Key

His partner's life at stake. No dilemma. This time he has to go.

Nearly a year has passed since Joseph Crane, hardware store owner, husband and father to a small daughter has left the safety of Bronze Canyon. Hearing that his old partner is wanted for murder and is missing, Florian Fooks as he is uncomfortably known outside Bronze Canyon, crosses the Mississippi for the first time.

Way outside his comfort zone, in Boston, he discovers that the murder victim was the uncle of the woman, his partner Tobias Swan, ran away with. With Tobias as the last person to see the victim alive and the police closing in on him, Fooks is in a race against time to prove his partner innocent. The more he discovers about the dead man's murky life, the more convinced Fooks becomes that there is more to his death than appears at first glance.

The Elusive Key is the second in the Florian Fooks murder mystery series.

IN THE PIPELINE

The Essential Condiment

Left an inheritance. But only if he can solve a murder in time.

With three boisterous children and a wife, living in a tiny house, reformed outlaw, Florian Fooks is desperate to improve his lot. Out of the blue, his former mentor, David Culley, asks him to visit. David drops a bomb shell when he forecasts his imminent murder. Fooks first instinct is to disregard the prophecy as the ramblings of an old man. Yet when the death occurs, Fooks can no longer ignore the possibility that David was right.

At the reading of David's Will, Fooks stands to inherit a large sum of money, which would solve his current problems and more. But to inherit, he has to solve David's murder within three months. Otherwise, the fortune is shared amongst the other beneficiaries, none of whom showed any fondness for the old man. Hostile would be a better word and Fooks finds himself with a ready-made list of suspects.

The Essential Condiment will be the fourth in the Florian Fooks murder mystery series.

297 | THE EMBEZZLEMENT LEDGER